Caribbean Adventure Series
Book 5

MUDDY WATERS

A Rick Waters Novel

ERIC CHANCE STONE

Printed in the United States of America

ISBN: 978-1-959020-01-1

First Edition

10 9 8 7 6 5 4 3 2 1

MUDDY
WATERS

MUDDY WATERS SYNOPSIS MUSIC CD COMING SOON

ERICSTONE.GUMROAD.COM/L/MUDDYWATERSMUSIC

CHAPTER ONE

An eerie, thick fog wafted over the dying cornfield as the car slowed down. The crackling of dead grass and gravel under the tires was the only sound in the stagnant air. Tyler stepped out of the car and slung a black Fender Strat over his shoulder. He walked to the center of the crossroads and looked up at the blue moon. It was five minutes to midnight on October thirty-first. It was the first full moon on Halloween in seventy-five years. He couldn't believe he was really doing this.

Tyler had just returned from a gig in Fort Walton Beach, Florida, where he was booed off the stage. The echoes of the people's laughter rang in his ears and tortured his mind. He was determined to never let that happen again, and he had only one chance to make it happen.

"Hello? I'm here," said Tyler, looking around.

This was the same spot where Robert Johnson, a famous blues musician, had sold his soul to the devil in exchange for fame, fortune, and talent. Robert had definitely gotten the talent and later the fame, but he'd died far too young at the hands of a jealous husband before he had the fortune.

Tyler wanted to be a famous musician, too. A respected one. He was willing to try anything, but now that he was here, unease curled in his stomach. Every little sound around him was amplified, and he looked over his shoulder and all around him, in anticipation and fear.

He glanced down at his watch. The second hand struck midnight.

A silhouette of a man stepped into view. He was wearing a long trench coat and had a briefcase in his right hand. He moved toward Tyler in a manner that almost seemed as if he were floating. A cloud of fog and mist surrounded the man as he approached.

"What is your desire, young man?"

"I want to be the best blues guitarist in the world and get a record deal."

The man looked at Tyler without speaking. He opened the briefcase and pulled out a single piece of yellowed paper. He closed the briefcase, put the paper on top of it, and held it in front of Tyler with a quill pen dripping red ink. Tyler took the pen in his hand and looked down at the paper. The contract appeared to be written in blood, and the wording was hard to understand. Most of it was too small to read or in a language he'd never seen before.

"What am I signing here, exactly?" He squinted his eyes. "I can't understand the details."

"You want to be a famous guitar picker, don't you? It's just a contract between you and I, so you can achieve that dream," said the man.

This can't be real, thought Tyler. But he was so desperate, he decided to give it a shot.

He quickly signed the paper and handed it back to the man. The man began to laugh. He laughed from deep within, and his laughter echoed over the cornfields. It gave Tyler the creeps. Suddenly, a gust of wind from behind the man hit Tyler's face, and a heavy fog engulfed the man. Tyler could no longer see him. The wind died down, and the man was gone.

Tyler walked back toward his car. *Did it work?* His hands were itching to find out. He leaned against the hood, slung his Strat forward, and plugged it into his battery-powered pig-nose amp that was hanging from his hip. He played a simple blues riff, but it seemed different. His fingers seemed to know where to go without thinking. He went into a minor pentatonic scale he had played a thousand times, but his speed was much faster than he had ever been able to play it before. He tried a Dorian scale that he had played a few times, and his fingers played the notes as if they already had muscle memory. He slid into the Dorian-Mixolydian-Hybrid scale, then into the Lydian dominant, followed by the Locrian scale, and back to the standard blues scale with ease.

"What the fuck?" he said out loud.

He hadn't even played some of these scales before, but now he could play them without effort or even thinking. He pulled out his phone and played along to a backing track of a Joe Bonamassa song that he'd always tried but failed to play well. He played the entire song note for note with more finesse and taste than Joe himself. He played a few more notes and looked at his fingers in amazement. He began to laugh with excitement. He felt as if he had won the lotto.

The moon began to fade away behind a dark cloud. Out of nowhere, a hot pain shot through Tyler's back. His eyes got blurry and he passed out.

Deputy Sheriff Ron Dalton drove down Highway 8 toward Dockery Farms, a route he had driven many times before on patrol. For some reason, he took a right at the old dirt and gravel road toward Lead Bayou, past the True Life Church and cemetery. When he got to the next intersection in the road, he spotted a car sitting off to the side.

Many people believed this was the true crossroads where Robert Johnson had supposedly sold his soul to the devil. Others claimed it was where Highway 61 and Highway 49 met. There was a huge memorial sign at that location claiming to be the exact spot. No one agreed on the exact location or if it even actually happened. It was mostly folklore and a tourist draw.

Deputy Dalton pulled off to the side behind the empty car. He assumed whoever had parked here was fishing over at Lead Bayou. As he approached the car, he realized it was still running. Dew covered the car's roof, and it was obvious it had been here overnight. He checked for clues around the car that might lead him to the vehicle's owner. A gray nylon guitar pick was sitting in the gravel beside the front tire. He picked it up—Dunlop. He put it in a clear evidence bag and tucked it into his pocket. He looked for footprints and there seemed to be two sets. There were none heading toward Lead Bayou, so whoever's car it was, they weren't fishing. He reached into the car and turned off the ignition.

"Hello? Is there anyone here?" he called out.

He waited, but only silence answered. He walked back to his cruiser and repeated the same thing over his external PA mic on his radio. Nothing. He decided to run the plates. An uneasy feeling stirred in his gut, a feeling that something bad might've happened here the night before.

"Dispatch, this is Deputy Ron Dalton, Car C2442. I need to run plates on an abandoned auto. Are you receiving?"

"Ten-four, Ron, this is Dawn at dispatch. Please give me the plate."

"It's a Harrison County plate, AGF-257."

"Stand by, Ron."

A few minutes passed, and the dispatcher got back on the radio.

"That car belongs to Tyler Raynes of Biloxi. Come back."

"Tyler Raynes? Any relation to Jack Raynes who owns that big casino down there?"

"Please hold. Let me text you his driver's license."

Deputy Dalton's phone pinged, and he looked at the photo. He did a quick Google search and confirmed that this Tyler was indeed the son of Jack Raynes, owner of the Red Ruby Casino in Biloxi.

"Dawn, I'm gonna need a tow truck and forensics unit out at Highway 8, by the old Dockery Plantation. Take the first right on the dirt road toward Lead Bayou. Wait, let me just share my location to your cell. It'll be easier."

"Ten-four, Ron. Standing by."

Ron shared his Google Maps location and waited.

About an hour passed by, and he saw the lights of a tow truck kicking up dust in his rearview mirror. He stepped out of the cool air-conditioning and waved the driver over to the front of the car. The forensics unit arrived a few minutes later. Ron had already taped off the area. A man with a white coat stepped out of the forensics van.

"Hi, Ron, what you got?"

"I'm not sure, James. I found this car left running, no owner in sight. I have a gut feeling some foul play went down here last night."

James Watson opened his forensics bag and put on some vinyl gloves. He took several photos of the area, including any tire tracks and footprints nearby.

"Do you find this odd, Ron?" asked James.

"What?"

"Follow me. You see these tracks leading to and from the car?"

"Yeah, so?"

"Look at the other set of footprints facing these tracks."

"Yeah, it looks like two people were facing each other. That's not odd," said Ron.

"Not by itself, but look at the other prints. There are only three steps, and they start in the center of the road. No tire tracks, and no footprints coming from the side of the road. There are no more going in the other direction. How did the person facing the other man leave? It's as if he was here and then gone with no exiting prints. I can't wrap my head around it."

"I see what you mean. That is odd. I'm sure there's a perfectly good explanation for it."

"Yeah, maybe he's a Martian who dropped down from outer space." James chuckled.

James continued his forensics dance and got prints off of the car. He only found one set of prints, and they most likely belonged to the owner.

"Do you need me anymore?" asked Ron. "I want to head back to the station and contact the father."

"Nah, go ahead. I'll let you know if I find anything interesting."

"Oh, hang on." Ron reached into his pocket and handed James the guitar pick he'd found. "I almost forgot. I found this near the driver's side front tire."

"Okay, I'll log it into evidence."

Deputy Ron headed to his cruiser and started his trip back to the Sheriff's Department in Bolivar County. He often worked in the Sunflower County jurisdiction under a concurrent agreement. It was a short drive. Ron went inside to his desk and searched for Tyler's father's contact info. He was unlisted, so he called the Red Ruby Casino. After going through several automated messages, he finally got a human.

"Reservations, how may I help you?"

"Hi, this is Deputy Ron Dalton of the Bolivar County Sheriff's Department. I'm trying to reach the owner, Jack Raynes. It's an urgent matter. Can you patch me through?"

"Please hold, Mr. Dalton."

After a long pause of some elevator music, she came back on the line.

"Mr. Dalton, I'm going to patch you through to the GM, Don Jacobs."

Another pause came on the line.

"Hello, this is Donald Jacobs. I understand you are trying to contact the owner, Jack Raynes? What is this is about, exactly? Jack is a very busy man."

"It's a private matter, Mr. Jacobs, and it involves his son."

"Okay, I will take down your info and personally give it to Jack. I'm sure he will return your call as soon as he's out of his meeting."

Ron gave Donald his cell number and the landline number of his desk.

"I'll run this up to him now," said Don. "Is there anything else I can do for you?"

"Nah, just make sure he understands this is urgent."

"Will do. Thank you."

Ron returned to his computer to check the social media of Tyler Raynes. He had a fairly large following on Facebook and Instagram. Luckily, most of his posts were public, so anyone could see them. Ron scrolled his Facebook page to October twentieth and saw he had played a gig in Fort Walton Beach, Florida, at a place called The Green Door Music Hall. He read a few of the comments people had left. Some were obviously from friends who praised his musical prowess, but there were actually more negative comments than positive ones. He read them out loud to himself under his breath.

Tune that fucking guitar!

Get some lessons, you need them.

Decent song selection, but please, for the love of God, don't ever butcher an Eric Clapton song again.

He scanned the Instagram posts and the comments were all similar. Then he saw a video Tyler had posted of a Keb' Mo' cover song. He put on his headphones and turned up the volume on his computer. He winced as the song started. Now he understood what everyone was talking about. Tyler was trying so hard to sound good, but he just didn't. He was struggling with chords and his vocals were off-key. The poor kid had all the desire in the world but not a whole lot of natural talent.

Ron's cell phone rang, and he looked down to see a 228 area code. It was probably Tyler's dad from Biloxi.

Damn, that was fast!

"Hello, this is Deputy Ron Dalton."

"Deputy Dalton, this is Jack Raynes. I'm returning your call."

"Hi, Mr. Raynes. I have some information about your son, and I hope you can help."

"Call me Jack. What did he do now? How much is bail?"

"Uh, it's not like that, Jack. This morning, we found his car abandoned and left running over near Dockery Farms on a side road. He was nowhere to be found. When's the last time you spoke to him?"

"Let me think… I believe it was October twenty-fifth. He had gone over to Fort Walton the week before to play some little bar, and he was telling me about it. He was kinda depressed and wanted to borrow some money for guitar lessons. I'm not stupid; guitar lessons were an excuse for drug money. He had gotten into coke a while back. We sent him to rehab and he was clean for a while, but I think he fell off the wagon again. He would disappear for days at a time. I was getting pretty fed up about it. I assumed when you called, he was arrested for possession again. I haven't seen or spoken to him since that day, but it's not that unusual. Do you think something bad happened to him?"

"I have no idea at this time, but I'm treating it as a kidnapping. Since you haven't heard from him since October twenty-fifth, I'm going to list him as a missing person. Do you know if he had any ties to anyone over in Fort Walton?"

"I know he had a friend in Destin he crashed with sometimes when he'd play over there. I can't remember his name, but if you look on Facebook, you can figure it out. He's the guy with the sleeve tattoos and bleach blond hair. I think he's a drummer or something. Maybe he has some info for you. Did my number show up on your phone?" asked Jack.

"Yeah, I'll go ahead and store it. And please, if you can think of anything else that might help us track down his whereabouts, don't hesitate to call me any hour of the day."

"I will. I'll have my daughter ask some of his friends. I'm willing to bet he got on a bender and was high as hell and left with someone to score more coke. He probably didn't even know he left his car running. He's been a bit of a disappointment to us all lately." Jack sighed. "Don't get me wrong, I love my son and he has so much potential, but all he wants to do is play that damn guitar and he ain't that good. I tried to bring him in to the family business—I let him play at the casino twice a week with his little blues band, and his friends came and spent money, so it was a wash for me. But it didn't last long 'cause his heart wasn't in it. He started talking about wanting to fly out to California to take lessons from the same guy who taught Keb' Mo'. He's been obsessed with Robert Johnson and the Delta blues. I was a guitar player myself in my younger days and steeped in the blues. The problem with Tyler is he lacks motivation, and I'm always afraid any money I give him'll end up getting used for drugs. It's a vicious cycle."

"Thank you, Jack. I will keep you posted on our end. The car has been brought to impound, and forensics will go over it in great detail. We are a small department with limited resources, but I'll call down to Okaloosa County and see if they have anything that will help. I'll let you go now. Gotta get back to work."

"Me too, Deputy Dalton."

"Call me Ron, Jack."

"Okay, Ron it is. Goodbye for now."

"Bye."

After hanging up, Ron called the Okaloosa County Sheriff's Department for any info they had on Tyler Raynes. Turned out he had been arrested for possession of cocaine and released on bond back in May. He pleaded out of the case and was given probation. He had moved his probation visits to Harrison County and had no outstanding warrants. He was about to be released from probation in November. His next scheduled visit was November twenty-third, and his last was on October twenty-sixth, which he showed up for.

Ron faxed the missing person info to Okaloosa and then called the probation officer down in Biloxi. He left a voicemail and went back to his computer to send an email to the probation officer. He was still on call, and dispatch sent out a 10-16 over the radio—a domestic disturbance.

"Dawn, this is Deputy Dalton. I'll take that 10-16. What's the address?"

"It's the Gillard Farm."

"Oh, again? I'm on it."

Ron knew exactly what it was. Old Man Gillard was drinking again and probably yelling at his wife, and she was yelling back at him. This was almost a weekly occurrence. He'd go out to the farm and try to calm them down, and if he couldn't, one of them would end up in the drunk tank. It was usually Old Man Gillard. Ron was beginning to think the guy enjoyed getting locked up, just to get away from his ornery wife. It was a routine call and never violent. Ron normally hated domestics because they were usually very unpredictable and full of emotion. They were considered one of the most dangerous calls, in fact. Not this one though.

Ron was getting into his cruiser when his cell rang. He switched it to his hands-free and took the call.

"Deputy Dalton, this is Jeff Smith. I'm Tyler Raynes's probation officer. What can I do for you?"

"Hi, Mr. Smith. Tyler has gone missing and I was wondering if you had any insight into his behavior lately. Anything strike you as odd? Has he been clean and sober?"

"Missing? That's not good. He's been on time for all his visits, and I did two random drug tests on him and he was clean. I think that time he spent in jail woke him up. He seemed to be very motivated to advance his music career. That's all he ever talked about during our visits. I love the blues and I actually enjoyed seeing him when he'd come in."

"Is there anything you can think of that seemed unusual or anything he said that made you pause?"

A short silence fell on the line.

"Well, last time he was here he kept going on and on about selling his soul to the devil to become a better guitar player," said Jeff. "I just blew it off. I mean we've all hear the rumor about Robert Johnson selling his soul at the crossroads. It's just silly folklore. The last thing he said was that he was dead serious and planned to do it."

Deputy Ron felt the hairs on the back of his neck stand up, and a shiver went down his spine.

"I just laughed and told him to go for it," continued Jeff. "He seemed agitated that I didn't believe him. How could I? I finally just went along with him and pretended to get it. I doubt that helps though."

"You'd be surprised. We found his car idling at the very place many believe Johnson did that. I don't believe in that crap either, but apparently Tyler did."

"Wow, his car was found at the crossroads?"

"Yep, exactly. That's the last place he was, as far as we can tell. Thanks for your help, and if anything comes up, I'll holler at you."

"Sounds good."

"Catch ya later," said Deputy Dalton.

"On the flip side, my man. I hope Tyler is okay. I really like that kid."

"I'll keep you in the loop."

They both hung up, and Ron proceeded to the Gillard farm, trying to shake off his uneasy feeling. There was no way Tyler could've sold his soul to the devil. It was just folklore.

But the kid was still missing.

CHAPTER TWO

Johnie polished the stainless-steel rails of *Nine-Tenths* in the warm afternoon sun of Destin Harbor. He would polish for a while, then stop and gaze out over the harbor at the tourist boats bustling about. He was just happy to be a free man. Not more than a week ago, he was still facing the possibility of life in prison, or maybe even the death penalty, due to false allegations brought about by a devious woman. But with the help of Rick Waters and the crew, the charges were dropped and the woman and her husband in question were brought to justice.

Johnie had been Rick's first mate and engineer for almost two years now. He didn't need to work. He could easily retire and move to some island in the middle of the Pacific, but he loved taking care of Rick's fifty-five-foot sport fisher. Rick had purchased the massive yacht after solving a murder a few years back and collecting the reward. It had been his dream to own and captain a great fishing boat, although he spent more time solving cases than he did captaining. Johnie was just happy to be a part of it. He would've worked for free to be a part of this crew. Rick knew that too, but paid him handsomely.

Johnie's cell rang. "Nine-Tenths Charters, this is Johnie McDonald. How can I help you?"

"Hey, Johnie, it's Rick. You busy?"

"Not really, just polishing the rails a bit. What's up?"

"Jules and I are heading to Mississippi tomorrow. I just wanted to see if you needed anything for any upcoming charters."

"Let me think, hang on."

Johnie jogged into the salon and looked around, trying to remember if he needed anything for the boat.

"We're a little low on Flor De Caña. We did a number on it the other day."

"Oh yeah, I can pick some up at ABC. I have to swing by Walmart too. Are we good on paper towels?"

"We can always use a few of those, and maybe grab a few shop rags."

"Okay, I'll grab a box," replied Rick.

"Why are y'all headin' to Mississippi?"

"Remember when Carson met with the D.A. after they dropped the charges against you?"

"Of course, how could I forget. Y'all saved my butt," replied Johnie.

"Well, after he met with them, he was going through some new open case files and found one about a missing kid, a guitar player actually. His dad is the owner of the Red Ruby Casino. I'm gonna go there, throw a few bones, and see if I can talk him into hiring me to find his boy. I'm gonna search for the kid regardless, but maybe I can get paid too. It's worth a shot."

"Good idea, Rick. I'll hold down the fort here. I have three captains on speed dial now, so no worries there."

"Okay, I'll swing by the boat and drop off some supplies. We'll be taking Chief with us. He hasn't done a road trip with us in a while. We're gonna take the new Bronco. I need to break it in. The new car smell is annoying. Haha."

Gary Haas, one of Rick's sidekicks, had recently purchased the entire crew brand-new Badlands Broncos in everyone's favorite color. Gary had won Powerball a few years back and invested wisely, and his fortune had grown ever since. Dropping a few hundred thousand bucks on brand-new Broncos didn't even faze Gary. It was pocket money to him.

"Sounds good, Rick. I'll be here polishing away," said Johnie.

Rick and Jules headed to ABC Fine Wine & Spirits on Harbor Boulevard to refill the Flor De Caña and also get some other supplies for their road trip. As they walked into the ABC, a woman was standing behind a makeshift tiki bar offering a free sampling of Cruzan's new Hurricane Proof rum.

"Like a sample?" asked the nice lady in a flowery hat.

"Free sample of Cruzan rum? Twist my arm, haha," replied Rick.

She poured two fingers of the rum into paper cups and slid them toward Rick and Jules. They both downed them and began to cough.

"Wow, that's got a bite. What can you tell me about it?" asked Rick.

"I have to be honest with you, I was just hired today. The normal girl who does the tastings got sick, so the rep called me. I don't know a lot about this rum, sorry. I do know it tastes great with pineapple juice. Wanna try?"

"Sure! My favorite rum is free rum."

She reached under her bamboo bar and pulled out two red Solo cups, filled them halfway with rum, and added some pineapple juice and two large ice cubes.

"Here ya go. Y'all enjoy. We have bottles available, and here's a coupon for two dollars off."

Rick put a bottle in his cart and took the coupon. They proceeded to the rum section and grabbed two bottles of Flor de Caña for the boat and some beer as well. Jules chose a bottle of Aguardiente Amarillo de Manzanares, her favorite liquor from her native Colombia. It had a hint of coffee and was extremely smooth. Rick didn't care for it but loved to indulge Jules any chance he could. They had met at a casino in St. Croix where she was a dealer. Rick had swept her off her feet and they had been in love ever since.

Rick grabbed an extra bottle of Flor de Caña 25 for the road. They finished their cups of rum and pineapple juice, paid, and were headed out the door when the girl behind the bar hollered, "Roadies?"

"Sure, why not," replied Rick.

Jules waved another one off.

The girl poured an extra heavy one for Rick and gave it to him. He thanked her and they headed to Walmart. Jules grabbed a shopping cart once inside Walmart, and Rick put his left hand on it for balance.

"I can push it, Rick."

"I know, Jules. Trust me, I need to hold on to this. I can't believe it. I'm drunk in Walmart!"

Jules nearly fell over laughing. "Rick, you only had three drinks."

"I know, I don't understand."

"What was that rum called again?"

"It was Cruzan Hurricane Proof."

Jules pulled out her phone and googled it. "*Ay, Dios mío*, Rick! That rum is 137 proof. No wonder you are drunk. I'm feeling kinda lightheaded myself, and I had way less than you."

Rick rolled his eyes then put both hands on the cart. Jules relented and let him push it. They picked up some supplies for *Nine-Tenths* and their road trip, and Jules grabbed some red grapes for Chief.

After leaving the store, they headed down to Destin HarborWalk to drop off the supplies. Jules drove the Bronco. Rick was definitely legally drunk at this point. He devoured a Walmart sub on the way to the boat and was feeling better and not slurring anymore.

"We're here," Rick yelled up to Johnie, who was way up on the tuna tower polishing. Johnie climbed down and helped Rick put away the stuff.

"How long y'all gonna be gone?"

"Not sure, my man. Depends on if I get the case or not, I guess. Possum headed back to Houston. Gary and Carson took Gary's new jet joyriding out to the Bahamas. I'll touch base with them tomorrow."

"That Gary is something else. I bet you anything that fucker buys an island while he's out there," said Johnie, shaking his head.

Rick snorted. "That wouldn't surprise me one bit!" He went over to Chief. "You ready for a road trip, boy?"

Chief hopped up and down on the top of his cage, encouraged by all the excitement. He could always tell when something was about to happen. Partly because Jules had carried in his travel cage and partly from Rick's tone of voice. He jumped over to Rick's shoulder, nearly falling off. His wing was still in a soft cast from the injury he'd received after someone took a shot at Johnie and broke the glass sliding doors on *Nine-Tenths*. Chief had nearly died from loss of blood but was recovering nicely now.

Jules took Chief off of Rick's shoulder, placed him in the travel cage, and gave him a couple of red grapes. He munched on them and looked up at everyone as if he wanted them to be jealous of his treats.

"Okay, we are out of here," said Rick. "Call me if you need anything, or just put it on the company card. Oh, wait, did Gary say anything about when he was going to put the new travel trailer on the harbor for the business bookings?"

"He sent me a text message that it would be next week. I'll forward the photo to you. He may have already sent it to you as well."

Rick took out his phone and, sure enough, saw a message from Gary. His phone had been on silent mode and he hadn't even felt it vibrate. He blamed the rum.

They stepped off of the boat and set Chief's travel cage on the back seat of the Bronco. That was the only thing Rick didn't like about the new Bronco, that it didn't have a bench seat like his old '62 Ford. The ride was so smooth, though, that he could overlook it.

They took the scenic route on Highway 98 past Navarre and Pensacola. They continued hugging the coast all the way to Orange Beach. Normally, they'd head north on I-10, but Rick was craving a blackened fish sandwich, and he was friends with the chef at Fisher's Dockside at Orange Beach Marina. Chef Jonathan Tibbs had taken up residency there after leaving the Keys where Rick had originally met him. They had been fast friends ever since Rick helped him dock his sailboat at the now defunct Smuggler's Cove restaurant and marina. Even though blackened fish sandwiches weren't officially on the menu, he knew Chef Jonathan would gladly make him one with grouper or snapper.

Jonathan approached their table after they sat down. "Rick, how are you? Long time no see. Who's this?"

"Chef Jon, this is Jules, my girlfriend. This of course is Chief, but you already knew that."

Chef Jon shook Jules's hand and waved at Chief. "Well, what brings you my way today?"

"We are headed to Biloxi and thought we'd swing by for a quick meal."

"Let me guess. Blackened fish sandwiches?"

Rick grinned. "You know me too well, my friend."

"I have a treat for you today. I know you like grouper— today I got some grouper cheeks in. They are to die for."

"Man, my mouth is watering just thinking about it," replied Rick.

"You gotta try this new beer we got on tap too. It's called Surrender Cobra from Big Beach Brewing just down the road." Chef Jon walked behind the bar and poured a pint of the dark nectar. "Jules, I'm sorry, what would you like?"

Jules waved off his apology with a smile. "I'll just take a club soda and lime. I'm driving."

"Coming right up."

The chef placed both drinks down on the table and disappeared into the kitchen. He returned fifteen minutes later with two piping hot blackened grouper cheek sandwiches. He stood tableside and waited for them to take their first bite.

"Oh man, that is good!" said Rick with a full mouth.

"You like it, Jules?" asked the chef.

She nodded aggressively while still chewing.

"Okay, I'll let y'all eat. I gotta cook for a little longer before my shift is up. I'll join you if you want in a little bit."

"We'll be here," said Rick.

They scarfed down their sandwiches, and Rick ordered another beer. Chef Jon sat down with them and ordered a round of appetizers. The pimento cheese app was amazing. It came with homemade pork skins. They sat around the table for a couple of hours reminiscing about the Keys and all of the dive trips they had been on. It was getting dark, and Biloxi was still two hours away. They decided to call it a night.

"You're welcome to crash at my place, if you like," said Chef Jon as they all stood up.

"Thanks for the offer, but I think we'll get a hotel room." Rick clapped his friend on the shoulder before they parted ways.

It was a beautiful night on the Gulf, and after they checked in at their beachside hotel, Rick, Jules, and Chief took a long stroll down the beach. Chief sat on Rick's shoulder the entire time mocking seagulls. The beach was magical.

Rick had gotten them a one-bedroom suite at Hotel Indigo. It was a lovely boutique hotel and it was pet friendly. Once they returned from their beach walk, Rick set Chief on top of his travel cage in the living room and gave him some grapes. He could hear the shower running in the bathroom and walked in to find Jules already in the water.

"Join me?"

"You don't have to ask me twice."

Jules scrubbed Rick's back with her gentle hands, and Rick did the same to her. It wasn't long until they were making love. They started in the shower and finished on the couch. Afterward, they were both tired and lay in bed and drifted off to asleep. It was the perfect ending to a perfect day.

The morning sun broke through a sliver in the curtain and fell right into Rick's eyes. Although he had drunk quite a bit the night before, he didn't have a hangover. Most likely because Jules always forced him to drink a large bottle of water before bed and gave him a cherry-flavored BC Powder. She was always on his ass to drink more water. She wasn't bitchy; she just loved taking care of him. He loved it too.

"Good morning, sleepyhead," said Rick.

Jules yawned and wrapped her arms around Rick's neck, kissing his cheek. She ran to the bathroom and brushed her teeth. Rick did the same, and they kissed afterward and hugged for a long time. Rick had never been this happy in his entire life. The love of a good woman made him a better person, and he intended to keep her around.

Rick made a pot of coffee, and Jules ran downstairs to get some bagels from Hunters Bend Restaurant in the lobby.

"Rick, come eat!" called Jules from the living room when she came back.

Rick stepped out of the bedroom carrying his laptop. He had been researching all he could find out about Jack Raynes. He could smell the bagels when he walked in.

"Here, Rick, I got us this quiche too. Try it! It's cheese and spinach."

"Jules, real men don't eat quiche," snarked Rick.

"You will eat it, and you will like it!" demanded Jules as she airplaned a forkful toward his mouth.

He reluctantly took a bite.

"Mmm, mmm," said Rick with a mouthful.

"I told you!"

"Okay, don't tell anyone I like quiche."

"You are silly, Rick Waters."

After breakfast, they decided to hop in the pool for a bit before heading to Biloxi. Rick immediately made a beeline for the little waterfall on the edge of the pool. He let the cool water run over his head and waved Jules over. They were the only two people in the pool. He tried to coax her into fooling around under the waterfall, but she wasn't having any of it. She pointed up to the windows of the hotel, indicating they weren't truly alone. Rick kissed her and then dunked her for fun.

Once they were showered and back in clean clothes, they loaded up the Bronco and headed north through Foley toward Interstate 10. The route dumped them off at Buc-ee's, which held the world record for the largest convenience store in the world, at 66,335 square feet at their New Braunfels, Texas, location. Even the store in Alabama was a sight to behold. Jules was blown away by the size of it. Rick topped off the gas tank, and they parked to go inside and shop. Jules bought a Buc-ee's t-shirt and forced Rick to get one too. He bought a new Buc-ee's forty-ounce thermal mug and a small bag of beef jerky.

"Let's roll, baby. We're burning daylight," said Rick.

They hopped back in the Bronco, and Rick put Chief's flight harness on, set him on top of the travel cage, and lowered the ragtop down. The warm air was nice as they continued their journey toward Biloxi. They drove over the bridge into town, and Rick pulled into the parking lot of the Red Ruby Casino. Jules carried Chief, while Rick pulled both of the big bags to the front desk.

"Good afternoon, sir. How may I assist you?"

"We need a room for four nights, please. What's the best room you have in the casino?"

"We have the executive suite—oh wait, we also now have the presidential suite, which is not quite ready but will be by two o'clock. It's $1,497 a night. Will that be okay?"

"Is there a weekly rate?" asked Rick.

"I can knock off thirty percent if you book a whole week. It also comes with a butler and an official welcome visit from the owner, Jack Raynes," said the man behind the counter.

"We'll take it."

The man took Rick's ID and credit card and waved over a bellman to help them with the luggage.

"If you'd like to use the pool, we can store your bags until your room is ready, or you can visit the casino or one of our restaurants. We have three fine-dining restaurants in the resort and a food court."

"We're kinda all pooled out today, but I may play some craps while we wait."

"Do you need a marker, sir?"

"Nah, I'll just buy some chips. Hopefully you'll owe me a marker when I'm done," said Rick with a chuckle.

"Well, good luck, sir."

He handed Rick his key to the room, looked at his watch, and said his bags would be in the room by two o'clock. Rick tipped the guy twenty bucks to let Chief into the room early and another twenty to the bellman who would carry him up.

"We'll see you in a little while, boy." Rick patted Chief on the head and placed the cage in the bellman's cart.

Rick put his hand in the small of Jules's back and led her to the casino.

"Let's roll some bones, baby."

CHAPTER THREE

Rick and Jules strolled hand in hand into the casino. A red-headed man was throwing the dice as they approached the table. The winning number was six. The man softly tossed the dice, and they bounced off the back of the felt, landing on snake eyes. After the man's throw, Rick placed two crisp hundred-dollar bills and his driver's license on the table. He wanted to get a player's card and it was customary to just drop your ID.

One of the standing dealers pushed over five twenty-five-dollar chips and the rest in five-dollar chips toward Rick. Rick placed two five-dollar chips on the come line. The man threw a four, and one of the standing dealers moved Rick's chips to the four spot. Rick asked for double odds on the four and put another ten dollars on the come line. The shooter took the dice in his hands, whispered to them, and blew on them before tossing them. He rolled a three and a two.

"Five, five, a no-field five!" hollered one of the dealers.

The dealer across from Rick moved his ten dollars to the five spot, and Rick again asked for double odds. He doubled his come bet to twenty dollars. On the next throw, the shooter threw an eleven.

"Yo-lev!" yipped the stickman.

"Yes!" whispered Rick as the dealer paid him twenty on the come bet.

"Parlay," said Rick.

The dealer picked up his twenty-dollar win and placed it on top of his other twenty, doubling his come bet yet again. The man then threw an eight. The dealer moved Rick's forty-dollar bet to the eight and was about to place double odds on it again when Rick said, "Ten-X that bet."

The table's maximum odds were ten times odds. That meant he would need four hundred dollars to play ten odds. Rick had a good feeling. He pulled out his wallet and placed four hundred-dollar bills on the table.

The dealer picked them up, counted the bills out loud, and said, "Four hundred dollars on the eight. It's a bet."

The man's next throw was a five. The dealer paid Rick his bet plus odds on the five. Rick decided to not bet on the come bet for the next throw. The shooter threw a four, and the dealer again paid Rick on the four and odds. Rick stacked up his chips and asked for some hundred-dollar chips. He placed eight hundred dollars on the come bet. The man then threw another eleven. The table erupted with cheers. The dealer paid Rick even money on his eight hundred dollars.

"Parlay."

The man then threw another eleven.

"Holy shit!" said Rick.

The dealer paid Rick even money again, and he parlayed it on the come line. He now had $3,200 sitting on the come bet alone. Rick only had three bets on the table now. Ten dollars plus double odds on the original six, and ten dollars plus ten odds on the eight. Rick felt that a seven was coming soon.

"Take my odds down," said Rick.

The standing dealer picked up Rick's twenty on the six and the four hundred dollars on the eight and handed it to him. Now all he had on the table were two place bets: the six for ten and the eight for forty. He couldn't take down his $3,200 on the come line. The shooter took the dice in his hands, did his usual habit, and tossed the dice.

"Seven-out!" shouted the stickman.

The dealer picked up Rick's money on the eight and six. Rick was bummed at first, then remembered that seven was a winner on the come line.

"Seven-out, pay the come and the don't pass," said the stickman.

The standing dealer placed $3,200 on the come bet line. Rick pulled all the chips toward him. A crowd had gathered now and hooted and hollered.

"Color out," said Rick, as he placed all his chips on the table.

The stickman exchanged most of the greens and reds with a few whites and some blacks. The whites were worth a thousand dollars and the blacks were worth five hundred dollars. He put all the chips in his pocket and placed two crisp Benjamins on the table.

"One for the dealers and one for me on the twelve."

"It's a bet!"

It was Rick's turn to throw, but he passed and asked Jules if she wanted to do it. She gladly accepted and picked up the dice. She said a little prayer and tossed them. The first die landed on six. Everyone held their breath. The second die landed on its corner and began to spin. As if the world had turned into slow motion, it just slowly spun on its axis. Then it fell over and landed on the one. She looked up at the dealer, who was about to yell seven when the die flipped over one more time, landing on the six. The crowd erupted in cheers. Rick and the dealer had both just won three thousand dollars on the single throw. The twelve paid thirty to one.

"Woohoo!" yelled Rick.

The dealers were all hollering and cheering, and the Pit Boss walked over to Rick to thank him and gave him a coupon for free dinner for two in the casino's steakhouse. He handed Rick back his driver's license and new player's card.

"Mr. Waters, that was some session you just had there. On behalf of the Red Ruby Casino and all the dealers, we'd like to express our gratitude. That three-thousand-dollar tip bet is the biggest we've had in months. That was quite impressive. Why twelve?" asked the Pit Boss.

"Well, we had seen a couple of elevens and many other numbers, but no twelve yet, and I just thought it was due."

"You got that right. Are you staying on the property?"

"Yes, as a matter of fact, our room should be ready soon. We are staying in the presidential suite."

"Oh wow, well I guess I can't upgrade you then. But please enjoy dinner on us and come back and play anytime. Uh, wait a second, I have something else for you." He stepped away for a second and came back and gave Rick his business card. "If you are interested in a couples massage, we have an excellent spa here. I called guest services and added two free massages to your account. If you need anything else during your stay, I wrote my cell number on the back of my card. I mean it, anything. Suggestions on what to do while you're in Biloxi or recommendations for dinner or whatever."

"I sure... ahem, *we* sure appreciate it. This is my girl-friend, Jules. She used to be a dealer in St. Croix. She was a stick girl when I met her."

"Oh, that's too cool. If you ever want a job..."

Jules smiled. "Thank you, but I'm retired from dealing now. I do miss it sometimes."

"If you get bored during your stay and wanna work the stick for fun, just let me know. We also have a morning craps lesson for the guests. You're welcome to join us and be part of the team. Once a dealer, always a dealer, right? I assume you're not licensed in Mississippi. But it would be our little secret." The Pit Boss winked.

Jules glanced down at the business card. "Thank you, Mr. Castro. Why, we have the same last name. I am Juliana Castro."

"Ah interesting, Juliana. Are you from Cuba?"

"Somewhere down the line, I think. I was born and raised in Colombia though."

"Well, it's nice to meet you both and I hope to see you again."

They both shook his hand, and Rick carried his chips over to the change window. The lady behind the cage counted out the winnings. In a little over twenty minutes, Rick had won close to fifteen thousand dollars. Rick looked at his watch. It was only 1:15 p.m. Their room wouldn't be ready for another forty-five minutes, so they decided to check out the rest of the resort.

A tall, scraggly-looking guy was pulling the handle on one of the slot machines and eyeballing Rick as he got his cash from the cage window. Rick kept his eye on him without him knowing. They walked past him and when they rounded the hallway, Rick told Jules to stand behind him. He put his shoulder against the wall and waited.

Sure enough, like clockwork, the scraggly man turned the corner. When he did, he was staring Rick squarely in the eyes.

"Something I can help you with?" asked Rick.

The man looked shocked. "Uh, no, I was heading to my room."

"Why are you following me? Hoping for a quick score?"

"Uh, uh…" He just stuttered, not really saying anything.

"Let me save you some time and teeth. If you turn around right now and walk away, that would be your best decision. Otherwise, I'm gonna have to give you a little attitude adjustment. Don't let me catch you stalking us again. Do you understand?"

The man nodded and turned around and disappeared.

"What the hell, Rick?" asked Jules.

"I spotted that guy watching me cash in my chips. I've heard of people getting robbed in casinos, even killed after cashing in large amounts of chips. That's why it's always good to get a check instead of cash, but I figured we could use some running-around money. Don't worry, I doubt we'll see him again."

They looked at the pool and spa and checked out the menus at two of the restaurants. It was past two o'clock now, so they went to their room. Once inside, there was

Chief, sitting on top of his cage by a big-screen TV munching on grapes. The room was massive. Rick pushed a button on a remote control, and all the curtains on the huge wall-length window rolled up, revealing a breathtaking view of the beach. Jules wandered off into the bathroom and came back yelling.

"Look, Rick, look!" She came out carrying two plush white robes. "They have our names embroidered on them. Look, it says Juliana in red."

"Wow, that is some service."

There was a massive mahogany dinner table in the dining area with seats for twelve people. A giant bedroom on one end and an even larger master suite on the other. A gift basket sat on the table with a chilled bottle of Cristal and two glasses, plus a welcome card. Rick read it aloud:

"Welcome to the Red Ruby Casino. We hope you enjoy your stay with us. Please feel free to call the number on the back. It's my direct line. I'd love to welcome you both in person. Sincerely, Jack Raynes."

Rick picked up the bottle of Cristal. "Shall we?"

Jules just shook her head up and down like a little girl. Rick poured them both a glass and decided to give Jack Raynes a call. It was what he was here for in the first place anyway. He picked up on the second ring.

"Hello, this is Jack."

"Hi, Jack, it's Rick Waters calling from the presidential suite. I wanted to thank you for the fine service and gift basket."

"Oh, that's my pleasure. Do you like good cigars, Mr. Waters?"

"Call me Rick, and why yes I do."

"Excellent. I just got a case of Fuente Don Arturo Gran AniverXario, which basically is their one-hundred-year anniversary cigar. I'd be honored to share one with you. One of my Pit Bosses told me about your extraordinary session at the craps table today. We are all impressed."

"Just the right place at the right time, I guess," said Rick humbly.

"When is a good time for me to stop by the suite?"

"Anytime, really, we just need to unpack."

"Will three o'clock work for you?"

"Perfect, we'll see you then. Can you also bring Jules a cigar? I'll gladly pay for it. She's quite the connoisseur."

"Nonsense, they are on me. I'll see you both at three."

Rick ended the call. "He's sure a likable guy, Jules. He's bringing us some cigars."

"Yay!" replied Jules.

She opened the sliding glass door onto the balcony. The view was amazing. She put Chief's flight suit on, attached a safety leash to it, and brought him and his travel cage out to the balcony table. Chief loved being outside and the cool fall air was pleasant. The three of them sat on the balcony, taking in the scenery.

Soon, Jules got up and unpacked all the clothes into the beautiful hand-carved cherry dresser and walk-in closet. One thing that Rick loved about Jules was that she never left their clothes in the luggage, even if they were only staying in a place for one night. She had told him that if you put your clothes in dressers and put away the suitcases, it was as if you were home, even if you were far away. She had even gotten Rick into that habit when he traveled alone.

The doorbell rang. Rick glanced at his watch and it was three o'clock on the dot. He walked over to the door and peeped through the eyehole. Standing there was a dapper-looking man in a three-piece suit. Rick opened the door.

"Mr. Raynes, I presume?"

"Call me Jack. Mr. Raynes was my dad."

"Aha, okay, I say that all the time. Then call me Rick. This is Jules, by the way. And way over there on the balcony is Chief, our beloved cockatoo."

They all shook hands, and Jack was taken aback by Chief. He kept staring at him and saying hello over and over.

"As a boy, I had a pet bird too. It was a myna bird. His name was Gungadin. I got him as a gift from my grandfather. He loved to mimic all the animals on my granddad's farm. He'd say, *Hello, Gungadin,* then start mooing like a cow." He chuckled to himself at the memory. "Does Chief do any animals?"

"He does a few dogs and seagulls mostly," replied Rick.

"How cute! Ready for a cigar?"

They all agreed, and Jules offered Jack a glass of champagne. He took it and passed Jules and Rick each a cigar. They were exquisite. Jules moved Chief back inside away from the smoke. They enjoyed the cigars for a few minutes. Then suddenly, Jack's eyes got a little misty.

"I have to apologize. I'm not normally like this, and champagne is for celebrating, but I don't have anything to celebrate at the moment. You see, my only son Tyler has gone missing. It's a very new development and the police are stumped. I'm not sure what to do next. I purchased a billboard with his photo on it and a $250,000 reward for any info to his whereabouts," said Jack.

"I have a confession to make, Jack. That's actually why I'm here. I came to help you. I'm a private investigator and I specialize in finding people. A friend of mine named Carson who is retired from the FBI came across the case file and told me about your son's disappearance. I felt drawn here to help you. I'm not doing it for the money, but I really think I can help."

"I must say, Rick, just like at the craps table, your timing is impeccable. I was seriously just about to start looking for a private eye. Then boom, you stepped into my casino. What's your going rate?"

"Like I said, I'm not here for the money."

"I understand that, but time is money, and your time is just as important as anyone else's. How about this? There's a $250,000 reward for info on my boy. If you can find him, I'll match that. So, five hundred thousand dollars, plus I'll give you three hundred-dollar-a-day per diem. I'm also not charging you to stay here now. I'll have your card refunded. Sound fair?" asked Jack.

Rick's eyes widened at the offer. "That's beyond fair. In fact, it's too much."

"I insist. My son is a little misguided, but I still love him, and I don't want anything bad to happen to him."

"I understand completely. I'll do everything I can. Do you want me to sign a contract?" asked Rick.

"A handshake is as good as a contract to me, if you're okay with it?"

"I'm perfectly fine with that, Jack."

They shook hands. On his way out, Jack told Rick he'd get some current photos of Tyler and a list of his friends and recent gigs. Half an hour later, the room butler delivered the documents and introduced himself.

"Hello, Mr. Waters, my name is Gino. I will be your butler. Mr. Jack told me to take good care of you. Is there anything I can get you?"

"No, Gino, I think we're good at the moment. We're gonna chill in the room a bit before dinner."

"Very good, Mr. Waters. I'll leave you to it. Here's my number if you need me, twenty-four-seven." He handed Rick a card and let himself out.

Rick opened his MacBook and began to do an inventory of Tyler's friends and create a timeline. Starting a database was a good way to begin the case. After an hour of logging names and searching for phone numbers, he felt he had done enough to take a break.

"You wanna nap or go get a massage, Jules?" asked Rick.

"I think nap. I know your naps, Rick, and the answer is yes," she said with a wink.

She moved Chief into his own bedroom and turned the TV on for him. Rick and Jules settled into the master bedroom and put some soft music on, made love, then fell asleep in each other's arms.

CHAPTER FOUR

It was dark outside when they awakened. They'd both slept longer than they wanted to. They planned on going to the steakhouse, so Jules jumped up and made a reservation for 8:30 p.m. She went to check on Chief and returned a few minutes later.

"Rick, can I see the keys? Remember his new chew toy we got him at the pet store? It was meant for a dog, but he loves it. I think it must've fallen out in the back seat of the Bronco. I wanna run down and get it before we go to dinner."

Rick tossed her the keys, and she threw on a pair of shorts, a cute tank top, and her jogging shoes. The outfit she usually wore to the gym.

"I'll be right back."

"Okay, baby. I'll get dressed for dinner."

Rick stepped in the shower. He took his sweet time, and by the time he was ready to go, she still hadn't come back. He looked at his watch and realized she had been gone almost twenty minutes. He grabbed his iPhone and texted her.

> You get lost? LOL

No response.

> Baby, we're gonna be late for dinner.

Still no response.

He frowned. Something was wrong. She was always quick on the draw with her texts.

He put on his shoes and got in the elevator to look for her. He walked through the entire casino, then the shops. He decided to see if maybe she had just finally gone outside to the Bronco and her cell was on silent. He went out to where he had parked and stopped in his tracks.

The Bronco was gone.

What the fuck?

He walked to the parking spot and spotted something shiny. In the grass beside the lot was her cell phone. It was shattered.

Rick ran as fast as he could into the casino as he simultaneously dialed 9-1-1. He reached the front desk.

"Hello, sir, how can I help you—" started the man behind the desk.

"I need you to call Jack. Right now, please. It's an emergency."

The receptionist's brow furrowed, but he nodded and did so. Jack was still on the property and came down quickly to see Rick.

"Jack, something's happened. Jules is gone and so is my Bronco. I need to see your surveillance cameras ASAP. There is no time to waste."

Jack called his head security officer, and he and Rick followed him into the camera room. One thing casinos had were a lot of cameras.

Rick looked at his watch. "Can you go back to 7:40 and scan the parking lot? Especially the north side by the main entrance."

The officer pulled up the appropriate tapes, and they all watched. Jules came into view as she walked toward the Bronco. Thirty seconds later, a man walked out in her direction. He looked around.

"Can you pause it and zoom in?"

"Sure," said the security guard.

"Stop!" said Rick, narrowing his eyes. His heart was pounding fast. "That's the son of a bitch I encountered in the casino earlier today. He was bird-dogging me."

The security guard let the video continue, and the man approached the Bronco. Jules was half in and half out of the car, reaching for something in the back seat. The man moved fast on her and stuck something in her back. It looked like the barrel of a gun, but when they zoomed in on it, it was just a stick. He said something to her, and she handed him her phone. He smashed it on the ground and forced her to the driver's side with the stick in her back. She climbed in and he got in the back seat right behind her.

"If that fucker hurts her, I will kill him with my bare hands," said Rick through gritted teeth.

Two Sheriff's Department units arrived at the entrance and took Rick's info. Rick just paced and paced. He needed to find her. He remembered something and quickly called Gary.

"Gary, it's Rick. Didn't you say you put some kind of tracker on the Broncos?"

"Yeah, it's an Apple AirTag. Each one has one. Why?"

"Someone carjacked Jules. Do you have the app?"

"Yeah, let me check," said Gary. "I'll also forward you the app link, so you can track it in real time. Okay, the Bronco is traveling west on Highway 90 toward Bay St. Louis. It's going the speed limit. If you speed, you might be able to catch up."

"Thanks, buddy. I downloaded the app, I see it. I'll keep you posted."

Rick ran over to where Jack was. He was speaking to one of the deputies and telling him he would have photos of the perp printed shortly and brought down from the camera room. Rick told Jack about the Bronco and the tracking device.

"Do you have a fast car I can borrow?"

"Screw that; follow me."

The two of them jogged toward the elevators and took one to the top floor. Once there, Jack led Rick through another door and up a set of stairs to the roof. There sat a shiny EC135 helicopter.

"Jump in. Let's cut this fucker off at the pass," said Jack.

"You know how to fly?" asked Rick.

"Let's hope so, since we're the only two on board."

Rick followed the Bronco as it drove west on Highway 90. As they got closer, he started to look for it on the highway, out of the massive chopper windows. His app said they were within five hundred yards of it.

"There it is!" yelled Rick.

Jack pulled the chopper lower, and they could clearly see Jules driving. Rick knew she was being forced to drive but couldn't make out the man in the back seat from that distance. The map showed a bridge up ahead.

"Can you land on that bridge? It says it's the Bay St. Louis Bridge. You need to pass the Bronco and land a few feet in front of him."

"Hell yeah I can!" said Jack.

Jack sped up as the bridge approached, and hovered low over it. As the Bronco neared the bridge, it was slowing down. Jack slammed the helicopter hard into the concrete, and sparks flew off of the skids. The Bronco was in full brake lockup, and the wheels were bouncing and smoking. Rick braced for impact, but the Bronco came to a stop inches from the chopper. Jack killed the engine, and the propellers slowed as Rick jumped out and yelled at the top of his lungs, "He doesn't have a gun!"

Jules jumped out of the Bronco, and the man ran at her. With all her might, she kicked him dead square in the crotch. He folded over. She kneed him in the face, and blood exploded from his nose. He hit the concrete like a sack of potatoes. She kicked him three more times in the ribs for good measure. She collapsed to her knees, clearly shaken from the ordeal. Rick ran up to her and gave her a huge bear hug. She was trembling in his arms. Several police cruisers and an ambulance pulled up.

"It's over, Jules."

She began to cry uncontrollably. Rick continued to hold her. An EMT ran up and took her vitals.

"We'd like to take her to the hospital and make sure she's okay."

She tried to protest, but Rick insisted. The carjacker was taken away as well, and Rick was allowed to drive the Bronco. He followed the ambulance to the Ochsner Medical Center in Hancock. The EMTs wheeled Jules into the Emergency Room. By the time Rick met her inside, a nurse had already taken her vitals. Jules started to break down when she saw his face again.

"Is there anything you can give her to calm her nerves? She's been through a lot."

The nurse informed him that the doctor would see her shortly. A room became available, and they pushed her in the wheelchair to the curtained room in the ER. They allowed Rick to follow. They gave Jules a gown, and she changed into it and sat on the paper-covered bed. Rick sat on the chair right next to her and never let her hand go. She was still trembling but seemed to be calming down.

"That guy was crazy, Rick. I truly think he was gonna kill me or at least try. If I had known he had a stick and not a gun in my back, I would've taken him out before we left the parking lot. I know I've told you I'm not super fond of guns… but I think I want one now, and maybe some Mace and a Taser."

"As soon as we get back to Destin, I'll sign you up for a gun safety course and get you a carry permit. I promise, baby." Rick kissed her on the forehead. "Then we'll go out and find you a nice Springfield Hellcat nine-millimeter. It's perfect for your purse and has some real knockdown power. I think there's a gun show next week in Pensacola. We can go check some out there and do some shooting."

The doctor came in and looked at her chart. He had a charming bedside manner. He was dark, tan, and looked Latin. He looked over at Jules and spoke Spanish.

"¿Cómo se siente señora Castro?"

"Please call me Jules, and if you don't mind, speak English so my boyfriend Rick can follow along."

"Duly noted, Jules. The nurse said you might need something for your nerves."

"I think I'm okay now. I did some deep breathing. Rick's been helping me."

"Hello, Rick, I'm Dr. Rodríguez. I'll be taking care of Jules."

Jules interrupted. "Are you from Colombia?"

The doctor smiled. "Yes, I am. I went to the National University of Colombia in Bogotá, and medical school in Pontificia Universidad Javeriana, and also the Miller School of Medicine in Miami."

Jules looked closer, squinting her eyes. "Ricky Ticky, is that you? It's me, Juliana Castro. I was roommates with your girlfriend at U of C. My hair was much shorter, and I think I was in my blonde phase then."

Dr. Rodríguez seemed to search his mind and then a light went off. He let out a laugh. "I haven't been called Ricky Ticky since college. I apologize, Rick, I guess you're out of the loop. My real name is Ricardo, but Jenny, Jules's roommate and my then girlfriend, started calling me Ricky Ticky for some reason. What a small world."

"How did you end up here?" asked Jules.

"Quite by accident actually. I flew to New Orleans to celebrate finishing medical school, and I rented a ragtop car and decided to drive down the coast toward Florida. I got in a small fender bender in Bay St. Louis, and I was brought here and fell in love with a nurse. She's now my wife. I did my residency in New Orleans and commuted to see her every chance I could and eventually landed a position here on the staff. I've been here ever since."

"That's a great story," said Rick.

"Well, Jules, as much as I've enjoyed this reunion, I'm sure you're ready to get out of here. You're in perfect physical health. Would you like to speak to a counselor? That carjacking may haunt you for a while. I highly suggest you speak to someone."

"I'll be fine. If I change my mind, Rick can help me find someone in Destin. That's where we live now."

Dr. Rodríguez signed her chart and gave her a clean bill of health and discharge papers. They all traded cell numbers and promised to stay in touch.

Rick pushed Jules to the exit and helped her climb back in the Bronco. The stick the carjacker had used was still on the floorboard behind the driver's seat. He pulled out a clear baggy and put the stick inside it while wearing disposable latex gloves. It was just one more piece of evidence that would seal the man's fate. He wouldn't see the light of day for some time.

It was too late for dinner back at the casino, and Jules wanted a drink, so Rick made a pit stop at The Blind Tiger in Bay St. Louis. The kitchen was still open, so they took a seat at the bar and Rick ordered them doubles. He called Jack, then Gary, to update them on Jules.

"You want shrimp tacos, baby?" asked Rick.

"Whatever you think, Rick," she replied as she took a huge swig of her rum and soda.

Rick placed two orders for shrimp tacos and some smoked tuna dip while they waited for the entrées. The lights on the Gulf twinkling under the night sky calmed Jules down even more. Rick rubbed her back often and sat closer to her than normal. She needed comforting, and Rick was the man to do it. They closed the place down, and Rick let Jules have more to drink than he did, as he planned on driving.

On their way back to Biloxi, Jules fell asleep. Rick drove with one hand and kept another on her side the entire trip. Once they arrived at the casino, he held her hand all the way back to the room. She climbed into the shower while Rick checked on Chief and got ready for bed.

Alone in the bathroom, Jules curled up like a baby on the floor of the shower and cried. She realized the trauma was more than she could handle alone. She shook it off as she got dressed, put on the best happy face she could conjure, and climbed into bed. She would tell Rick the next day what was going on in her head. She was a strong woman, but a traumatic event like that would try anyone's confidence. She wanted to face it head-on.

"You okay, baby?" asked Rick.

She kissed him on the shoulder. "I will be. Thanks for helping me, Rick. I don't know what I'd do without you."

"And you never will because you'll never be without me."

Rick kissed her forehead and turned off the light.

CHAPTER FIVE

Rick awakened before Jules and put on some freshly ground coffee. He quietly called the butler and asked him if he could put together a special breakfast for them, with an emphasis on fresh fruit and some flowers. Jules started to wake up once she smelled the coffee. Rick brought a cup to her in bed and told her to continue to rest, and that he had a surprise for her. The beds had electric adjustable frames, so Jules grabbed the remote and propped up the bed. She turned on the TV and scrolled to the music channel and played an easy listening channel.

A few minutes later, there was a knock on the door. Rick jogged into the living room and tipped Gino for the spread he had just delivered. He made Jules a tray on the bedside table and delivered it with a lit candle and a single red rose. Her eyes lit up with tears of joy.

"What's the occasion, Rick?"

"No occasion. Just because I love you."

Her lips tightened, and she tried to hold back her emotions. She let out a little whimper. Rick sat down beside her and took her hand.

"We'll get through this together, baby. Okay?"

"Thank you, Rick. I feel so vulnerable. I think I need to talk to a therapist or something."

"I think I know someone who can help."

Rick scrolled through his phone and found the number of a woman he had spoken to before who focused on PTSD. He gave her a quick call and found out she was now doing Zoom sessions, and she had an opening this afternoon. He asked her to hold on and covered the phone.

"Jules, I have Tamara on the phone. She helps people with PTSD. Would you like to meet with her today over Zoom at 1:00 p.m.?"

Jules thought for a moment. "Yes, Rick. Please and thank you."

Rick made the arrangements and then stepped into the living room and called Jack.

"Hi, Jack, you told me to call if I needed anything. Well, I do. Actually, it's for Jules."

"Whatever you need, Rick, shoot."

"Haha *shoot*, that's exactly what I need. Do you know where I can get Jules a Springfield Hellcat nine-millimeter with a three-day waiting period?"

"Are you free now, or soon?"

"Yeah, let us finish breakfast."

"Okay, when you're done, can the both of you come to my office?"

"Sure, we'll see you in about thirty minutes."

Rick joined Jules and made himself a plate of sliced mangos, papaya, and bananas, with two hard-boiled eggs on the side, and a half an avocado. They both finished at the same time, and Rick told Jules they needed to go meet Jack. They got dressed in beach casual clothes and took the special elevator to Jack's office.

"Good morning, y'all. How was breakfast?" asked Jack.

"Amazing," replied Rick.

Jules agreed and rubbed her belly as if she was stuffed.

"Jules, Rick tells me you are interested in getting a small pistol for protection. He mentioned a Springfield Hellcat nine-millimeter, a nice little handgun. There are also other good options and if you'd like, I can show you a few," said Jack.

"Yeah, Rick said we might go to the gun show. Do you know a nearby store instead?" asked Jules.

"You could say that. Follow me into my study."

They followed Jack into an extensive study with an entire wall of old books, and a large desk against the window with a polished humidor sitting at the edge of it. Jack walked to the center of the bookshelf and pulled down the top corner of *War and Peace*. The wall suddenly began to open, and bright lights came on, revealing a huge stainless-steel room with a felt-covered table in the center. Once their eyes adjusted, Rick saw what could only be described as an army arsenal. The right side of the room was covered with semi-automatic rifles and machine guns as well as military-grade weapons. Rick's eyes lit up when he recognized the Barrett M82 Sniper Rifle. It wasn't just extremely valuable; it was super rare to own, especially for a civilian.

"Holy fuck, are we at Gun City?"

Gun City of New Zealand was rumored to be the largest gun store in the world.

"Close, but this ain't a store." Jack grinned. "Just my personal collection."

Jack opened the glass, took down the Hellcat, and handed it to Jules. She took it in her hand, and Jack showed her how to hold it.

"How does it feel?"

"It's good, I think."

"What else catches your eye?"

She scanned the wall and pointed. "I like that one."

"Good choice!" Jack reached up and took it down, laying the Springfield Hellcat on the felt. He handed it to her. "This is the S&W M&P Shield. It's also nine-millimeter with a thumb safety. Great little gun. Wanna shoot it? Hell, shoot both of them and then decide."

"Where? Is there a gun range near here?" Rick interjected.

"Yep."

Jack pushed a button under the table and the rear wall opened up, exposing a full-length double-lane firing range, complete with chain-driven return targets.

"Let's have some fun!"

Both Jules and Rick just stood there with their mouths hanging open.

"Are you Jack Raynes or James Bond?" asked Rick.

"I prefer to go by Jack Reacher." Jack winked.

"Touché."

"Ever shoot a machine gun?" asked Jack.

"I wasn't in the military. I've shot AR-15s but nothing fully automatic."

"Let's fix that."

He slid open the other glass and pulled out a Heckler & Koch MP5K and a classic Kalashnikov, better known as an AK-47. Rick was beside himself with excitement.

"Let's get Jules going first and then we can play," said Jack.

Jack led Jules into the shooting room. He grabbed a large box of ammo and handed them both ear protection. He closed the door to the gun room. It was dead silent inside. The walls were triple insulated and the entire room was soundproof.

"I was about to ask you if anyone in the casino could hear you. You answered that before I asked. How thick are the walls?"

"The floor is three feet of solid concrete, and the walls are two feet thick with shitloads of sound-dampening material. Trust me, no one outside of this room can hear anything," replied Jack.

He instructed Jules on the proper loading and safety on both handguns. He was incredibly gentle and thorough with her. It seemed he had done this before. His training gave Jules confidence. She began to shoot at the targets. She was way off at first, and Jack explained to her that she needed to squeeze the trigger rather than pull it. After several more magazines, Jules was getting more comfortable and accurate. With every magazine she shot, she got closer and closer to the bullseye.

After shooting many rounds with both guns, she told them she preferred the S&W M&P Shield.

"Is that okay, Rick?"

"Yes, Jules, you have to make the decision. It will be your gun," replied Rick.

"Thank you, Jack. I really appreciate you letting me try these. I love this one. I can't wait to get one of my own."

She held it up in the air beside her face, James Bond style, and blew on the chamber.

"It's yours, Jules. My treat."

"Huh?"

"I'm not only a collector, I'm also a dealer. I can also sign off on your concealed carry permit. We just need to fill out the paperwork. Consider it a one-stop shop."

"Oh my God, are you serious?" Jules squealed.

"Serious as a heart attack!"

Jack reopened the door to the gun room and slid open a drawer beneath the weapons. He handed her a locking case, a waist holster, and a cleaning kit, plus three boxes of ammo.

"I don't know what to say, Jack," said Rick.

"Don't give it a second thought. Now, Jules, you can't legally carry this concealed until your permit arrives and I also get your background check back. Just don't get caught with it, and I won't tell anyone if you don't."

Jack handed Rick the AK and took the MP5K for himself. He grabbed cases of ammo and showed Jules how the cleaning kit worked and set her up on a small work table beside lane one where she could clean her new gun. He closed the doors again to the gun room, and he and Rick took turns firing both machine guns. Rick had a huge grin on his face. Jules even took a turn but was way more comfortable with her new handgun. By the time they were done, a three-inch pile of casings lay on the floor.

"Let's eat lunch!" hollered Jack.

Rick helped Jack clean the machine guns and sweep up the casings. He placed them in a bin. Jack reloaded so he saved every casing. Jules placed the pistol in her purse, and they agreed to meet down in the café in thirty minutes.

Jack preordered his special off-the-menu delicacy. Jules and Rick joined him at a table in a small room beside the café. Jack took their drink orders and opened the giant silver serving tray, revealing three of the biggest lobsters Rick had ever seen.

"I took a chance and hope y'all like seafood. This is also Tyler's favorite meal. I figured we could eat and go over what we know so far about his disappearance."

"I think that's a great plan. I called my partners Gary and Possum, and they are meeting me tonight in Jackson. We'll rendezvous there and continue up to Dockery Farms. Gary is renting a forty-five-foot Prevost and we will make that the command center. There aren't a whole lot of hotels up there and if we all stay on the bus, we can put our heads together more often. It sleeps twelve."

"I spoke with Deputy Ron Dalton up in Bolivar County," said Jack. "He said there's nothing new he can add. I also told him I hired you. He seemed open to sharing info with you and working together, which is a rare response from law enforcement, as I'm sure you know. He doesn't seem to have the usual ego issues of other cops. Here's his contact info." Jack handed him a business card.

Jules listened and ate a few bites of lobster then excused herself so she could attend her one o'clock Zoom meeting.

"I'll have some lobster sent up to the room in a doggie bag, Jules. Enjoy your meeting," said Jack.

"Let's get down to brass tacks, Jack," said Rick once Jules was gone. "The first forty-eight hours are the most important. We're way past that. I'm sure you understand what I'm saying."

"Yes, Rick. I know the chances of finding my boy alive are slim. I want him brought home regardless. I also want the person responsible for this brought to justice. Even if I have to deliver that justice myself. You feel me?"

"I got you! What gives me hope is that you told me he had a drug problem, at least in the past, and you haven't received a ransom note. That is actually positive news. Maybe he wasn't taken. Maybe he's just lost. I mean, he was out there at night and may have wandered off in the cornfield. Even if the corn was dead and brown. Lord knows how easy it is to get disoriented in a cornfield. I've done it myself."

They continued to go over Tyler's disappearance, and Rick asked Jack about every person who'd had recent engagement with him. After a long lunch, Rick took his notes and Jules's leftovers back up to his room. She had finished her Zoom meeting and was sitting on the balcony with Chief.

"How was it, Jules?"

"She was great. She gave me some links to PDFs for some additional offline therapies I could try. Also, a link to a self-administered EMDR."

"EMDR?"

"Oh, it stands for Eye Movement Desensitization and Reprocessing. It's basically a light that goes back and forth on a screen, along with sounds. You use headphones and follow the light. It's pretty cool. It's supposed to take bad memories and relocate them so they don't affect you. It's worth a shot. She really put things into perspective for me. I'm gonna continue to meet with her every week. I really like her. Thank you, Rick. I'm gonna be fine."

"I'm so glad to hear that, Jules. Hi, Chief!"

Chief hopped up and down on Jules's lap, excited to be out on the balcony. Rick explained to Jules that they had to cut their casino trip short and head up to Jackson to meet Gary and Possum. She packed all the luggage and called the bellman.

After saying thanks to Jack, they loaded up the Bronco, bound for Jackson.

They arrived at Hawkins Jet Center just as the sun set. On the tarmac sat Gary's new private jet and a beautiful maroon and stainless-steel Prevost Tour Bus. As the Bronco approached the bus, out stepped Gary with a Busch Light in his hand. He waved them toward the rear of the bus. Rick parked the Bronco a few feet behind the bus, and he and Jules stepped out.

"You're the only multi-millionaire I know who drinks Busch Light!" said Rick with a grin.

"Old habits, Rick, old habits," replied Gary.

Gary walked over and gave Jules a big hug.

"You okay, girl?"

"I'll be all right. Wait until I show you my latest accessory."

A white truck approached the Bronco, and two men in work jumpsuits stepped out with tools. Gary waved them over and pointed toward the front of the Bronco. They quickly began to install the towing baseplate kit on the front of the Bronco. With the speed and precision of a NASCAR race team, one guy jacked up the Bronco, and the other guy slid under using a crawler. In no time at all, the plate was installed and they wired it all up for towing. With Gary's help, Rick maneuvered the Bronco closer to the bus, and they hooked it up to the Blue Ox tow bars.

"Let's roll!" said Gary.

"Aren't you forgetting something?"

Gary scratched his head. "Uhh... what?"

"Put the Bronco into tow neutral. And if you don't mind, can we get our luggage and Chief out first?"

"Oh yeah, good idea."

They boarded the bus, and Gary turned on the overhead LED lights and gave them the grand tour. It was absolutely beautiful. There was a rear master bedroom that had been converted from an entertainer's lounge to a bedroom which slept two, and lots of comfortable bunks.

Rick whistled. "I can't even imagine how much this costs to rent."

"Yeah, it was stupid. I did the math and it didn't make any sense, so I bought it."

"You bought it? Are you nuts?!"

"Nah, I always wanted one. It was on sale for $2.1 million. I talked them into $1.9 cash."

"You are one of a kind, Gary! Oh, where's Possum?"

"I sent him on a beer run. Well, liquor and beer run. The aviation center has free loaner cars. I also ordered food and staples from Instacart. They should be here soon, and we can get on the road."

As if Possum's ears were burning, he climbed onto the bus carrying two cases of Busch Light and balancing a bottle of Flor de Caña on top.

"Help, help, I need help getting all the liquor in."

"Y'all know this is a work trip, right? Finding Tyler Raynes is our top priority," said Rick sternly.

"Of course, Rick. I've already called Carson and he is bringing in the Feds. I also called Texas EquuSearch. They do search and recovery with horses, and they're bringing in a team from Dickinson. I had to make a large donation, but they are worth it," replied Gary.

Jules and Gary helped Possum unload the liquor, and once Instacart arrived, Jules put everything away. She was also the most organized of them all and used an app to file where everything was. The endless rows of cabinets and drawers were all assigned letters and numbers, and if anyone wanted to find something, all they had to do was open the app and type a few letters in the search bar.

Rick's phone rang. It was Jack.

"What's up, Jack?"

"I just got a call from my assistant and she told me that a few days before Tyler disappeared, he used his iris scanner to gain access to my vault at the mansion. I gave him access because he kept some of his guitars in there. It's humidity- and temperature-controlled. When my assistant did his monthly cleaning of the vault, he realized The Black Strat was missing. He went back and looked at the surveillance video, and Tyler removed The Black Strat and put the regular Strat he used for gigs in its place."

"Okay, so he disappeared with a black Strat! I'm taking notes."

"No, not *a* black Strat, *The* Black Strat. It's David Gilmour's famous Black Strat. It sold at auction to the Indianapolis Colts' owner Jim Irsay for $3.9 million. The money went to charity. Besides collecting guns, I also collect guitars.

I told you I used to play. Tyler knew that guitar was off limits. I paid Jim six million dollars for it. I can't even wrap my head around why Tyler would take it. I think whoever took Tyler, if he was even taken, may have known about that guitar. It's a major piece of the puzzle."

Rick took a huge swallow, trying to imagine a guitar worth six million dollars. He reassured Jack that his entire crew was already making strides.

"We'll find him, Jack, and that guitar. I have a gut feeling Tyler and the guitar are both still okay. As a matter of fact, I'm bringing in the FBI and Texas EquuSearch.

"Thanks, Rick. I have faith in you."

CHAPTER SIX

ows and rows of cornstalks as far as the eye could see reflected the moonlight as they approached Dockery Farms. There were no RV parks near the famous old plantation where many of Mississippi's blues players cut their teeth back in the day. Jules tried to find a dry camping spot using an app called Harvest Hosts. There was nothing close enough, so they decided to go directly to the last place Tyler was presumed to be: the crossroads.

Gary pulled the bus into the grass beside the cornfield, fired up the generator, and turned off the mighty diesel engine. They all stepped off of the bus. Besides the whisper-quiet hum of the Onan generator, it was dead silent. Low fog floated over the cornfield. It was incredibly eerie. Rick grabbed his metal detector and a headlamp.

After several sweeps near the area where Tyler's car was found, he gave up after not even a ping. They all returned to the bus, and Jules made everyone sandwiches. They talked about a game plan and decided after the sun came up, they'd search the area and then move their base camp to some-place other than a cornfield.

"You have any paper maps?" asked Rick.

Gary pulled out a roll of US and Mississippi maps and laid them on the dinette. Rick rolled out the detailed Mis-sissippi map and pinpointed their location. He drew a twen-ty-mile radius around their parking spot. The circle went almost to Rosedale to the west and Shellmound to the east; north was just woods and open fields, and Indianola was due south. Rick decided to focus on Cleveland, as it was the closest to the crossroads.

"Rick, Rick, I found one!" yelled Jules.

"Where?"

"Bolivar County Expo Center. It's first come, first serve, but they have hookups, and Cleveland at least has some infrastructure, and it's only 5.9 miles from the Bolivar Sher-iff's Department. Isn't that who first found Tyler's aban-doned car?"

"Great job, Jules!"

As if Jules had telepathically contacted the deputy in Bolivar County, a Sheriff's Department cruiser pulled up next to the bus with its blue lights on. Deputy Dalton stepped out and knocked on the bus door.

"Hi, who's the owner? Y'all can't stay here overnight. Someone over at Dockery Farms called it in."

"Hello, Deputy, I'm Rick Waters. This is Gary, Possum, and Jules. Gary owns the coach. Mr. Jack Raynes hired me to help with his son's disappearance."

"Oh, I'm Deputy Ron Dalton. Jack called me and told me y'all would be coming. Sadly, it doesn't change the fact that you can't camp overnight here."

"We found an RV spot at the Expo Center, but they don't open until tomorrow," piped up Jules.

"Y'all just follow me. I have the key. It's part of my nightly patrol. I'll show you where to park and hook up and you can pay in the morning. I'll leave a note and let them know."

Gary drove the Prevost though the double-gate cyclone fence. Rick and Possum hopped off, unhooked the Bronco, and helped him back up to the gravel spot, where they could hook up the shore power. Once plugged in, they thanked the deputy. He said he'd swing by the next day so they could share notes about the mission.

"Possum, did you bring that new drone you were telling me about?" asked Rick after the deputy was gone.

"Yep, it's in a flight case under the bus. Why?"

"What kind of range does it have?"

"Well, unlike consumer drones, this one has military specs and I control it through a sat phone, so, to be honest, I'm not sure it has a range, at least for control. Battery life would be the only holdback. It's supposed to fly up to two hours on a full charge though."

"What's the payload?"

"It'll carry about three pounds without really hindering flight time much. Whatcha got in mind?"

"Remember that thermal-imaging camera I bought?"

Possum stroked his chin. "Yeah, I think I know where you're going with this."

He stepped off of the bus, opened one of the big bays below, and pulled out his flight case and brought it inside.

"I charged the batteries before I left, but let me plug it in and top them off. We can figure out how to attach your thermal camera to the body in the meantime."

Rick retrieved his new thermal-imaging camera and some duct tape and wire ties.

"You can fix or rig anything with these two things, haha!" said Rick.

"True dat," replied Possum.

Jules and Gary gathered around them watching their redneck engineering project. Surprisingly, the camera was snug against the body and didn't hinder the props at all. They stepped outside, and Rick used his GPS to find the exact spot where Tyler was last known to be. Possum fired up the drone, which was virtually silent. Once it was about twenty feet overhead, they couldn't hear it at all. He turned off the running flight lights and took off at full speed toward the site. I agree with him there, I think it should be 'It was almost six miles away, but with a top speed of seventy-five knots, the drone was there in no time.

Rick instructed Possum to do a round square pattern from the center of the street to about five hundred yards out to start. They spotted a few blips of red, which were probably bunnies or gophers. A few large red objects moved, but they figured they were deer.

After about forty-five minutes, they spotted a rather large red object that wasn't moving. Rick thought it might be a cow. Possum lowered the drone for a closer look, thinking if it was a cow, it would spook and run off. As the drone got closer and the ground came into view, they could clearly see a pile of cornstalks lying over the warm object.

"Oh my God, let's go!"

Possum and Gary grabbed shotguns from the overhead compartment, and Rick grabbed his forty-five and three headlamps.

"Jules, stay here, baby. Lock the door behind us and monitor your phone."

Possum sat the drone down right next to the cornstalk-covered object and logged the GPS coordinates. They all feared it was a freshly killed dead body. Still warm. They jumped in the Bronco, and Rick sped as fast as he could. He knew if the person was still alive, they might not be for long. He prayed it wasn't Tyler. He doubted it was, but anything was possible, and he also knew criminals often returned to the scene of the crime. Maybe the heat got too much for him, and he returned Tyler to be found dead or alive and then fled.

Rick handed his phone to Possum.

"Call the deputy! Let him know what's up."

He locked up the Bronco's brakes and came to a sudden stop in the gravel. They all jumped out and strapped on their headlamps. Possum took the lead with his portable GPS. The drone and unknown victim were nearly at the edge of their round square pattern. They ran through the cornstalks, flanking each other and trying not to fall into a gopher hole.

"Stop!" yelled Rick.

They all stopped, breathing heavy.

"What is it?" asked Possum.

"If someone was murdered here and their body is still warm, then the murderer could be nearby. We could be running into an ambush."

"I have an idea," said Possum.

He pulled out his sat phone and flew his drone up three hundred feet.

"Rick, look at your thermal feed."

Rick opened the app and saw the now orange and yellow figure under the drone. Whatever or whoever it was had started cooling down. He saw their three red bodies on the screen.

"We're clear. Great idea, Possum."

Possum returned the drone to earth on auto-land, and they ran up to the spot where the drone had just been. In the center of the cornfield row sat a hump covered in cornstalks. They all held their breath. Gary approached the mound and used his shotgun to lift off the stalks. He leaned in closer and then laughed. Reaching down, he pulled up a huge pile of stalks.

"It's a fucking boar!" hollered Gary.

They all gathered round and put their headlamps on it. It had clearly been shot. A few minutes later, they heard an engine approaching. Headlights appeared coming up one of the cornfield rows. Someone on an ATV was coming their way. He pulled up next to them and stepped off.

"Hey, y'all. Huntin'?" asked the chubby redneck guy dressed in all camo.

"Uh, yeah, is this your hog?"

"Yeah, it's a bigun. I hiked back to my truck to get my ATV. I wasn't about to drag that sombitch through the field by hand."

"Why'd you cover it in cornstalks?"

"Damn coyotes. Last boar I shot was just bones and skin by the time I got back. I thought it was worth a try. I guess it worked."

"Let us help you get it on your ATV," said Rick.

They each grabbed a leg and pulled it toward the ATV. The man folded out what could only be described as a stretcher, they rolled the boar onto it, and he tied it to the rear of the ATV. Possum grabbed the drone, and they all hiked back to the Bronco. The deputy pulled up just as they were getting there.

"False alarm, Deputy Dalton. It was just a wild boar." Rick explained what had happened.

The deputy just sat on the hood of his car unfazed by the story, as if he'd heard similar tales many times before. "A dead boar, huh? Well, thanks for letting me know. I'm glad it wasn't a body." With that, he got back in his cruiser to continue his patrol.

Rick called Jules and told her it was a false alarm, and they headed back to the Prevost.

"That was a colossal waste of time," said Gary.

"Yes and no. At least we got to try the drone and see its potential. It could really come in handy if we are trying to track someone down at night," replied Rick.

"That's true."

Rick's phone began to vibrate. It was Johnie.

"Hey Johnie, what's happenin'? You're up late. No charter tomorrow?"

"I did have one but they canceled last minute. I kept the deposit. Listen, I was over at AJ's and ran into Captain Jim who runs *American Spirit*. We were having a few beers and started talking shop as usual. Anyway, he told me that a guy he knows needs money bad and he has been restoring a Corinthian Cat snorkel boat. He's ninety percent done with it and pretty much ran out of money to start his business. He's selling it for pennies on the dollar. I know we are doing well with *Nine-Tenths* running fishing charters, but most of my trips are half days, and I'm usually back at the dock by three o'clock."

"Go on," said Rick inquisitively.

"I've been watching these snorkel boats and harbor cruise boats go out every day full of tourists. There is a lot of competition, but I had an idea. I ran it past Captain Jim and he thinks it's a great idea."

"I'm listening. You mind if I put you on speaker, so I don't have to tell your idea again to the gang?"

"Go for it. Okay, so my idea is we buy the boat, tweak it out real tropical like, or tiki style, whatever. Then, hire a local musician to play on the bow. No one is doing live music on any of these charters. We could charge a flat fee for the charter and offer free rum punch, beer, and wine, and maybe some small appetizers, and do a sunset cruise for two hours. I could run the boat most days, and on days when I have late charters, I could hire a captain. We'd still be profitable even after paying a musician, captain, and first mate, and since I'm on salary, you'd make even more when I drive it."

"Do you know of any crew available?"

"Actually, I'm sitting right next to a tequila-guzzling chick and her captain husband as we speak. They run one of the snorkel boats but are looking for a change."

"Tequila guzzler, huh?"

"Haha, she's a fine worker and top-notch first mate, she's just blowing off steam tonight with us at AJ's. Her name is Missy, and her husband is Jason. I really think we should give this a go. I can only polish so much stainless on my time off. I get bored sometimes. What do you think?"

Rick was silent for a minute, pondering the possibility of starting a second charter. Johnie certainly sounded convincing, and he figured if it didn't work out, they could always sell the boat for a profit if they got a super good cash deal for it.

"Do you have any photos of the boat? How much are they asking?"

"Hang on; I'll text you."

Rick's phone pinged, and he looked at the photo.

59-foot Corinthian Cat—$92,000 OBO

"Ninety-two thousand dollars—that's a good deal?" asked Rick.

"Actually, it should be priced at around $125k, so $92k is a sweet deal, but Captain Jim told me he's almost positive we could pick it up for seventy-five cash. You want me to go see him tomorrow?"

"Yeah, go check out the boat and then have him call me. After I talk to him, I will make a decision. If I decide to go for it, I can call Samantha over at Synovus and have her get you a cashier's check for seventy-five thousand dollars. Keep me posted."

"Yahoo! We're getting another boat!"

"Wait, what?!"

"I know you, Rick Waters; you're already running in your head who you want to play on the bow. Don't worry, I have a list of solo guys and gals in the area and maybe some touring musicians who stop through here. That won't be a problem."

"Haha, okay, Johnie. We'll see. You're probably right. I am kinda stoked about the idea now. Chat with you tomorrow. Enjoy AJ's. Don't get too hammered. Ciao for now."

"Later, Rick. Call you mañana."

Possum and Gary had already settled into their bunks, and Jules had turned down the bed. Rick caught himself yawning and knew it was time to hit the hay. He took Chief out of his travel cage and let him sleep in the bed between him and Jules.

The smell of fresh coffee and bacon filled Rick's senses. He squinted to see his watch. It was 6:15 a.m. As usual, Possum was up making breakfast. Rick could hear Gary rustling in his bunk. He leaned over to give Jules a hug and realized she wasn't in bed. Neither was Chief. Just as he was about to panic, he saw a note.

Couldn't sleep, Rick. Took Chief for a walk around the Expo just before sunup. No need to worry. I'm packing!

xxoo
Jules

Ever since Jules got her new pistol, she seemed more confident than before. Rick wasn't sure if it was the handgun or the online therapy session. Either way, he was glad she was doing better since the carjacking. She was either actually doing better or faking it until she made it. Rick staggered up, made the bed, and washed his face.

"Mornin', Possum, hit me!"

Possum poured Rick a cup of piping hot coffee and handed it to him.

"Leaded, unleaded, or ethyl?"

Now to most people, leaded or unleaded coffee meant regular or decaffeinated, but the fancy lingo Rick and Possum used meant with or without Baileys, and ethyl meant add a shot of Jameson. If he had said super unleaded, that would've meant an Irish coffee. If he said it with a Spanish accent, it meant with a shot of Patrón XO.

"Unleaded. It's too early for all that funny business, Possum."

"I know, hombre, just seeing if you're paying attention. Oh, look, there's Jules and Chief."

Possum pointed out of the driver's side window at Jules walking toward the bus with Chief on her arm.

"At least some of us are getting exercise," said Possum.

"Buenos dias, boys," said Jules as she stepped up into the bus.

She reached behind her back, pulled her new handgun out of her waistband, and placed it in her purse sitting on the dinette. She did it with such nonchalance, as if she was putting her phone in her purse. Rick noticed how at ease she already was with her gun. He started to think she might be using it as a crutch to block away the pain and fear she had endured from her carjacking. He planned to find a way to bring it up to her in a comfortable way that wouldn't upset her.

"Breakfast is served," said Possum.

Gary stumbled into the galley and grabbed a cup of coffee without speaking. His eyes were bloodshot and he was barely awake.

"Didn't sleep well, Gare Bear?" asked Rick.

"Nah, I was up all night thinking about the missing kid and that guitar. I kept asking myself why the kid would take such a valuable guitar that his dad told him was off limits. I mean, the kid is really set for life because of his dad. Why would he risk upsetting his dad and being taken out of the will? Then it dawned on me. Maybe that's exactly what he wanted. Maybe he thinks the reason he hasn't broken through on the music scene is because he always knew he had his dad's money to fall back on. Maybe he wasn't kidnapped at all. What if he was trying to make it look like a kidnapping, but he really just wanted to disappear and reinvent himself, with no money and no rich family? He's a blues player, and the blues come from the deep south and despair. That could be what was holding him back, at least in his mind."

"That's really insightful, Gary. It's a definite possibility and we need to pursue all of them. You take that one and run with it. I'll stick with the obvious, that he was indeed kidnapped. Each day that goes by without a ransom note means anything could have happened. Hell, he could've been abducted by aliens for all we know," said Rick.

"Or even Bigfoot!" added Jules.

They all laughed and continued to finish their breakfast. Rick's phone rang. It was Deputy Dalton.

"Hello, Deputy, what can I do for you on this fine morning?"

"I have two things for you. We got some results back from forensics. We found several fingerprints on Tyler's car and a very small trace of blood. Most of the prints belonged to Tyler. We found one that belonged to one of his friends, but he had a rock-solid alibi and was hundreds of miles away in Pensacola and unable to travel. He was in jail for a drug charge. He's been cleared and is not a suspect. We also found a palm print belonging to his dad, which would not be unusual since he bought Tyler the car. As per most cases, the dad remains a person of interest. I don't see any reason why his dad would be involved, but we always check the family first."

"You said two things?"

"Oh yeah, the county of Bolivar will be picking up your tab on the RV spot. We appreciate your assistance in this matter."

"Well, thank you, and thank the county or whoever for me."

"No problem. Oh, one more thing. We got a hit on the two footprints we found in the center of the road near Tyler's car. One was a Converse, size eleven, Tyler's size and he was known to mostly wear those. The other was a wing-tip-style shoe, size ten and a half. The kind that old blues guys used to wear. What's interesting about the shoe is, we tracked down the manufacturer, and they told us based on the print on the bottom of the shoe, that those haven't been made since 1922."

"Nineteen twenty-two?! How would someone even get a pair of those?" asked Rick.

"They are indeed rare. I'd say maybe an estate sale or a vintage shop, but someone wearing something so valuable out on a gravel and dirt road is strange."

Rick thanked the deputy again and hung up and then told the crew about the conversation. They decided to split up the tasks. Possum would go about contacting all known associates of Tyler and getting alibis. Gary planned to head back to the original spot where Tyler had disappeared and do some metal detecting and see if they'd missed anything. Rick and Jules would drop Gary off for two hours then run into town to go over all the files the deputy currently had available. It was gonna be a long day for everyone.

CHAPTER SEVEN

The sun was warm on Gary's face as the Bronco took off, leaving in a dusty rush. Gary had brought his CamelBak backpack and some beef jerky. He started sweeping the center of the road where the original footprints were found and continued outward. He searched the entire road to the grassy edge then moved twenty feet forward and did the same circle again, making sure he overlapped by drawing a line in the dirt. He got a few beeps. He dug in one of the spots, as the signal was quite strong. It turned out to be an old square nail like the ones used to build the old plantations. He put it in his pocket; a treasure was a treasure, after all.

He moved to the center of the crossroads, about fifty yards from where Tyler's car was found, and he got another hit. Under some loose gravel, he spotted something shiny. He brushed if off and held it up to the sun. It was half of a cuff link with the initials *WB* inscribed on it. On the inside, there was a little diamond with the letters *VC* and what looked like a lighthouse, then the letter *A*.

Gary frowned. *That's a strange thing to find in the middle of a damn dead cornfield.*

He put it in his pocket with the nail and continued his sweep. It was probably nothing, but he would check the internet later to try and find the maker of the cuff link, just in case.

Jules and Rick arrived at the Sheriff's Department. Deputy Ron Dalton was sitting at his desk with a cup of coffee and a box of donuts in front of him. He picked up a glazed donut and took a big bite just as he looked up to see Rick and Jules.

"Come on over," he said with a mouthful of donut.

He slid over a file overflowing with papers. He methodically organized them in order of the date he received each tip.

"Look, Rick, unlike some cops, I don't have an ego. I just want to find the kid. As a matter of fact, you're welcome to make copies of the entire file folder and take it with you. I'm the closest thing you'll find to a detective in this small department. We sort of do all the jobs, pretty much wherever we are needed. There's only five of us here. No one else has had their hands on this case but me, so that will make it more efficient."

He pointed to the copy machine in the corner of the office. Jules nodded at Rick and took the papers over to copy them. Time was still of the essence, and the kid's life depended on them finding him as soon as possible. She had told Rick she would play secretary, gopher, whatever he needed. Rick's phone vibrated, and he picked it up and showed the name to the deputy before answering.

"Hi, Jack. I'm with Deputy Dalton at the sheriff's office. What's up?"

"Can you put me on speaker phone?"

"Done."

"I got a ransom note just now. I'm gonna text over a picture to you as soon as we hang up, Deputy Dalton. I checked my mail this morning and I saw a brown envelope addressed to me, but there was no stamp on it. It had to have been placed in my mailbox this morning. Unfortunately, I have no cameras pointing in that direction. I'll just read it. It's all words cut out of magazines and newspapers except the money amount, which was typed on a piece of paper and glued. It says: *I have your boy and his guitar. Want $350,000 by next Friday. Drop will be at crossroads. Put it in a burlap sack and hide near first corn row.*"

Jack paused for a long moment to let the words sink in. "What do I do? Pay it?"

Deputy Dalton interrupted. "First, I need you to get that original ransom note to me. How fast can you FedEx it to me?"

"I can do better than that. I'll just fly it up to you on my chopper. Can you send me coordinates for a good place to land?"

The deputy thought for a moment. "Yes, there's plenty of space at the Expo where Rick and his gang's bus is parked. We can rendezvous there as soon as you get here. Put the envelope in a large Ziploc if you can, and try not to touch it any more than you already have."

"Well, I have good news on that front. I was very careful not to handle it."

"That's awesome. We'll see you when you get here," replied the deputy.

"Bye," said Rick and Jack at the same time.

Rick knew that the cruising speed of Jack's EC135 helicopter was roughly 140 knots, so he estimated that he'd arrive in about an hour and a half. He told the deputy he'd meet him at the bus after they picked up Gary.

Gary was still metal detecting when they pulled up in the Bronco. He was way up the road past the crossroads toward a bayou. Rick honked the horn, and Gary's head spun around. He jogged up to the Bronco and hopped in the back.

"Find any treasure?" asked Rick.

"I did actually."

Gary pulled out an old Crown Royal bag and opened it wide. Jules and Rick peered inside.

"Noooice!" said Rick sarcastically.

"Yeah, it's mostly beer can tabs and old nails, but check this out." Gary reached into his pocket and handed Rick the broken cuff link. "That's not something you find every day."

Rick closely examined the cuff link then handed it to Jules.

"I wonder who owned this and when it was made?" asked Jules.

"Possum has a friend who works at the University of Houston. He's a historian and I'm sure he can identify its origins," said Rick. "When we get back to the bus, I'll have him contact the guy and arrange to have it FedExed there. It may not mean anything to the case, but you never know. Oh, there's been a ransom note sent to Jack. We're meeting him at the bus in about an hour. He's flying in on his chopper."

"Okay, great. That means the boy's still alive, right?"

"We hope so. You never know with things like this, but it's promising."

"I met some kids who were fishing over at Lead Bayou at the end of the road and asked them if they heard or saw anyone or anything on Halloween night. They said their mama only allows them to fish here during the day, but they told me there's an old man named Mudbone who fishes here every night. I'm gonna come back here tonight and ask him some questions. I can drive myself. Oh, I forgot to tell you—I hired a delivery company to bring my Bronco up from Destin. Should I get Possum's as well?" asked Gary.

"I think we'll be okay with two vehicles. We can always rent one if we absolutely have to," replied Rick.

Rick's phone vibrated. It was Johnie.

"What's up, Johnie?"

"I'm here with the Corinthian Cat and the guy is ready for an offer. Should I say seventy-five thousand dollars like we discussed?"

"How's the boat look? Are the motors good?"

"He repowered it last year with twin Honda four strokes. They are like new, almost no hours on them."

"Okay, offer him sixty-five thousand and go up to seventy-five if you need to. Call me back."

Rick hung up and they drove toward the bus. In his rearview mirror, he could see a car coming up fast. He was about to move over when the car bumped him and damn near knocked him off the road.

"What the hell?!" shouted Rick.

"What's going on, Rick?" said Jules, grabbing her arm-rests.

The car bumped him again. Rick sped up, and the car moved closer. He squinted in the side mirror to see who was driving but to no avail. He could tell it was a newer model Cadillac. He thought maybe one of those new CT5s, which were straight-up hot rods.

The Caddy bumped Rick hard, and the Bronco spun sideways off the road into a big ditch. It came to a sudden stop, jerking them all forward as Jules gasped.

"Is everyone okay?" asked Rick once the dust settled.

Then he saw Jules's forehead bleeding. It had hit the dashboard.

"Oh no, are you okay, Jules?"

"I think so." She gingerly reached up to touch her forehead, wincing. "It's just a little bump."

Rick handed her some napkins from the glove box and threw the Bronco into four-wheel drive. After a little rocking, they got out of the ditch. He sped down the road toward the Cadillac, but it was long gone and on blacktop now, so impossible to follow. They had no idea which way it had turned.

"Who the fuck was that and why did they just try to kill us? Did anyone get any numbers off the plate?"

"I only saw two, Rick—7C—but it was a Florida plate," replied Gary.

"Florida? Way up here in northern Mississippi?" Rick narrowed his eyes. "That's no coincidence. Whoever that was knew who we are. We need to run a trace on that car. Two letters are better than nothing to go on. I'll have the deputy run it. But first, we need to get Jules looked at. Bolivar Medical Center isn't far."

"I'm okay, Rick, I promise. Just a little headache."

"You could have a concussion, baby. It's too risky. Gary can take the Bronco back, and I'll stay with you until you get checked out."

Jules finally nodded in agreement.

Rick pulled into the ER parking lot and helped her inside. A young male nurse walked her to a room and took her vitals. Her BP was a little high, as expected in that situation. They did a CT scan once they got her into the back. Gary had already left to head back to the bus. After an hour, the doctor released her and gave her a script for some Tylenol 3. Rick called Gary, and he was parked outside when they exited.

"You gonna live, Jules?" asked Gary.

"Yeah, it's just a little bump. I'm fine."

"Listen, Jack just arrived in the chopper. Possum is entertaining him on the coach. I got the deputy up to speed on the Cadillac, and he's running a search now in coordination with the Bay County Sheriff's Department. Once I got back to the bus, I remembered seeing a sticker on the Caddy that said *Bill Cramer Cadillac*. I googled it and found out it's a dealer in Panama City. I'm gonna call them when I get back to the rig."

"Great job, Gary!" exclaimed Rick.

"I forgot to tell you, EquuSearch arrived and in light of the ransom note, it's not being considered a murder case yet, but they are gonna search the area regardless. Deputy

Dalton said the FBI is coming in tonight. They are bringing down a forensics RV and another large mobile unit. I guess they are turning the Expo Center into a command post."

Rick let Gary drive back, and Jules sat up front with him. Rick held Jules's hand the whole way. He was anxious to talk to the deputy and Jack back at the bus.

When they arrived, the Expo grounds were bustling with excitement. Two large horse trailers pulled by Ford F-350 duallies were parked close to the bus, and Jack's helicopter sat a few yards away. Men were walking the horses around on the grass behind the coach, to stretch them out after the long ride in from Texas. Rick helped Jules out of the Bronco and talked her into lying down and closing the master cabin door for at least a few minutes.

Rick stepped back out of the bus to meet the Equu-Search guys. He gave them a map of the area they'd already searched. Possum was on the phone with his friend from Houston and asked to borrow the Bronco to make it to FedEx before they closed in order to send the cufflink. Rick gave Possum Jules's prescription, and he said he'd pick it up on the way back.

"Deputy," said Rick as he shook his hand.

"Call me Ron, please. We're gonna be working together closely, it looks like, along with the Feds."

"Okay, Ron it is. Any hits on the plates yet?"

"No, but Gary is on the phone with the dealership in Panama City now."

Jack was also on the phone and hung up when he spotted Rick.

"Rick, I heard about your car adventure. Is everyone okay?"

"Yeah, a little shook up, but all in all we're good."

"I gave the ransom note to the deputy, and he will be handing it over to the FBI forensics unit once they get here. This thing is heating up. Whoever has my son and The Black Strat has no idea what its value is. If Tyler can keep his wits about him and keep his mouth shut, it'll stay that way. He likes to brag, so I'm not holding my breath, just crossing my fingers and toes."

They all climbed into the bus and sat around the big dinette. The only thing they could do now was wait for the FBI. Gary hopped on and joined them.

"I have good news and bad news."

"Just spill it, Gary," said Rick impatiently.

"Good news is I identified the Cadillac. It's a brand new CT5. It had just been transferred from Georgia to Florida. The two letters I saw on the plate were dealer tags. The car had literally just been taken off the delivery trailer and was sitting behind the dealer's building."

"The bad news?" asked Rick.

"It was stolen. It was actually idling as they were gonna bring it in to service for its fourteen-point check. Whoever took it knew what they were doing. The surveillance cameras show a man wearing a devil's mask and dark gloves hop in and drive off. That's all they've got so far. It could be anybody."

"Shit!" exclaimed Rick in frustration.

After the meeting, Jack flew the helicopter back to Biloxi. Gary and Possum planned to head over to Lead Bayou around ten o'clock to see if they could locate Mudbone and determine if he saw anything on Halloween night.

They were all hungry, so Jules made a large, tasty pot of Goat Water, a recipe she knew from the Caribbean. It was basically some diced-up goat meat and whatever veggies she could get and some special seasoning. Finding goat meat was actually no easy task. They didn't have it in any local stores, but Deputy Dalton knew a farmer who had dozens of goats and had him slaughter one. She also made some fry bread, which they were all fond of from the time she'd made shark-n-bake back in Destin. It was the same recipe minus the fried shark fillets.

They hadn't been eating long when Gary's cell phone buzzed. He glanced at it. "Oh, it's the auto delivery company." He answered it. "Hello? Yeah, I'll run up to the gate and open it."

Gary grabbed the extra set of keys the deputy had given them in case they needed to get off the Expo grounds after five, and headed outside.

When he came back, Jules asked, "Anyone want seconds?"

Gary got half a bowl. The big salad bowls Jules used were massive and filled everyone else up to the brim.

"I find it odd that the kidnapper is only asking for $350k. Either he truly doesn't have any clue what The Black Strat is worth or he's an idiot," said Rick.

"Maybe he does know, Rick," replied Jules. "Maybe he plans to get the money and then pawn the Strat or already has."

"You make a valid point, Jules. Could be a joke on his end, sort of a bonus double cross. Or… what if the ransom note actually came from Tyler and it's basically a 'fuck you' to his dad?" interjected Possum.

"I'm pretty sure he and his dad have a good relationship though," said Rick.

"According to who? The dad, Jack?" replied Possum.

"That's true, we've only heard one side of the story. I'm gonna question some other people in regards to Tyler and Jack's relationship."

After they finished eating, Possum and Gary loaded up in Gary's Bronco bound for the crossroads and Lead Bayou. They were bringing a bottle of Crown Royal and another bottle of Buffalo Trace in the hope of persuading him to talk if Mudbone got tightlipped.

Rick and Jules sat on the folding chairs outside of the bus for a while. The moon was half full and the sky was cloudless. With the lack of light, the stars were sparkling in the heavens and the Milky Way could clearly be seen.

"It's so romantic, Rick."

Jules looked over at Rick, and he knew that look. It was the first time they'd been alone since they'd arrived in northern Mississippi. He took her hand and led her to the bedroom. They made love and sipped on some port wine Jules had found in one of the cupboards. It was a perfect night. Afterward, they curled up and fell asleep, awaiting Gary and Possum's return.

With Possum as navigator, Gary parked the Bronco close to the small bridge over Lead Bayou. A rusty old Chevelle was parked there, and through the headlights they could see a man fishing on the center of the bridge with two cane poles. Gary turned off the lights, and they both walked toward him.

"Hello, are you catching anything tonight?" hollered Gary so the man wouldn't feel like he was being ambushed.

"I gots me two channel cats and a gaspergou. Don't really eat the gaspergou but they makes a good soup base," replied the man as they got closer.

He was sitting on a small Igloo ice chest and had a lantern propped up above him with a shepherd's hook. He was an older black man with crusty skin and more gray than black in his beard.

"Hi, I'm Gary and this is Possum. We're just out here trying to help with that missing boy. Some kids we saw here the other day told us you might have been here on Halloween night fishing. Did you hear or see anything? I mean, if you are Mudbone, that is? I forgot to get your name," continued Gary.

"Yep, I'm Mudbone, but I can't help you. I just fish."

"Are you positive you didn't even hear anything? You like whiskey?"

Mudbone's eyes opened up a little when Gary said that. "Yeah, I like whiskey. I still didn't hear anything."

Possum handed Gary both bottles of whiskey.

"Well, you mind if we sit a spell and have a few drags off of this bottle? Which one do you like better?"

"Free country, I suppose." Mudbone shrugged, and then he pointed at the bottle of Crown Royal.

"Hey, Possum, can you grab those folding chairs and three plastic cups from the back of the Bronco? I'm gonna sit here and see if I can learn a thing or two about catching catfish. Worst-case scenario, I catch a buzz!"

That made Mudbone chuckle a little. He handed Gary a cane pole sitting beside the cooler.

"Too bad y'all ain't got no Black Velvet. That's my kinda whiskey."

Dammit, I have some on the bus. That thought gave Gary an idea though. He quickly texted Rick and told him to secure a bottle of Black Velvet to the drone. He sent over his exact GPS coordinates.

"Listen, Mudbone, if I can make Black Velvet fall from the sky, will you tell us what you heard and saw on Halloween night?"

"Hahahaha, sure thing. If'n you can make Black Velvet fall from the sky, I'll tell you whatever's you wanna hear. Now, let me show you how to hook that crawfish on the line."

Gary had been catfishing for years with Rick but went along with Mudbone's instruction. He seemed to take pride in teaching how to fish. Gary texted Possum about the plan, and he gave Rick a quick drone flying lesson over the phone while he was getting the chairs and cups. The drone was sitting in the lounge fully charged, along with the sat phone. Possum returned to the bridge just as Gary unscrewed the cap off of the Crown Royal. He poured three fingers in each cup and passed them out. They all took swigs.

"Not bad, it ain't Black Velvet, but it'll do," said Mudbone.

They continued to fish and make small talk. Mudbone liked to talk about his family and growing up in Mississippi. Every time Gary tried to change the subject to the night of the disappearance, Mudbone would look away and fidget with his cane pole. Gary became more and more certain he had seen something that night, but something was holding him back from sharing it. After about forty minutes, Gary got a text from Rick.

> In position, wave when you
> want me to drop.

"All right, Mudbone, you promised to talk if I could make Black Velvet fall from the sky."

Mudbone looked up and saw the stars shining above. If he had turned around, he would've seen the bottle dangling from the drone in the sky, about fifty feet above and a little behind Gary. The propellers were just out of earshot from that height. But Mudbone never got off his ice chest. Gary made sure he was looking at him as he waved his arms and said, "Kalamazam!"

Rick moved the drone directly above Gary, and the bottle fell from the end of the tether line. Gary caught it as Rick quickly pulled the drone back fifty feet, out of sight. Mudbone's eyes were fully wide open, and he almost tripped over the cooler to get away.

"What the hell? Is you some kind of devil?!"

Gary texted Rick to lower the drone down beside them. He slowly lowered it as Gary pointed to it. It softly landed, and the props quit spinning. Gary pointed his flashlight at it and began to laugh. Mudbone cracked a smile.

"You got me. A deal is a deal. But first, let me have a swig of that flying devil juice."

Gary took Mudbone's cup and poured out the Crown. He refilled the cup half full of Black Velvet. Mudbone took a big swig and walked over to the drone.

"I ain't never seen no little helicopter like that."

"It's not a helicopter; it's a drone and it's controlled by a friend of ours, Rick, back at the bus."

"Drone, huh? I ain't never seen nuttin' like that either."

"It's state of the art. So anyway, let's sit down and talk about Halloween night."

Possum put the chairs around Mudbone's cooler and hit record on his iPhone.

"I fish 'ere pretty much e'rry night. Been for as long as I can remember. Halloween night I had two channels and a flathead in my cooler, and I was just about to pack it up for the night. I looked at my watch and it was ten minutes to midnight. I started packing my car when I heard a car pull up down there. It gets kinda spooky out here at dat time of night. It made me a little nervous."

He pointed toward the crossroads.

"Still, I didn't think much of it, being Halloween and all. They's always kids coming down here on Halloween tryin' to follow in the footsteps of Robert Johnson. It's foolishness. So, when I closed my trunk, I heard two men talking, then there was a huge flash of light. It was almost as if it became daytime at night for just a few seconds. I ran down the road, thinking someone's car blew up. When I got to the crossroads, all I saw was a car sitting there and no one else around. The car was still running. I got spooked and ran back to my car and drove home. I didn't come back for a few days as I was really skeered. I then heard about the boy missing. I didn't wanna get involved. I still don't.

I gots me enough enemies as it is," said Mudbone with a stern look on his face.

Gary was listening closely, his brow furrowed. "Who do you think took the boy?"

"I don't know. Maybe a little flying helicopter, ahem, drone as you call it."

"Why would you say that?

"Because even in the moonlight, I could see the boy's footprints coming to the center of the road one way and no other prints. Made no sense, that's why I got spooked. I thought maybe a Martian came down and got him. I seen me some strange lights in the sky out here at night by my lonesome."

"Wow, that's quite a story, Mudbone. Anything else you can recall? Anything at all?" asked Gary.

He thought for a minute and gazed up at the stars.

"Nah, not really. I will say this. They's lots of kids go missing up in these parts. Someone or something's taking them. Always young and full of life. That's why I came back to fishing. They don't want nothing from a broken-down old man like me. I just mind my own bidness."

"Thank you, Mudbone. If I think of any more questions, I know where to find you."

Gary patted him on the back, and Possum shook his hand. Possum handed him the rest of the Black Velvet bottle, and they headed back to the Bronco. They began the drive back in silence.

"What do you think the bright light was all about?" asked Possum.

"I have no idea. Another piece to the puzzle."

They drove the rest of the way back without talking.

CHAPTER EIGHT

Gary and Possum got Rick caught up on Mudbone's recollection of Halloween night, and they all called it a night around two in the morning. But Possum didn't fall asleep right away. He put on headphones and listened to Mudbone's recording over and over, taking notes. He kept thinking about aliens snatching the kid, as farfetched as it sounded. Unlike Bigfoot, Possum was a firm believer in UFOs. He refused to believe that earth was the only intelligent planet in the solar system. It just didn't make mathematical sense. As weird of a possibility as it was, he would follow up on any sightings on Halloween in the morning.

He finally dozed off around 3:15 a.m. He dreamed of alien abductions all night.

Knock, knock, knock.

Possum jolted awake in his bed. For the first time in a long time, everyone was awake before him. He heard Rick going to the front of the bus to answer the door.

"Come in, Ron." Rick's voice traveled into Possum's room. "We're just about to have some coffee. Wanna cup?"

"Sure, sounds good."

Possum stumbled out of his bunk, washed his face, and joined everyone in the main lounge. Ron was sitting on the couch admiring the drone Possum had plugged back in to charge before going to bed.

"Good morning, sleepy head," said Jules, as she handed him a cup of coffee. He took it with a grateful smile.

"Listen, I spoke with the FBI this morning and they are considering paying the ransom and setting up a sting," said the deputy. "The area where the kidnapper wants the drop done is real close to where the abduction took place. They want to hide some motion-detection field cameras in the cornfield a day before the drop. They asked me to enlist you for help. They know about your drone and want to utilize it."

"They know about the drone?" said Rick. "How?"

"Well, they are the FBI."

"Actually, it's no big secret," interjected Possum. "I had to register it with the FAA. Of course, they know about it. I'm not sure why they don't use their own though."

"I think because of time," said Ron. "You're already here and the drop is two days from now. Since you're already proficient at flying it and have the thermal-imaging capability, I guess it's just easier all around. They want you to fly above the drop zone and cue them when you see heat heading toward the money, then they will pounce."

"No problem," replied Possum. "Glad to help."

"Whoever this guy is, he's creepy. He sent another message and wants them to tie a long nylon line to the money bag and fly a big red helium balloon to it like in the movie *IT*."

"That is weird," said Rick.

"He wants to pick up the drop after dark. They are going to position cameras all around the money facing every possible direction a person could come to get to it. Between that and your drone camera, there's no way he can snatch that money and get away. They will circle the entire area and roads with units. If he grabs it, they'll grab him," said Deputy Ron.

"Sounds foolproof," replied Rick.

"Let's hope so. A boy's life is at stake."

The gang met with the FBI and went over the game plan. If all went well, they'd have the kidnapper and Tyler back within days. Friday couldn't come soon enough.

All day Thursday, the team prepped for the big night. Possum would do the flying, and Rick would control the thermal-imaging camera and communications with the Feds.

Possum was still intrigued by Mudbone's Martians comment. He decided to do some research and see if there were any sightings on Halloween night. He scoured the internet and found a Facebook Group called ALIENS IN MISSISSIPPI. He scrolled back a few days and saw several references to a bright light in the area that night. They were all ruled out and debunked as nothing more than the moon's reflection off of a silver weather balloon. Nothing too interesting.

He called the deputy and asked if he could send over any reports of stolen aircraft or any other unusual thefts.

He figured he was spinning his wheels, but between what Mudbone had said and the crazy dreams he'd had the night before, he couldn't put it out of his head. He didn't share his curiosity with the rest of the crew, though, as he knew they'd razz him forever and make him wear a printed t-shirt with the saying: *I saw an alien and all I got was this lousy t-shirt*. Still, he felt like he was onto something. A gut feeling mostly. If they caught the guy on Friday as planned, it would be all for naught, but he followed his lead anyway.

"Hey y'all, Jules and I are gonna make a food run. How's fried catfish sound?" asked Rick.

"Hell yeah, and get some hushpuppies too," replied Gary. "I'm gonna take a walk to stretch my legs. I'll be back soon."

While the others were gone, Possum continued his UFO investigation online. His phone vibrated. Deputy Ron was calling.

"Go for Possum."

"Hey, Possum, I checked all open case files for any aircraft thefts or sightings. We got a few calls on Halloween, but those were ruled out as a weather balloon, as we discussed. The only aircraft-related theft even remotely close to here was at a trade show down in Jackson last month. I don't have a lot of info and it doesn't really fit the bill. A couple of drones were stolen. I guess they settled with insurance because the cases are closed now. I wish I had more for you."

"What kind of drones?" asked Possum.

"I have no idea; that's not in the report. You'd have to follow up with the insurance company or contact the guy they were stolen from. I can't legally give you his name, but if you go back to the trade show website, there is only one drone company listed. It was a convention for surveillance stuff, so there were all kinds of spy gadget companies and whatnot there."

"Okay, thanks, Ron. I'll follow up on it. I appreciate the info."

Possum searched for the trade show listing and finally found it. It had happened the first week of October. He scrolled through the list of companies and found Danford Drones. They were an outfit from Chicago. He looked up their website and it listed all types of drones. He decided to call the company and see if he could speak to the guy who was at the trade show.

"Danford Drones, for all of your drone needs, how may I help you?"

"Hi, this is MJ." He used his real name so he wouldn't have to explain the Possum nickname. "I was trying to find the person in charge who was working the trade show in Jackson, Mississippi in October. I understand a couple of your company's drones were stolen? Is he or she available to speak to?"

"Oh, that would be Jacob, Jacob Danford, the owner. I'm sorry, he's actually on vacation for two weeks. Maybe I can help you?"

"I hope so. Do you know what kind of drones were stolen?"

"I'm sorry, who are you with? The police or insurance?"

"I'm assisting in an investigation in the area. I'm a civilian investigator, but we are working with the Bolivar County Sheriff's Department," replied Possum.

"I'm kinda new here, so all I know is that he settled with the insurance company. It was a rather large settlement. I can't really give you that info, but I overheard my boss talking to one of the techs. I heard him say that they can build a new one, and that one drone was a deployment drone, whatever that means, and the other was a recovery drone. They were prototypes. I know the tech is frantically building a new one in the shop now. It uses some sort of helium is all I really know. I wish I could be more help."

"Do you know how big it is? I mean, is it like handheld or larger?"

"Oh, way larger. It takes two guys to load it into the truck."

"Is there any way I can speak to Mr. Danford?"

"He'll be back in a couple of weeks. I can take your info and forward it to him and see if he can call you. I'm not comfortable giving you his cell number, but if you give me yours, I'll share it with him."

"Fair enough, and thank you."

Possum gave the girl his number and email info, then went back to the website to look at different drone models. He clicked on the recovery drone page but got a 404 error code, so the page was linked wrong apparently. He looked at a couple of videos of drones on the page and one that actually flew with a man. It had five drone motors and a seat in the center. It was quite impressive. He'd seen drones like that on YouTube before.

When he clicked on the deployment drone page, it was about the kind of drones that could deliver small packages to people. He had read that Amazon was looking into the technology. It was similar to the one he already had. There was a link for a hunting drone, but it only said, *Coming Soon.*

Gary returned from his walk just as Jules, Rick, and Chief came bounding through the door with boxes of fried catfish. It smelled otherworldly. The aroma made Possum take a pause, and he closed his laptop to join the others for dinner.

"Okay, we got catfish, hushpuppies, baked beans, and macaroni salad. Also, sweet iced tea!" exclaimed Jules.

Rick let Chief hop onto a makeshift PVC stand he'd built and placed on the kitchen counter. He gave the bird a corner of the catfish. Chief ate it and shook his head a few times from the heat. The group all sat down and chowed down on the catfish and sides.

"Where'd you get it?" asked Gary with a mouthful of macaroni salad.

"At a place called Catfish Cabin down in Boyle," said Rick. "We should all go there one day. They have a killer salad bar. The place is cool inside with lots of old photos of Mississippi on the wall. They even let Chief come inside and wait for the food. He was a hit with the kids, as usual. I don't think a single person in there ever saw a talking bird before. His photo will be on that wall soon, I bet."

"After we eat, can we go over the plans tomorrow night one more time so we are all on the same page?" asked Possum.

"Sure thing. I'm stuffed now anyway, so let's begin." Rick set his fork down and sat back in his chair. "Possum, you will be flying the drone. I will operate the infrared camera and have a direct link to the FBI and the rest of the team. They will also position motion detector cameras hidden in the corn facing away from the money in all directions. So, if this son of a bitch thinks he can just waltz in there and take the money, then haul ass on some ATV through the corn, he has another thing coming. The FBI will have a team surrounding the area far enough away not to scare him off but close enough to nab him. All roads leading away from the crossroads will be blocked about a half a mile away. Even if the motion detector cameras miss him, he'll show up on thermal imaging. He's as good as in jail already."

Rick pulled out a paper map of the area and drew the circle that the FBI planned to make around the area and put an X where the money would be placed.

"What kind of bag or case are they putting the money in?" asked Possum.

"He requested a standard burlap sack, like the kind you get at the feed store or Tractor Supply. I guess because it's lightweight, easy to carry, and they are everywhere so it won't raise an eyebrow. Nothing usual about that, I guess."

Possum kept his research to himself. It was just a theory he was working on, and it might not amount to anything. After of couple Cruzan rums over ice, they called it a night. They wanted to get a good night's sleep to be on top of their game for the next day.

Morning came early, not because they were ready to get up, but because Chief started crowing at 6:15 a.m. Apparently, he had learned to mimic roosters since they'd arrived in Mississippi. Possum jumped out of his bunk and made coffee and eggs for the crew. Rick and everyone else eventually staggered into the main lounge, still yawning.

"Thanks, Chief!" said Jules sarcastically.

She kissed him on the beak anyway. Rick's phone rang, and it was Deputy Ron.

"Hey, Ron, good morning."

"Morning, Rick. I'm with the FBI guys and they wanna meet at Dockery Farms around ten this morning to go over the plan and place the cameras. Will that work for you?"

"Sure, Ron. You want the whole team there?"

"Yeah, that would be best."

They hung up, and Rick told the others to get ready to meet the Feds.

"We never discussed my job, Rick," said Gary.

"Oh, I'm sorry. You will assist Possum with the drone and keep an eye out for him. He will be so focused on flying the drone, he'll need an extra set of eyes on him in case someone tries to ambush. Bring your tactical rifle and night scope."

"And me, Rick?" asked Jules.

"Jules, you'll have my six."

"Your six?"

"You'll be back-to-back with me while I focus on the thermal camera. Just like Possum, my eyes will be on one thing only, so I need you for protection with your new pistol."

"I got you, Rick!"

After breakfast, they headed over to Dockery Farms and put the plan in motion. Once the cameras were all set up, all they had to do was wait. The Feds had set up a base behind the main farmhouse, out of view of the crossroads but close enough.

As soon as the sun disappeared behind the horizon, everyone got into position. Deputy Ron placed the burlap sack inside the first row of corn and tied the red balloon to it, then drove off as instructed. The motion cameras caught him coming and going. It was go time.

Possum flew the drone high above the site and then hovered directly above the money bag's GPS coordinates. He lowered it to three hundred feet. It was dark, and he couldn't see anything with the drone's 4K camera.

He kept the drone hovering there for almost an hour and forty minutes. Still, he didn't catch sight of anyone or anything coming to the drop point. The drone was getting low on battery by now. Possum had extra charged batteries, but if he left, he might miss the guy. He didn't want to crash the drone either.

Deputy Ron was starting to get a bad feeling in the pit of his stomach, the longer this went on and nothing happened. Someone should've come for the money by now.

"Something's wrong," he muttered.

He called the lead FBI guy, who agreed. They decided to go back to the drop site. Deputy Ron drove a four-wheeler over and changed into a camo jumpsuit so as to not raise suspicion in case the guy showed up. Hopefully he'd just assume Ron was boar hunting.

He stopped the four-wheeler about fifty yards from the drop site and peered through the scope of his rifle to spot the red balloon. He couldn't see it. He frowned. *Did it get busted on one of the cornstalks?* He drove closer, then jumped off of his four-wheeler and ran over to the spot where the burlap sack was supposed to be.

His stomach lurched with worry.

"It's gone! It's gone!" yelled Ron over his radio.

Rick could clearly see Ron on the thermal camera, as the Feds all pulled up at the same time. The money bag was gone.

Dammit, thought Rick.

"That's impossible!" said Ron. Rick could still hear him over the radio.

"Are you sure this is where you dropped it?"

"A hundred percent sure."

He pointed to a nearby cornstalk where he had used a permanent marker to put a small X on one of the leaves. No one would've seen it if he hadn't pointed it out.

"All these damn corn rows look alike. I put the X there in case something went sideways, which apparently it did."

"Stupid question, but how much helium did that balloon have in it? Could it have floated away?" asked one of the Feds.

"Hell no, that balloon couldn't even hold up the top of the burlap sack, let alone fly off."

They all stood there with their hands on their hips, pondering what had happened. Rick clenched his teeth. This didn't make any sense. How could it have just disappeared?

"We'll need to see the footage from the drone and thermal right now," said the lead FBI guy.

"No problem."

Bring it down, Rick texted to Possum.

He and Jules hurried to meet the Feds at the drop zone. They could see Possum lowering the drone to the ground. By the time they got there, Possum and Gary were pulling up in the Bronco.

Rick removed the SD cards from both the drone's camera and the thermal camera and gave them to the FBI.

"You won't see anything in there except for a few rabbits and a deer or two. Nothing got near the money until Ron came back to check."

"We'll decide that."

"Have at it, Hoss!"

All the teams powwowed for a while, trying to figure out what the hell had happened to the money. There were no stops of cars, trucks, ATVs, four wheelers, or anything on the perimeter. It completely defied logic, as if the money had just magically vanished.

"Maybe the devil from the crossroads did it," said Possum sarcastically.

As ridiculous as it sounded, that explanation fit the scene. A forensic team gathered around the drop spot of the ransom to search for footprints or anything to indicate someone or something had come into the zone. All the motion cameras except for one didn't even fire one frame. The one that did was just a stalk of corn blowing in the wind. Nothing unusual whatsoever. All the team could do now was go home and wait for a call or, God forbid, a dead body to be found.

"I'm beginning to think this guy is toying with us," said Rick, as he and his pals walked away from the Feds. "Do you think Deputy Ron never placed the money? Is that even a possibility?"

"Unless he's a magician, he dropped it," replied Possum. "The motion cameras videoed the drop and him leaving empty-handed. I'm sure they'll question him, but the video will most definitely exonerate him quickly."

"I just can't fathom how the money disappeared into thin air! There has to be a logical explanation," said Rick.

"Let's all go back to the bus and put our heads together," said Gary.

CHAPTER NINE

Two days passed, and there was no call or no movement on the disappearance of Tyler or the money. Everyone was getting tense and somewhat bored with the stagnation of the case. Rick consoled Jack a few times on the phone, but with each passing day, the grim reality that Tyler might never return was becoming evident.

A little after lunch on the third day since the ransom drop, Rick's phone buzzed with a call from Deputy Ron.

"Hi, Ron, any news?"

"I'm afraid so. This is hard to believe and even harder to say, but a small box was delivered to the Sheriff's Department today. The surveillance cameras spotted a young local kid who dropped it off. He was questioned and released. He said a man in a fancy Cadillac paid him a hundred dollars to drop off the box. He didn't get a good look at the guy because he was wearing large sunglasses and it was dark out. He did say he could see there was a patch over one of his eyes though. The box was wrapped tightly in twine. The kid had no idea what was inside of it."

"Dammit, the suspense is killing me. What was it?"

"It was a severed finger. It also had a note—well, sort of a poem, I guess—wrapped around it. The class ring on the finger belonged to Tyler Raynes. We can't be a hundred percent sure it's his finger yet, but we are waiting for fingerprint files from Okaloosa County to do a match."

Rick's eyes widened. "Oh my God. Does Jack know yet?"

"Since you two have a closer relationship than I do, I thought I'd let you tell him. But let's wait until I get confirmation from the fingerprints. I'm gonna send you a screenshot of the note inside. Let's get together this afternoon after you've had time to analyze it. Forensics didn't find any prints on it, and the only prints on the box belonged to the kid who delivered it."

"Okay, Ron. I'll text you later after I go over the note."

Everyone had gathered around Rick during his phone call, trying to listen. He told them about the severed finger and the kid who brought it in. Jules gasped and put her hand over her mouth. Rick's phone whistled with the text of the note. He shared it to his MacBook so they could all see it larger.

You did your job and dropped the cash
Before your eyes I took the stash
That's just the first cuz I want more
Now Jack Raynes is my money store
The next drop will be from a civilian
Just Rick Waters and a cool five million
I'll return the guitar picker and singer
But for now, here's his right ring finger

"That's just fucking sick!" said Rick as he slammed his hand hard on the dinette, making the MacBook bounce.

"How the hell does he know you're on the case, Rick, and why did he call you out? It makes no sense," said Possum nervously.

"I know. Nothing about this case makes sense," replied Gary.

"Let's put all the clues we have on the table," said Rick, getting up and starting to pace. "The guy who gave the kid the finger was driving a fancy Cadillac. The car that ran us off the road was also a fancy Cadillac. It has to be the same guy. How fucking hard can it be to find a stolen Cadillac?! I'll bet a million dollars that finger belongs to Tyler. The kidnapper wants to provide proof of the kidnapping. That's one way to do it. He wouldn't take the risk of sending another person's finger. It's definitely Tyler's."

"Why five million, Rick?" said Jules, frowning. She was rubbing her arms nervously. "That's a big jump from $350k."

"That's a great observation, Jules. I was thinking the same thing, and why me?"

Suddenly, Rick went into a deep stare and his face went white.

"What is it, Rick? You look like you saw a ghost," said Jules.

"I think I may have. I just remembered something. Hang on."

Rick called Deputy Ron.

"Ron, did the kid who dropped the money say which eye had a patch on it?"

"Hold on, let me pull the file."

A minute went by, and Rick could hear rustling in the background.

"Okay, the report says the man had a thin beard, was wearing all black clothes and sunglasses. The patch was on the right eye. The kid was called over to the driver's side window, and he remembers clearly seeing the patch closer to the passenger's side. So, that's the right," said Ron.

"Thanks, Ron. Can I talk to this kid at some point soon?"

"He's a minor. I can bring him in with his parents and you can sit down with him. He's quite upset about what happened and even tried to give us the hundred dollars. My gut feeling is he's a good kid who got suckered into doing something he shouldn't have. There's no charges on him. I'm sure he'll come in. Why?"

"Just a hunch. Let me know when we can meet with him."

"Okay, thanks, gotta run."

"Bye, Ron, thank you."

Rick stood up as everyone looked at him with bated breath.

"Dale Fucking Clemens!" exclaimed Rick.

"What? He's dead!" said Jules.

"Is he? Is he really? They never found his body, and I speared him through his right eye. We took five million dollars from him, and he vowed to get it back. I know it seems like a stretch, but it could be him. My name never went out to the press that we were working this case. He knows who I am, and he wants his money."

"How did he find out you were on the case?" asked Gary.

"I'm not sure about that part yet. I'm not sure about anything yet, but the puzzle piece fits. Once I talk to the kid, I'll see if he can remember anything else about the man's description. Sometimes a new set of eyes and ears on someone can help them recall things."

"Recall!" blurted out Possum. "Remember that guy TC LeNormand we used on the Emily Davis case? He's the one who does hypnotic regression therapy. You think we can get the kid to do that?"

"He's in Houston, right? Do you think we can get him to fly here?" asked Rick.

"Hell, I'll just fly down in the jet and bring him here myself. Money talks and bullshit walks," said Gary.

"All right, Possum, can you contact TC and then maybe you and Gary can go pick him up," said Rick. "Jules and I will stay here and mind the fort, and I'll talk to the kid's parents and see if they are okay with that, assuming you can get TC to work with us."

"Consider it done," said Gary as he rubbed his thumb and fingers together to represent money.

"Plus, TC is a good guy and I bet he'd even do it for free," said Possum.

"Well, we're gonna take care of him anyway," replied Gary.

Rick and Jules drove down to the Sheriff's Department to meet with Deputy Ron. The FBI was also at the station when they pulled in.

"Afternoon, everyone," said Rick.

They all nodded, exchanged handshakes, then walked to the back of the office where the kid and his parents were waiting. Ron introduced Rick and Jules to the family, and they agreed to let Rick ask the kid some questions. Tommy was a typical-looking, skinny, thirteen-year-old kid wearing a Snoop Dog t-shirt and ripped jeans. His parents, Jules, and Ron stepped out of the room. They joined the FBI behind the one-way mirror. A surveillance camera and a camcorder were set up in the room, already running.

Rick sat down across from the kid and gave him a kind smile. "Tommy, as you know, my name is Rick Waters. I'm helping the police and the father of the missing kid. I love that band, by the way. My favorite album is *Ride the Lightning*. Most people like *Master of Puppets*, but I think the earlier album shows off their roots better. They weren't as polished and commercial then."

"Wow, that's my favorite Metallica album too. Cool!"

The kid seemed to relax quite a bit and slumped down in his chair.

"Now, I'm sure they told you that you are in absolutely no kind of trouble here. You are actually helping us tremendously. So, don't be nervous. Nothing you say here can hurt you. It can only help us."

"Okay, I get it."

"I want you to try and go back to the exact time you met the guy who gave you the box. You can close your eyes if it helps. I'll be right here. What can you remember about the man's face and clothes or anything else that might identify him?"

The kid gazed up at the ceiling, thinking. He finally closed his eyes.

"It was real dark and he was wearing all black, at least on top. I was sitting on my bike beside the car window, so I couldn't see his legs. He had a thin beard. I couldn't tell what color because it was dark. He was a white dude and he wore a baseball cap. It was also black and had some sort of emblem on it like a spear, kinda like the ones we use to gig frogs. He had glasses with thick, dark lenses, which I thought was odd at night, but then I saw his patch and thought maybe they were prescribed to him by an eye doctor or something. I didn't say anything about it to him."

"Can you remember anything else about him or the car?"

"I was a little high," whispered the kid, as he looked around the room as if someone would hear him.

"It's okay, Tommy, you're doing great. Closing your eyes worked pretty well, huh? I didn't see anything in the report about the cap. Would you be willing to go under hypnosis with your parents' permission to help remember more?"

"Sure, that's trippy, I'd love to do that. You promise I won't get into any trouble about getting high?" whispered Tommy again.

"You're fine, Tommy. It's not against the law here; it's been decriminalized statewide."

"Phew, okay. That's a relief."

Rick pulled out his iPhone and pulled up a photo of the Maserati trident logo and spun the phone around to Tommy.

"Did the logo on the cap look like this?"

"That's it! That's exactly it!"

A stern look came across Rick's face. His fear that Dale Clemens was behind this was becoming more and more real.

"You said he was wearing a black shirt. Do you remember what kind? Did you see any tattoos?"

Tommy thought for a moment. "Oh yeah, it was a cutoff black sweatshirt. You know the kind where people just cut the sleeves off and leave a little to hang over the shoulder? Now that you mention it, he did have a tattoo, but it was on his right arm, which I couldn't see very well. He did smoke a stinky huge cigar though. After he gave me the box and the money, he lit the cigar with a torch and took a drag off of it. The brightness of the lighter kinda blinded me for a second. That's when I noticed some sort of tattoo reflection in the passenger window, but I couldn't tell you what it was."

"Thank you, Tommy. You have been very helpful, and the little marijuana comment is between us. I promise," whispered Rick.

Rick stuck his hand out and the kid shook it. They both stood up as the deputy and his parents entered the room.

"Mr. and Mrs. Jones, I want to get your permission to have Tommy do hypnosis to help him remember more details about the night he got the box. Would you consent to that? Tommy is all for it. Talk it over and please let me know. I have a guy from Houston who may be able to come here who specializes in that, and he is the best in the business."

"Okay, Mr. Waters, we'll talk it over with Tommy over dinner tonight and call Deputy Ron back. If Tommy is okay with it, then I don't see a problem."

Tommy smiled and vigorously shook his head up and down. It was obvious he was stoked to do it. Now it was up to Possum and Gary to get TC to Mississippi.

Tommy and his parents left as Rick, Jules, and Deputy Ron went into another room to discuss the note. Rick's phone whistled with a thumbs-up text from Gary about TC. Rick sent a thumbs-up back.

"Rick, we just got the fingerprints from Okaloosa," said Ron grimly. "The finger we recovered is a match to Tyler's."

"Damn, I was afraid of that."

"The FBI is doing a DNA match. Apparently, a few years back Tyler signed up for a 23andMe account, so they can get a copy of his DNA on record."

"Okay, I think I know who the kidnapper is. It's a hunch, but all the pieces are coming together. What I'm about to tell you may be hard to believe, but hear me out. The guy's name is Dale Clemens. He had been attacking me and my crew back in Destin. He has some sort of grudge against me and thinks I stole five million dollars from him. That part is a long story and not relevant to the case. Let's just say he's a nut job."

Ron made an *mmm* sound, his brow creasing. But he said, "Continue."

"Some of the pieces don't fit yet, but here's what does so far: he wants five million dollars from me. That's the same amount he wants for the second drop. He has a penchant for Maseratis. The logo for Maserati is a trident. Tommy described a trident on his baseball cap. I'll bet you anything the tattoo on the mystery man's right arm is also a trident. He always had a small beard, and the kicker is, a few months back when he stabbed me, I shot him through the right eye with a spear gun in defense. His body was never found, and everyone, including myself, thought he was dead. The area where I shot him has a lot of alligators. I just assumed one of them tucked him in a gator hole to tenderize him and left him sitting as a bag of bones on the bay floor somewhere. But now I'm not so sure. There is also the sporty Cadillac that keeps appearing. We need to tie that together."

One of the FBI men interrupted. "Yes, he has been officially declared dead in our records. But you're right, a body was never found. You may be onto something. What's the connection to Tyler's abduction though? Why would this Dale Clemens kidnap him?"

"That part I haven't figured out yet, but I will. Trust me, I will!"

"Men, I think we can officially name Dale Clemens a person of interest," said the lead agent. "We've started a statewide search for that Cadillac. I'm gonna run a BOLO with Dale Clemens's last known photo. We have one from a fake passport on record. I'll have one of our sketch artists add an eye patch to the pic as a possible likeness, and another one with dark glasses. We'll try to get some local press to air it."

"That's a great idea," exclaimed Rick.

"We'll catch this sick son of a bitch one way or the other."

Everyone left the room. Rick and Jules thanked the deputy and headed for the Bronco to grab some dinner for the crew and rendezvous back at the bus. Rick's phone buzzed and he synced it through to the stereo.

"Hey, Rick, it's Johnie."

"Hi, Johnie. You're on speaker with me and Jules."

"Hi, Jules."

"Hi, Johnie."

"Rick, I just wanted to update you on the new booze cruise business. I got all the licenses secured. I have a captain and first mate lined up, and with your permission, I'd like to do a big launch this weekend with a great singer who's traveling through. Her name is Erica Sunshine Lee. I heard her at an Emerald Coast Parrot Head Club event at the Elks Lodge over on Okaloosa Island. She can do the first three days starting Friday night, then I can bring on some local guys to play the spots. If this goes over, we can have special events when these Trop Rock musicians come to town. The local Parrot Head Club alone will fill the boat. What do you think?"

"I like it, I like it a lot," said Rick, in the voice of Jim Carrey in *Dumb and Dumber*. "Can you stream her performance? We'd all like to see it."

"I'm sure I can. I've got very good cell coverage in the harbor and over by Crab Island. I'll get it set up. Oh, and I bought a small PA system for the boat. It's an EV Evolve 30. Very compact and easy to operate. You actually mix the sound with a phone app. It takes up a tiny footprint on the boat but really bumps. That will also be enticing for musicians, so they don't have to lug a PA on and off of the boat."

"Great idea, Johnie. Sounds like you've got it all under control."

"Yep, and *Nine-Tenths* has been steadily booked. When y'all get back, if we can set up that sales booth—the little travel trailer Gary got—that will really boost things."

"Okay, Johnie, we'll get that rolling soon. You just keep doing what you're doing, and we will too. Oh, wait, you're not gonna believe this. I think the kidnapper is Dale Clemens."

"What?! That fucker's dead!"

"Maybe, maybe not. Time will tell."

"Well, if he's not dead, he needs to be, after all the crap he did to us. If he ain't dead yet, maybe you can lend him a helping hand."

"My thoughts exactly, Johnie. All right, keep me posted on the new boat project."

Rick disconnected just as he pulled into the parking lot of J&W Smokehouse.

"Ribs tonight, Jules?"

"Yes, please!"

CHAPTER TEN

Rick dreaded the call he was about to make. How was he to tell Jack that his son's finger was severed and dropped off at the Sheriff's Department? He was afraid Jack would lose all hope. He decided to start with a positive part of the case then get to the finger. Jack picked up on the third ring.

"Rick, talk to me. What's going on with my son?"

"Jack, I have good news and bad news. Don't get too excited, we're still on the hunt for him. We are sure he's still alive. After the $350k was taken, we got a new ransom note poem asking for five million dollars. I know that's crazy money and we aren't gonna pay it. Well, you aren't gonna pay it. We are, however, gonna set a trap and make him think we are gonna pay it."

"What's the bad news?"

"This is hard to say, so brace yourself. In the box with the ransom note was also your son's right ring finger. It had his class ring on it, and we've confirmed a match with fingerprints from Okaloosa. They're still gonna run DNA, but it's just a formality. It belongs to Tyler."

A long silence followed. Rick waited for Jack to respond, giving him time to absorb the news.

"Let's get that son of a bitch! I'll kill him with my bare hands."

"I know, Jack, I know. He's one twisted sick fuck. We're doing everything we can to get Tyler back. We have some new leads, and it's a lot to go over. Too much over the phone. I can come to you if you wish."

"No, I'll come there in my chopper tomorrow. I think I'm gonna rent a little room nearby. I need a break from the casino. Hell, I can't even think lately. I'm just taking up space here. I wanna help if I can. Do you know of anything I can rent nearby?"

Rick thought for a second. "Do you have an RV?"

"I do actually. Why?"

"We've sort of set up a base camp here at the RV park at the Expo grounds. Even the FBI has a big rig here. It's the same place you landed before, but it's grown now with more Feds and people from EquuSearch. There's plenty of spots and it's basically the command center now."

"Okay, I'll have an assistant deliver my coach there and I'll fly in tomorrow morning. He can leave right away and drive overnight."

"Okay, Jack. Hang in there, buddy. We're gonna get Tyler back."

"Thanks, Rick. I appreciate everything you've done."

Gary and Possum had spent the night at Possum's place in Houston and planned to send a car for TC around two o'clock the next day, then swing back by and take all three of them to Houston Hobby Airport. Gary's jet was being fueled and serviced there on the private jet side of the airport.

Possum was glad to be home, even for a short bit. He took Gary on a tour of his little part of Houston, which included a quick drive-by of the place where Rick had rescued Chief from gangbangers in Houston's notorious Greater Third Ward.

"It's that house right there." Possum pointed to it.

"What a dump," replied Gary.

The old house was now covered in MS-13 gang signs and other graffiti. The area looked even worse than he remembered.

Once back at his place, Possum cracked open a bottle of Brugal rum he had ordered, and they did the "ha-ha clink-clink" for a couple of hours. It was good for them to bond. They'd known each other back in school, and Possum knew Gary and Rick had been good friends before Gary moved out to Port Neches. That's when Possum had stepped in and Rick and Possum had become thick as thieves. Gary had sort of lost touch with everyone until recently.

"Possum, when I won the lottery, my life was forever changed. I'm really glad we've had this time to talk. I've thoroughly enjoyed hanging out with you and Rick again."

"Me too, hombre."

Possum was proud of how Gary had turned the winnings into more money. Some people who won the lottery had to file bankruptcy within a few years because of bad decisions, but not Gary. Everything he touched seemed to turn into gold—or diamonds.

They stayed up until the wee hours shooting the shit and drinking. It was a good night.

The Town Car pulled up to Possum's place at exactly 2:45 p.m. Possum climbed in and introduced Gary and TC to each other. The drive to the airport only took about eighteen minutes. Gary's new full-time pilot, Clay, greeted them on the tarmac. TC scoped out the plane and seemed impressed as he was offered an assortment of cheeses, wine, and crackers for the short flight to Jackson.

"How long have you been doing the hypnosis thing?" asked Gary, as he strapped on his seatbelt.

"For more than twenty years now. Some people used to think it was hocus-pocus, but strong scientific evidence now proves otherwise. I've helped break some big cases open."

"I sure hope you can help us on this one. We have some leads, but not enough yet. Hopefully the boy you are going to put under will remember more than he has so far."

"You can count on that. Hypnotic regression therapy always brings things closer to the surface. Some things people block for their own protection, and some are just misplaced in the brain. Either way, they come out."

Gary's Bronco was fueled and clean when they arrived. The drive to the Bolivar County Expo Center took a little over two hours. They all climbed out, and Gary showed TC his new bus.

"You can either stay here in one of the bunks, or if you choose, we can get you a hotel. The Cotton House is pretty nice. It's historic."

"This bus is extremely opulent and I appreciate the offer, but I need to prepare for tomorrow's session with the boy, and I need total quiet and isolation for that. I hope you understand and are not offended."

"I get it. No worries at all. I'll drive you over in the Bronco. If you have a few minutes, Rick and Jules will be here. He just texted me from the Sheriff's Department. You know Rick already."

"Sure, I can relax a bit."

TC took a seat on the big leather couch, and Gary poured a few glasses of wine. TC waved his off as he wanted a clear head for the hypnosis in the morning.

After TC met Jules and went over what the kid already knew from Rick, Gary took him to the historic 3.5-star hotel in Cleveland. It had been a long day, and Possum excused himself to a bunk. It wasn't long before Jules and Rick also headed off to bed with Chief in tow.

Everyone met at the Sheriff's Department at nine o'clock the next morning. Rick introduced TC to Tommy and his parents and then let the two of them take seats in the main interview room. Rick and the crew sat behind the one-way mirror, watching and listening. TC talked calmly and quietly with Tommy. He explained to him how the procedure worked, and Tommy seemed quite fascinated.

"All right, Tommy, let's begin. Close your eyes. I want you to relax all your muscles. Start at the top of your head.

Imagine calm waves flowing down the side of your temples. Now feel your neck relax into your shoulders. Warm tingles flowing from your shoulders down your arms to your fingertips. Now take a deep breath and hold it. Now slowly exhale. Imagine the air leaving your nose as your chest falls. Do it again. Now breathe in for six seconds with me, hold it, and slowly exhale for four seconds. Feel the muscles in your chest relax and let it flow down to your waist. Your legs are now melting into the chair and your feet are weightless. I'm going to count to three and on three, you will be sitting on your bicycle next to the man who gave you the box. One... two... three. What do you see?"

"I see a silver Cadillac pass me on my bicycle and stop on the side of the road in front of me. I'm feeling nervous because I've never seen this car before. I'm way out in the cornfields. I stop and wait for him to leave. He waves me forward and says he has a job for me."

"What do you see on the back on the Cadillac? Plates? Bumper stickers?"

"I see old-looking Mississippi plates and a sticker."

"What is on the sticker? Is it a bumper sticker?"

"No, it's an emblem. It says, *Bill Cramer Cadillac— Panama City, Florida.*"

"Very good, Tommy. What's the man doing?"

"He's holding out a hundred-dollar bill and waving me forward. I'm scared but I've never had a hundred-dollar bill before. I push my bike up slowly with my foot on the pedal, ready to blast off into the cornfield if he tries anything weird. He seems like a nice guy though."

"What does he say?"

"He says if I bring this box to the Sheriff's Department, he'll give me a hundred dollars. I ask him why he can't do it and he says because he has a ticket there and inside the box is a check to pay for the ticket and he is late to drive out to Tunica. He hands me the box and the hundred-dollar bill."

"Okay, what's he wearing?"

"He has a black sweatshirt on with the sleeves cut off and a black baseball cap with a frog gig logo on it. A fancy frog gig. He's wearing dark thick-rimmed sunglasses and he has a patch over his right eye. He thanks me for helping out and pulls out a cigar to light it. It's bright in the darkness of the cornfield."

"Does he have a tattoo? What is it?"

"Yes! I see it in the reflection of the passenger side glass. It's the same fancy frog gig like on his hat. This guy must really like to gig frogs."

"Anything else, Tommy?"

"He peels out, throwing gravel in my eyes. I don't think he meant to because he was so nice. I tuck the box under my arm and head for the Sheriff's Department. I just set the box by the front door and leave."

"All right, Tommy, I'm gonna count backward from three and you will immediately be back here and conscious with me. Three... two... one. Awaken."

Tommy opened his eyes and looked around the room.

"Did I do good?"

"You did great, Tommy. Thank you."

TC shook Tommy's hand and led him out of the room, back to where his parents were waiting. They all thanked Tommy for his help. After he and his parents left, the FBI and Rick's crew assembled in the war room Deputy Ron had started.

"I think we have to name Dale Clemens as a main suspect now," said Rick.

"Not so fast, Rick. All we have is someone who might fit the description of a supposed dead guy," replied Deputy Ron. "A tattoo and a ball cap of a trident don't mean it's Dale Clemens."

"That's true, I guess. I just feel it in my gut. It's definitely a guy in a stolen CT5 Cadillac from Panama City. That much we can conclude."

"I'd have to concur with that," said Ron.

"So, where do we go from here?"

"We have an APB out for anyone matching Dale Clemens's description. We have artist renderings going out on all the local news affiliates, and we're waiting for instructions to set a trap for the five-million-dollar drop. All we can do now is wait for him to make his next move," said the lead FBI agent.

"This is bullshit!" yelled Rick. "The kid could be buried in a small grave with little oxygen to survive. Who knows what this sick fuck will do! We need to find this kid!"

Ron patted Rick on the back to try and calm him down.

"We also sent the box to Quantico, and on one of the strings that tied the box together, we found a tiny strand of DNA," said the agent. "It's not enough to make a full DNA report, but it's known as mitochondrial DNA. That basically means if it is Dale Clemens's DNA, we can match it to one of his relatives, and if it's a match, it'll go back to fifty-two generations. That'll make the chances that it's either him or a close relative. Still won't prove it's him, but it'll get us a lot closer."

Rick was upset, confused, and concerned. He had been so certain Clemens was dead, but the more he learned about this kidnapper, the more he was convinced Clemens had survived and was involved in this mess. An uneasiness settled over Rick.

The crew headed back to the bus, and Gary arranged for TC to fly back to Houston. He told his pilot to drop off TC, arrange for ground transportation for him, and return the jet to Cleveland Municipal Airport instead of Jackson. It didn't have all the same facilities and services as Jackson, but it was much closer and offered fuel. Gary had just had the jet fully serviced, so he thought it would be better to keep it close by.

Once back on the bus, it was obvious to everyone that Rick was antsy. He was pacing back and forth from the lounge to the master bedroom as if he was trying to set the pace for a brisk workout.

"Hombre, have a seat. You're making me nervous," said Possum.

"I can't. I can't sit. All I can think about is that kid, Tyler. I keep seeing him gasping for his last breath in some shallow grave just below the dead, decaying cornfield. I should've never watched that damn movie *Buried* with Ryan Reynolds. It's driving me nuts and giving me claustrophobia. I need to get off this bus for a couple of days."

"That's a great idea, Rick," said Possum. "Why don't you and Jules head over to Tunica for a couple days and clear your head? They have Vegas-style casinos there, and the Gold Strike has a pool, golf course, and a nice spa. I went there once for a treasure hunters convention a few years back. It's real swanky."

"Is it pet friendly?" asked Jules.

"Let me check." Possum googled the Gold Strike Casino. "No, it's not, but that has never stopped Rick before. You really need to clear your mind, Rick. I think it would do you some good. It's only an hour north of here. Gary and I can hold down the fort, and if we need you, it won't take any time for you to get back."

Rick sighed, running a hand through his hair. "Maybe you're right, Possum. Jules, you up for a little road trip?"

She grinned and clapped her hands together. "I'm gonna go pack!"

Jules put together a single suitcase for Rick and her to share. He let her pick out his clothes. She was better at it than he was anyway. They left before sunset. Chief was extra excited. He must've been getting cramped inside the bus himself. Rick had called the casino after Possum gave him the idea, and they'd told him they had plenty of rooms.

The drive was nice and mostly flat through dead brown remnants of corn and beans, beans and corn. It had been one of the driest years in history, and most of the fields lay in ruin. It was cheaper to just call the crop a loss than to try and harvest it. The farms were subsidized, and in the spring, they would all be cut and replanted in hopes for a better season. The brown fields all ran together like a sea of dead plants. It seemed so odd that all they saw were flat cornfields and almost no houses or stores except for the occasional gas station. And then, boom, out of nowhere sprang up a massive gold-window-tinted, thirty-one-story, high-rise casino. It looked so out of place.

Jules stayed in the Bronco with Chief while Rick went inside to check in. Jules would transfer Chief to the clever JanSport backpack Rick had designed with a perch and stainless screens. Anyone seeing her with the backpack would have no idea an umbrella cockatoo was sitting inside. As long as he had grapes, he was silent.

"I need a room for two, King, non-smoking please," said Rick as he passed his ID and credit card over to the man behind the check-in desk.

"Ah, Mr. Waters, you already have a paid-for room. It's the Hawthorne Suite. All room charges, taxes, and amenities have been paid for by Mr. Gary Haas. How many keys?"

"Two, please."

"Will you be needing any help with your luggage?"

"No, we only have one bag and a couple of backpacks. We're good."

Rick took the keys and headed back to the Bronco. He chuckled to himself. *That Gary is something else!*

"All right, Jules, you ready? That sneaky Gary prepaid for a suite for us. I gotta do something nice for that guy. He's always showering us with gifts."

"He is, Rick. He's a good friend."

They made their way through the casino to the elevators and up to their suite. It was expansive and featured a small bar, couch, and a widescreen TV. The view was nice as the sun went below the horizon. On the desk sat a large gift basket. The card read:

Enjoy y'all's stay. It wasn't easy getting a bottle of thirty-two-year-old Flor de Caña in the middle of nowhere, but I did it. Put all meals and spa or whatever on the room. I got you covered. Y'all have fun.

Gary

There was also a bag of macadamia nuts, red grapes, two bottles of Caymus Cabernet, and assorted cheeses and crackers. Jules put together the PVC perch stand that Rick had built for short trips when a cage wasn't possible. She set it on the center of the small bar far enough from the wall that Chief couldn't get himself in trouble by chewing the wallpaper. Chief was high enough up that he would just stay on the perch. He still had his brace on from surgery. Someone had caused Chief's injury, and Rick was pretty sure that someone was Dale Clemens. One more reason he wanted to nail that son of a bitch to the wall.

"You hungry, Jules?"

"I'm famished. What's good here?"

Rick opened the hotel directory. There were four main restaurants in the hotel, plus a pastry shop and a Topgolf Swing Suite where you could drive balls into an indoor screen and eat a burger with beers while you played. Rick definitely wanted to do that, but for now he chose the Chicago Steakhouse.

"Cow, Jules?"

"Moo-moo!"

"We should bring a bottle of this Caymus and just pay the cork fee. I doubt they even have wine this good," said Rick.

"Let's bring two!"

Rick took his laptop and other electrical gadgets out of his backpack and put the two bottles inside. He secured the PVC feeding and watering bowls for Chief, patted him on the head, and they were out the door. He had forgotten to make a reservation, but when he got there and gave them his name, Gary had already secured a private room for them to dine in. He knew Rick too well and knew the first place he'd eat at was the steakhouse.

The hostess directed Rick and Jules to a small, quaint room with a candlelit table. The waiter came in and introduced himself as Tony. He opened a bottle of the Caymus with a raised eyebrow and poured two glasses for them.

"Nice wine," said Tony.

"Thanks, it's from a friend."

Jules scanned the menu, mainly to see what sides she would get. Rick knew she would go for a rib eye. He sipped on his wine and clinked his glass with Jules's, and finally opened his menu. He chose the porterhouse, and they ordered a couple of crab cakes for both of them as an appetizer.

He was surprised by how good the crab cakes were, out in the middle of a field of corn. Both his and Jules's steaks were perfectly prepared, and the twice-baked potato and creamed spinach were exquisite. They were both soon stuffed and opted to take the unopened bottle of Caymus back to the room.

On their way back, Rick heard some hooting and hollering at the craps table.

"Go, Rick, I'll take the bottle up. I wanna try the Jacuzzi. Don't use all your energy on the craps table. You're gonna need it tonight!" Jules winked at him.

Rick kissed Jules on the forehead. She knew how much he loved to play craps, and he loved that she wanted him to. She was the perfect girl. Never jealous and never smothering. She had no reason to ever be jealous anyway. Rick was enamored with her.

She disappeared into the elevator as Rick pulled out two hundred-dollar bills. He played the pass line with double odds and won a little, then lost a couple of throws. He just wasn't into it. The thought of Tyler being in a coffin with just enough oxygen for a few days haunted him. He knew it was all in his head and he was associating it with the movie, but still, it bothered him. He cashed in his chips after just fifteen minutes at the table and headed up to the suite.

Jules was covered in bubbles in the bathtub when Rick stepped inside their room.

"The water is magnificent," she called out to him. "Join me, Rick."

Normally, he would've been all in, but he hesitated. "I think I'm gonna shower instead," he said. "Sorry, Jules, I'm just feeling pretty anxious about everything. In a bit of a funk."

She understood. After Rick's shower, Jules dried off too and walked Rick over to the bed and sat down beside him.

"Do you wanna talk about it, Rick? I'm a good listener."

"Not really, Jules. I just feel out of control, like he's winning and we can't even get a leg up. I'm afraid the kid is gonna be murdered if he hasn't been already."

Jules rubbed his hands with hers and put her head on his shoulder. She just listened and tried to comfort him. She was worried about Rick. She had never seen this side of him, except once when he found out another guy he was looking for was murdered in St. Croix. He'd snapped out of it pretty fast though. This time seemed different.

"Listen, Rick, I know it's all gonna turn out fine. There's no way a scumbag like Dale Clemens can outsmart the great Rick Waters!" she said with excitement, trying to cheer him up.

She stood up and straddled him on the bed, wrapping her legs around his waist. Her robe came open and her bare breasts were pressed up against him. She started kissing him. Soon they were making love. It was passionate and tender. Afterward, they collapsed together in each other's arms.

"Thanks, babe," said Rick with a long sigh, and she snuggled into him. "I'm feeling better already. I promise I'll be more fun in the morning."

CHAPTER ELEVEN

"Cock-a-doodle-doo! Cock-a-doodle-doo!" belted out Chief at 6:13 a.m.

Rick and Jules both jumped out of their skin. Rick bolted out of bed and grabbed Chief and came back to bed, placing him in between himself and Jules.

"Shhhh, Chief, you're gonna get us thrown out of here."

Chief nuzzled Jules under her chin and cooed like a baby.

"He's so cute, Rick. Don't be mad at him. He just wanted to be near us."

"I know, but at 6:13 a.m.?"

Rick glanced down at his watch and noticed the date. He picked up his iPhone and opened his Notes app.

"Today's the day, Chief!"

"What, Rick?" asked Jules.

"Today Chief can take off his wing brace. We should celebrate!"

"Yay, Chief! Yay, Chief!" exclaimed Jules, sending Chief into full excitement mode.

His crest was fully raised, and his eyes were dancing. He was squirming under the covers like a newborn puppy.

"Well, since we're up, we may as well get some coffee. Bagels, Jules?"

"Si, señor."

Rick called room service. When they knocked on the door, Jules scooted into the bathroom with Chief and gave him a grape to keep him quiet. After the room service waiter left, she came out and put Chief back on his PVC perch. He seemed content and relaxed now and hopefully wouldn't do his spot-on impersonation of a Rhode Island Red rooster anymore.

"Hey, Jules, I was thinking. After breakfast, how about we try out that Topgolf Swing Suite for an hour? If I can still swing the old clubs, maybe we can book a round at the course for early afternoon. Or we could hit the pool or try out the spa?"

"Sounds like the perfect day. I used to be pretty good though, Rick." She smirked at him. "Don't get mad if I beat you."

"Haha, I don't care either way. As long as we can get some cold beers on the course and enjoy the day, I'll be happy."

"Let's do it."

After breakfast, Rick slowly removed the Velcro tabs that were holding the brace on Chief's wing. He still had a small bald spot on his chest and wing from the surgery site. Once Rick pulled off the brace, Chief spread both of his wings outward and started flapping slowly at first, then fast. He stood on one foot and spread out his previously damaged wing. It looked as though he was doing some sort of fancy bird yoga pose. He hopped up and down on the perch and looked relieved to finally get the brace off.

Rick gave him fresh water and a few grapes and some of the macadamia nuts in his PVC bowl. He gave Chief the whisper sign with his finger in front of his lips, and he and Jules took off for the Topgolf Swing Suite. It had just opened, and they were the first customers of the day.

"Two, please?" asked Rick.

"We don't normally open until eleven, but I came in early to do some calibrating on one of the video screens. We don't have our bar staff here yet, but I think I can get room service to bring you something, if you'd like. I'll set y'all up with a bay. Play as long as you like. Just give me your room number."

The man led them to a beautiful room adorned with leather couches and a wall-sized video screen. They were given two full sets of clubs and even two hockey sticks in case they wanted to hit like Happy Gilmore.

"Just use the house phone if you want room service. My name is Gill. I'll be in bay three doing nerdy tech stuff if you need me."

"Thanks, Gill. We'll take it from here."

Rick gave Gill his room number and called room service. He covered the phone with his mouth.

"Bloody Mary, Jules?"

"Can I get a mimosa instead?"

"Sure, baby, whatever you want." He asked the guy on the phone, "Can you bring us some mimosa setups and two spicy Bloody Marys? Yes, that's correct, to the Topgolf Suite Bay One."

Rick hung up and checked out the drivers with Jules. She picked up the hockey stick and looked confused.

"That's pretty funny," said Rick.

"Hockey?"

"Nah, it's from a movie. I'll have to show you sometime."

They took turns driving balls into the screen. The screen was flexible and the balls just softly bounced back to the ground even with the hardest swing. The technology was impressive. The ball would hit the screen and enter the simulated golf course with no delay. The flight of the ball was just as if you had struck a real ball on a real course. Dual-tracking technology used cameras and infrared tracking to measure the ball's speed and trajectory. Then they could go back and replay their swing on the big screen from above to judge how well they'd hit. There were eighty-four world championship courses to choose from. They started with a driving range then played a small par three nine-hole course. Rick scrolled though the choices and actually did find hockey. He felt a little embarrassed for thinking the hockey sticks were for hitting golf balls. They tried their hand at hockey, and Jules beat the crap out of Rick.

"How did you get so good at hockey, Jules? You are from Colombia."

She grinned at him. "We have a national team, men's and women's, but no arena. They practice with roller hockey until it's time for the games and then they fly up to Florida to get as much ice time as they can before the tournament. In college, I worked with the women's team one year. I got school credit for it. I flew up with them, and after they'd get off the ice, I had to put away all the gear and clean up.

I always got an hour or so to shoot at the net for fun once everyone left."

"Wow, Jules, you never cease to amaze me."

After two heavy rounds of mimosas and Bloody Marys, they decided to check on Chief and then head to the pool for a while. Rick texted Possum to see if there was any movement on the case.

Nada, came the reply.

He also thanked Gary via text for the great room and well-needed getaway for him and Jules. They took their swimsuits down to the pool and changed in the dressing rooms so they'd have some street clothes to go to lunch in. Rick got in the hot tub and realized his arms were sore from swinging the clubs so much. They opted to pass on a round of nine holes on the real course, figuring they might be able to do it the last day.

After an hour in the pool, they grabbed lunch at the buffet and then went into the spa for a couple's massage. It was glorious. They were close enough that they could hold hands, which they did often.

It was only two thirty when their massage ended. Chief waking them up early had made for a great day full of activities and more time left to play.

"Now what, Rick?"

Rick thought for a second. "Have you ever been to Beale Street?"

"Nope, I've never even heard of it."

"It's a cool street in Memphis, only about forty-five minutes from here. It's kinda like a little Bourbon Street, but with more emphasis on blues. They have B.B. King's Blues Club there."

"Oh, I love him. My daddy used to play his records all the time when I was a little girl."

Jules started humming "The Thrill Is Gone."

"All right, it's settled. Let's get cleaned up and we can grab Chief and head up in the Bronco. They have some great restaurants there too. It's pretty laid-back. Chief will not be a problem there."

Chief was being extra quiet in the JanSport backpack as they entered the elevator down to the lobby. Once in the Bronco, Jules took him out of the makeshift carrier and put him on her lap. Rick set the GPS for Beale Street. It said the drive would take them fifty-one minutes with traffic.

They arrived and parked in a covered parking garage right off of Beale Street on Second Street, only a three-minute walk to B.B. King's place. They decided to walk the entire street for exercise and sightseeing, plus it was only a little after five thirty.

"You want a Big Ass Beer, Jules?"

"Just a regular."

Rick just laughed and pointed to a kiosk up ahead with a huge sign that read, *Big Ass Beer.* Jules laughed and they both got one for fun. They were *big*—thirty-two ounces. Rick chugged his and helped Jules finish the last quarter of hers. She just couldn't fit it in. They kept walking and doing the tourist thing. Jules carried Chief on her arm for a while, then the bird hopped onto Rick's shoulder. Several people stopped to take photos.

Around seven o'clock, they entered B.B. King's Blues Club. They could hear the live music all the way down the street. Chief was snug as a bug in a rug in the back-pack, munching on his allotted grapes. It was fairly dark inside, and no one was the wiser. A guy was playing piano and ripping it up. Rick walked up and tipped him a twenty after his set. He thanked Rick and introduced himself as Mitch Woods.

"I'm the original boogie-woogie piano guy," said Mitch.

"Nice to meet you, Mitch. Not only did you tickle those ivories, but I think you sent them into a tickle frenzy!"

Mitch laughed, stepped off the stage, and joined Jules and Rick for a drink. Another act was setting up on the main stage. Mitch talked about a Blues Cruise he did every year in the Caribbean and told them they should consider going on it sometime. They exchanged cards, and when Mitch saw Destin, Florida, on Rick's card, he got excited.

"Man, I love playing down there. I usually roll through there on my way to or from New Orleans. I play at the Funky Blues Shack. Well, I used to. I heard they closed."

"That's true, they did. I tell you what, now that I know what kind of music you play, I'll shoot you a text if I find a venue you might like."

"I sure appreciate that, Rick. I wish I could stay longer, but I need to head to Nashville. I'm playing a little show at 3rd and Lindsley tomorrow night."

"Okay, Mitch, be safe out there on the road and keep doing what you do."

Mitch left, and Jules and Rick ordered another round of drinks called the Hoochie Coochie Man. They listened to most of the next trio's set then decided it was time to head back to Tunica. It had been a long day. Since it was dark and the area felt a little sketchy, Rick jogged down to get the Bronco while Jules and Chief stayed inside the entrance to B.B. King's. He pulled up, and she hopped in and buckled up and placed Chief in his backpack on the back seat.

The road to Tunica was dark. Once south of Memphis and past the bad neighborhoods, it was almost all corn. There was a fair amount of traffic but it was spread out.

About thirty minutes into the trip back, Rick noticed some headlights coming up pretty fast behind him. Once the car got right behind him, he assumed they would pass, but they didn't.

"Jules, take my piece out of the glove box."

"What is it, Rick? Who is it?"

"Probably some drunk asshole, but just to be safe, I wanna tuck my gun in the door."

Jules handed Rick his gun, and he stuck it in the drink holder next to his left leg. Jules instinctively pulled out her new pistol, and Rick waved her away to put it back in her purse. She did as he asked even though she didn't look happy about it.

The headlights were blinding, and he couldn't get a make on the car. With no warning, the car lunged forward and slammed into the rear of the Bronco. Chief flew forward in the backpack and almost hit the dash with the recoil. Rick fumbled to keep control of the Bronco. He reached down for the gun and *bam*—the car slammed into him again. This time hitting the far-right corner of the back, spinning the Bronco sideways. Once it hit the gravel, the Bronco spun completely around. It slid backward and slammed into a culvert, and went airborne. All Rick could do was hold on. It only took a split second, but it felt as if time moved in slow motion.

The front hood of the Bronco hit the grass and bounced again end over end before landing hard upside down next to a large live oak. Chief's backpack was on the roof and lying sideways. Jules and Rick just hung there in their seatbelts upside down. No one was moving. Rick was stunned. His pistol was lying below his head on the roof of the car, still in the holster.

Rick looked over at Jules, and she began to move and groan. He looked out of the window and saw someone approaching the Bronco. He could only make out a silhouette of an arm but could clearly see the stranger was carrying a shotgun by his side. Rick reached for the pistol. With his left hand, he unsnapped the holster, spun it around, and unloaded it, shattering the driver's side window. The man ran off and Rick heard his tires squeal. He started to smell gas. On Jules's side of the Bronco, he could see a puddle forming.

"Jules, Jules, are you awake?"

He reached for her. She was conscious, but out of it.

"We've got to get out of here. Now!"

He wriggled his seat belt clasp and it finally let loose. He fell to the roof of the Bronco. The door was jammed in the grass, and at the angle of the dirt berm they had created, he couldn't get through the side window. His only option was to kick the front windshield out. He used all his might and kicked. It cracked more than before, and he kicked again. On the third try, the window came loose from the frame.

He crawled out and ran to the passenger side. He was standing in a puddle of gas. He pulled on the door and it opened. He reached across and with all his might unbuckled Jules's seatbelt. He gently pulled her from the wreck, carried her about thirty yards away, and leaned her against a tree away from the Bronco. He felt her neck. She had a strong pulse and was breathing. She slipped in and out of consciousness. Blood dripped from her forehead.

Rick's hands were shaking violently, and he ran with all his speed back to the Bronco. He reached in and grabbed the backpack. He started running toward Jules and felt a compression against his body like he had never felt.

The explosion threw him forward. He landed nearly ten feet away face down in the dirt and grass. Chief's backpack was ripped from his arms and landed even farther away.

CHAPTER TWELVE

Rick squinted at the dome light above his head. He was moving.

"Where am I?"

A man in a white jumpsuit looked down at Rick.

"He's conscious. Hurry up," said the man to someone else.

"Mr. Waters, I'm Bryan. I'm the EMT. You were in a crash. We are headed to Baptist Memorial Hospital. Are you in pain?"

"Where is Jules, my girlfriend?"

"The girl who was with you is in another ambulance ahead of us. We had to stabilize you before we could leave. We brought you back three times."

Rick was confused and scared and only grasping some of what the EMT was saying.

"Where is Chief?"

"Who's Chief? There were only two of you at the accident when we arrived. Was there another person?"

"No, Chief is my bird. My cockatoo. Is he okay?"

"We didn't find any bird, sir."

A gush of heat rushed into Rick's face, and everything went black.

He awoke at the hospital. He was still in a daze and unclear about what had happened exactly. It all started to come back to him slowly. He reached for the call button. A nurse came in a few minutes later.

"Mr. Waters, you're awake. How are you feeling?"

"Where is Jules?"

"If you are referring to the woman who was with you in the accident, Miss Juliana Castro is in a room downstairs. You are in the ICU."

"Is she okay?"

"She'll be fine. She sustained a concussion and had a few small contusions. We kept her here for a few days. She is scheduled to be released today or tomorrow."

"A few days? I've been here for a few days?"

"Mr. Waters, you are lucky to be alive. You took a massive blow from the explosion of your SUV. We thought we lost you a couple of times. We induced a coma until your brain swelling went down. It came down a lot last night, and we have just been waiting for you to be responsive. That's a good sign. I've already called the doctor."

"What about Chief?"

"Yes, Mr. Waters, Miss Castro was going on and on about Chief—a parrot, apparently?"

"Yes, he's my cockatoo."

"I'm afraid you'll have to talk to Miss Castro about that. Do I have your permission to give her the code to call your room? She had no ID on her whatsoever."

"Yes, please. I need to see her."

Rick finally was conscious enough to feel pain, and the headache he had was worse than any hangover in history. Thirty minutes later, Rick's phone rang. It was Jules. She was crying.

"Rick, Rick, I thought we lost you. I have to get out of here. I have to see you. They said they won't let me see you until you are out of the ICU. Rick, they can't find Chief. I'm sorry. Gary and Possum have been to the crash site three times calling for him. His backpack was busted open and a few feathers were strewn on the grass, but there is no sign of him. I'm so sorry."

She started crying again, unable to keep it in.

"I've spoken to the police and told them everything I could remember," she continued. "The Bronco was burnt to a crisp. My purse was inside along with both of our guns. I don't care about that stuff though. I just want to be with you, Rick."

"Okay, baby, please contact Possum and tell him to keep searching the area for Chief. He has to be alive still. He probably just flew off and is scared somewhere. I'll try and get out of here as soon as the doctor lets me. I haven't even spoken with him yet. I don't have my cell phone. It was on the magnet on the dash of the Bronco. It's probably melted to nothing now. I did see the car lights behind me, but if the rear camera recorded it, it's long burned up now. I couldn't tell in the rearview or the video screen what kind of car it was."

"You just get well, Rick. We'll worry about the car later. I'm gonna find our bird! I'll call you again after I talk to Gary. I love you, Rick."

"I love you too, Jules."

Rick hung up. Anxiety was welling up in him about Chief. His head was pounding and his body ached everywhere. A few minutes later, the doctor arrived.

"Mr. Waters, I'm Dr. Nicca. I was here when you came in. You are one lucky guy."

"Yeah, people keep saying that."

"From what I understand from the police, you took a blast in the back that launched you several yards in the air onto the ground. A blast like that is equivalent to getting hit by a Mack Truck. You landed face first in soft dirt and grass, which probably saved your life. When the brain is jolted like that, it can cause swelling. If it swells too much, it can cause an aneurysm and even death. You were on the fence, Mr. Waters. We induced a coma to reduce swelling. Thankfully, it worked. Amazingly, you didn't break any bones and only have a few contusions on your face and the back of your arms. We just have to watch your brain. I will be ordering some more CT scans soon and another MRI. You are gonna be sorer than you've even been in your life, but if we can keep your brain from swelling and test your cognitive skills in a few days, I think you'll make a full recovery."

"And Jules?"

"Oh, Juliana Castro. She's fine. She did have a small concussion, but she will be right as rain soon. I'm probably gonna release her later today. That girl really loves you. All she ever did was ask about you and carry on about a bird. It didn't make sense to us at first, but a fellow named Possum called us and explained about your cockatoo. I guess he and another guy are trying to find your bird now. I wish you luck. I know how it is to lose a pet. I lost my spaniel Dixon last year. He was twelve. Do you have any more questions for me before I leave, Rick?"

"When can I get out of here?"

"Depends on the CT scan and MRI. If those look good, we can transfer you to a regular room for at least a couple days' observation. I don't wanna make any promises, but I'd say three to four days?"

"Thanks, Doc. I appreciate it."

The doctor left, and a slew of nurses and other people came in and wheeled Rick to a couple of different rooms for a CT scan and then an MRI. Now all he could do was wait. He was still foggy, but his memory was back and his fingers seemed normal. He wiggled them a lot and made sure everything was syncing on time. His brain was talking to his toes, and he could move his arms, although he was tremendously sore. He tried to sit up in bed, but the pain was too great. It would take him some time.

All he wanted to do was get out of there, hug Jules, and go find Chief.

A while later, a smiling man in dark blue scrubs came into the ICU. He grabbed a folder on the wall and walked over to Rick.

"Mr. Waters, I'm Anthony. I'll be taking you to a new room. You are being moved out of the ICU. That's always good news."

Rick thanked him as he wheeled him to the elevator and into a new room. A couple nurses assisted in getting him from the gurney onto a new bed. It felt like his muscles were on fire.

"Mr. Waters, on a scale of one to ten, what is your pain level?" asked the nurse.

"Twelve!"

"Okay, let me get you something to take that down a little."

He'd already had an IV in his arm with a saline drip for days. She left and then returned with a hypodermic syringe and injected something into the IV port.

"That should help quite quickly. How do you feel now?"

"I feel like I'm…"

He was out. The morphine hit him, and he felt euphoric as if he were flying. He was somewhere between consciousness and unconsciousness—in sort of a lucid dream. He was floating over a cornfield and hovering over a fresh mound of dirt. He flew down and began to dig. He hit something hard.

Suddenly, he was jolted back to reality and was staring at the ceiling light in the room. His TV was playing PBS on mute. He felt delirious from the morphine, but the pain was completely gone.

I could get used to this.

A couple of hours passed, and Jules came into his room. Her eyes were full of tears—a mix of tears of joy for Rick and sadness for Chief. She pulled up a chair next to Rick, took his hand, and kissed the back of it over and over. The look in her eyes was making Rick well up.

"Rick, my love, you are okay. I prayed to God to switch places with you, but He healed you on His own. I am a wreck. Between trying to find Chief and worrying about you, I think I've aged ten years."

"You look beautiful as always," slurred Rick. He thought he was speaking normally, but the morphine was making him sound drunk.

"Rick, Possum and Gary are still searching for Chief," continued Jules. "I printed out a picture of him and took it to several of the farmhouses with Gary's number on it, since neither of us have cell phones at the moment. Today is the day the FBI has to do the second drop with the five million. Gary knows more about it than I do. He will call you later. They can't wait until you get out to do the drop. Possum will fly his drone again, and he gave Gary a lesson on your thermal camera. I know you want to be there, but there is just no way. It's tonight after dark. I will stay with you. Gary has your room number and promises to call and let us know what happened."

Rick gritted his teeth in frustration but knew there was nothing he could do. He was still a day or two from getting out of here and even then, he would be limited in mobility. It would take quite a few weeks for him to get back to full strength and lose most of the pain. Rick mumbled a few more times, and Jules just put her finger gently across his lips.

"Just rest, Rick. I'll be here."

Nurses came in and helped Rick to the bathroom and made him walk around some to prevent atrophy. His legs seemed unfazed by the blast. His upper body was a writhing nightmare though. After a few trips to the bathroom and short hall walks, he dozed off, and Jules never left his side.

About ten that night, the phone in the room rang, jolting Rick awake. Jules picked it up. It was Gary. The morphine had worn off and Rick's speech had come back, but so had the pain. He would stick to Tylenol if he could.

"I'm going to put you on speaker, Gary," said Jules.

"Rickster, the man with nine lives. How are you?"

"I've felt better. What went down with the drop? Did they get him?"

"You're not gonna fucking believe this. Once again, the package vanished into thin air. No motion cameras caught anyone coming or going. But we do know how he did it this time. It backfired somewhat, and now we are on pins and needles until we hear from him. The FBI planted a tracking device in the package. They also planted an exploding dye pack in it. Their plan was to fire it off and then catch the little blue bastard in the act. But there was one problem. He didn't take the package."

"What do you mean? I thought you said it was gone."

"Oh, it was gone all right. When we drove up to the scene, the package was moving northwest parallel with Highway 8. The Feds were tailing it and then they exploded the dye pack. It suddenly stopped moving by Lehrton Cemetery, about two and a half miles outside of the drop zone and just past the perimeter they had set. No cars ever came through there until the Feds did."

"The package didn't just walk to the cemetery on its own!"

"That's right, Rick. It flew there."

"What?!"

"The Feds tracked the signal into the center of the cemetery, and scattered on the ground were pieces of a balloon drone. It's kinda like a Goodyear Blimp, only smaller and silent. The fucker used the claws on the balloon drone to snatch both packages from above without ever being seen by the perimeter cameras. If they had only faced one camera toward the money, they would have figured it out the first time. But no one considered—except for Possum, of course—that an alien could take the money. Possum told me about some research he had been doing. He found out about some drones that were stolen from a trade show down in Jackson, but he had no idea what size or scope they were. Now we know."

After a short pause, Gary continued, "Now here's the rub. He only knows that his drone went down. He has no idea about the dye pack causing it to crash. So, he's either gonna hightail it out of here because I'm sure he'll know his drone will be found eventually, or he's gonna try and recover it. The FBI wants to do a stakeout of the cemetery and see if he shows up for it. They will remove the dye pack and leave a new package a few feet away and scatter some hundred-dollar bills all in the area. If he doesn't show, he might just think it crashed on its own and the money got blown away. All we can do is wait."

"Wow, what a shit show. So, what now? What about Chief?"

"Well, I was just about to go there. I have a question though. Your thermal camera can pick up little rabbits and whatnot, right?"

"Yep, I like what you are thinking," said Rick.

"I thought you might. Possum is charging the drone and the thermal camera. We are gonna take the bus up to the crash site. There's a farm across the highway, and I talked the man into letting us park there for a few days to search. It's literally walking distance to the crash site. He's the one who called 9-1-1, so you might wanna meet him. He may have saved y'all's life. He's a sweet old black guy name Tungsten, like the steel. Cool name. I tried to pay him and he refused. I'll get some money to him somehow. Anyway, we are leaving soon with my Bronco in tow. Oh, I already ordered you a new red Bronco. You can give me the insurance money from the wreck. The new one is coming out of West Memphis, Arkansas. It should be here in a couple of days. I'm adding a roll bar to it since you like to flip them so much," said Gary with a huge laugh.

Rick couldn't help laughing too. "You didn't have to do that, dude."

"You mean partner, right? We are in this together now."

"True dat!"

"Okay, get some rest. If we find Chief, I'll call you. I promise."

"Any hour, okay? I don't care."

"You got it, buddy. Bye, Rick. Bye, Jules."

They both said goodbye to Gary at the same time. Jules took Rick's hand again and assured him Chief would be fine.

Time stood still for Rick. He had been moved into a regular room and a couple of days went by. His mind paced, and he switched from worrying about Chief to thinking of the missing kid. He couldn't sleep and just stared at the clock and at Jules slumped over in her chair. She looked so peaceful.

"God, thank you for helping me find such a wonderful woman," he whispered. "She is the best thing that has ever happened to me. If you can find it in you, please help us find Chief. I know I ask for a lot of favors, but I've been pretty good since you saved Chief's life that last time I asked. Maybe one more?"

Rick finally dozed off around three in the morning. He was startled awake by a nurse taking his vitals at 7:15 a.m. He looked over to where Jules was sitting, but she was gone. Just as the nurse finished, Jules popped back in with two hot coffees.

"Dark and sweet like your women, Mr. Waters? I mean woman, as in me. I saw the doctor in the hall and he gave me a thumbs-up. I think you can get out of here today."

"That's great, Jules. Any word on Chief?"

"No, I used the phone at the nurses' station and woke up Possum. I felt bad. They were out all night using the drone to find Chief. Possum thinks he's an expert at finding barn owls now though. He said he got excited when he saw some white plumage but realized it was just an owl. Apparently, there are a lot of old barns in the area. On the farm where the bus is parked, they have three."

"Too cool. I hope the doctor shows up soon. Speak of the devil!"

The doctor walked in right then.

"Mr. Waters, I have good news. I can release you today. All your motor skills are good, according to the nurses. You're MRI and CT scans are perfect. Now you're just a walking bag of sore muscles. I've prescribed a few muscle relaxers and pain meds for you. Tramadol is my go-to, but I can also do Hydrocodone if you wish."

"Can I just use Tylenol, Doc? I don't wanna have to depend on those things. I've heard Tramadol can make you cray-cray and Hydrocodone is kind of addictive."

"When used in moderation, both drugs are highly effective with little side effects. It's your call though. I'll give you a prescription and it's up to you if you fill it. Thank you, Mr. Waters. I wish you a speedy recovery."

Rick shook the doctor's hand and thanked him profusely. He would be released within the hour. Jules called Gary, and he arranged for a car to pick them up and bring them to the farm where the bus was parked. It was a struggle for Rick to get off the bed and into the wheelchair. He knew if he kept moving, things would get better. The last time Rick was badly injured, back in Brazil, Davi Kopenawa, the highest-ranking shaman of the Yanomami tribe, performed a ritual on him and miraculously healed him. He wished Davi were here now to do some of his magic healing on his sore body, but he was on his own this time.

The ride in the Town Car wasn't as bad as he expected. Occasionally, a bump would jar him and he would squirm a little, but he was more excited to get back to the bus and assist in any way he could to find Chief. The car pulled up to the farm. Jules helped Rick out of the car, and Possum and Gary came over to help as well.

"I got this, y'all. I ain't useless just yet."

Rick walked slowly toward the bus, feeling pain with every step. Once inside, he sat on the sofa and Jules elevated his feet.

"Can I get you anything, baby?" she asked.

"Just Chief, oh and maybe a rum, extra rum, no Coke."

Jules poured Rick a stiff thirty-two-year-old Flor de Caña on a single round, clear ice cube Gary had ordered. She knew what her man liked, and she doted on him. Gary stepped off the bus and came back a few minutes later.

"Rick, I'd like you to meet Tungsten. He owns the farm here and, like I told you, is the one who called 9-1-1."

Rick was about to get up, but Tungsten waved him down.

"No need to get up on my account. I gots kicked by a mule some years ago and it took me months to be all right and get up ons my own. I can only imagine how sore you are."

"I can't even begin to thank you for what you did. Not only the 9-1-1 call but also for being so hospitable and letting us park the rig here and search for my lost bird."

"Aw, it ain't nothing but a thang. I don't gets much comp'ny here so it's been kinda nice. Ever since my Lucy passed on, it's just been me and my horses and mules. I keeps to myself mostly. I do like to roll them bones over in Tunica sometimes though."

"Oh yeah, you're a craps player?" asked Rick.

"Hell yeah, I've been chasing them dice since I was old enough to get inside."

"We should play sometime. I love craps."

"Sounds like a plan, Mr. Waters."

"Call me Rick, I insist."

"Okay, Mr. Rick."

"Just Rick."

"Okay, Rick. Rick it is. I best let you rest now. If y'all need anything or wants to come up the porch and visit, don't hesitate. I got some fresh sweet tea and a little somethin'-somethin' I made in the big barn to go with it, if you catch my drift."

Rick motioned doing a shot, and Tungsten smiled and nodded.

Moonshine.

After dark, Gary and Possum started their drone rounds again while Rick rested. He wanted to be out there but he needed to heal. They called it around three o'clock.

About 6:30 a.m., a rooster crowed, waking up Rick, and he immediately thought of Chief. He knew soon it would be a lost cause. Chief had never been out in the wild before, and between hawks, snakes, and other predators, he didn't stand much of a chance.

Rick felt bad not joining the gang on the porch the night before for some spiked sweet tea and decided to bring Tungsten a fresh-brewed coffee. Jules walked with him, and there sat Tungsten on his chair, whittling as he always did.

"Try this, Tungsten," said Rick, holding out the cup to him. "It ain't as good as your moonshine, I'm sure, but it's pretty tasty. I call it Super Unleaded, but it's really just an Irish coffee. Take a sip and let me know what you think."

Tungsten took a sip. "Woo-hoo, that's got a kick to it. No wonder you call it Super Unleaded. You sure is up early."

"Yeah, one of your roosters woke me up this morning. No big deal. I like getting up early when I can."

"Oh, I ain't got no roosters. Maybe it was one of them barn owls. They do make a ruckus sometimes in the morning."

Rick froze. "What did you say?"

"Them barn owls make a ruckus."

"No, before that."

"I ain't got no roosters? Well, come to think of it, I did hear one this morning. I hate them damn things. Stinky and nasty. I buy my eggs at the sto'! Like a civilized person. It's probably the neighbors. I think it was coming from that barn over there."

Tungsten pointed to the small red barn that was leaning from years of neglect.

"Jules, can you run to the bus and get my spotting scope? It's in the bedroom in my black bag in the rear cabinet." Rick's heart was pounding. He hoped his gut was right.

Jules hustled to the bus and came back.

"I'm sorry to ask, baby, but can you go back and wake up Gary or Possum to borrow their cell phone and grab that JBL portable speaker on the dinette?"

"No problem, Rick. Possum's making eggs, and Gary is sipping a coffee and was about to join us anyway."

"Bring the tripod too. Hell, just tell them all to come here."

Jules ran back to the bus and shortly after came out, followed by Possum and Gary.

"What's up, Rick?" asked Gary.

"Possum, can you help me set up this spotting scope and the tripod and face that barn?"

"Sure thing, hombre."

"Gary, is your phone still synced to the JBL? And can you unlock it and hand it to me?"

They all looked perplexed like Rick was doing some sort of weird experiment or something.

Rick pulled up YouTube and searched for a rooster crowing. He cranked up the speaker as loud as he could and pushed play. He stared through the spotting scope at the barn. After a few YouTube crows, he paused it and listened and looked.

Cock-a-doodle-do, cock-a-doodle-do rang out from the direction of the red barn. Rick stared through the spotting scope and saw nothing. He played the audio again. Again, *cock-a-doodle-do, cock-a-doodle-do* echoed it.

"Look, Rick, look!" Jules pointed to the very top of the barn.

Rick raised the scope, and sitting on the highest peak was Chief, as if he was the cock of the walk! The biggest grin spread across Rick's face.

"Chief, Chief!" yelled Jules as she started running toward the barn.

Possum and Gary tried to keep up, but she was too fast. Tungsten fired up his tractor and gave Rick a lift over to the barn. When Chief heard Jules and saw everyone running his way, he started climbing down the barn. Board by board, foot by foot. By the time Jules reached the barn, he was halfway down. Gary and Possum finally caught up, holding their sides and breathing heavily. Rick arrived a minute later with Tungsten driving.

"Well, I'll be damned," said Tungsten.

"Yeah, he thinks he's a rooster," said Rick as he rubbed a tear from his eye.

Chief made it down to where Jules could reach him, and she took him from the barn and spun around with joy, holding him close to her chest. She walked over to Rick, and Chief nuzzled Rick on the chin. It was a miracle. He had survived for days in an area full of hawks, snakes, and other predators, and instead of being scared, he'd decided to mimic a rooster to declare the day started.

He's something else.

"This is a sign, y'all. If we can find Chief, then we can find Tyler. Let's get to work!" said Rick with strong determination in his voice.

CHAPTER THIRTEEN

Jules made lunch for everyone and a few special treats for Chief. Except for missing a few feathers and being quite dirty, he seemed to have come out unscathed when the Bronco blew up. Rick figured it might've had to do with the weight of the backpack and Chief's own light weight and feathers. Maybe the blast just went around him somewhat. He didn't care why. He was just thrilled Chief was home and safe. Now it was time to find Tyler.

Rick invited Tungsten over to the bus, and they all had lunch. Tungsten explained to them that the farm had been passed down through his family for generations, but it had fallen on hard times. He only had one running tractor, and corn prices had dropped, so this year he hadn't even planted anyway. He was considering selling the place or maybe taking on a partner who had some money to inject into the place for a new tractor and other implements. If he did that, then next year, he would have plenty of cotton and soybean.

He showed Rick a guy on GoFundMe who raised a bunch of money to get his farm profitable again.

"Do you still wanna, Tungsten? What would you if you sold the farm and could do anything?" asked Gary.

He thought for a second, rubbing his chin and looking around at the bus.

"I'd probably get me something like this and see the whole United States. I love to travel but usually just go to Tunica or Memphis. I went to Nashville once, and Gulf Shores. The sand is pretty down there."

"You should come visit us in Destin sometime. I'll take you fishing," interjected Rick.

"I'd like that. Maybe I'll take you up on it."

They all finished lunch, and everyone shook Tungsten's hand. Jules gave him a big hug.

"What a great guy. I'm gonna do something for him soon. I did put a fat envelope in his mailbox. It was just some fun money. Five thousand dollars. Maybe he'll make a run on the craps table and be able to buy that new tractor. Who knows," said Gary as he fired up the diesel pusher and pulled out onto Highway 61 headed south.

Gary drove as Rick navigated back to Gold Strike Casino, where his luggage was being held. Gary had arranged for them to store it and told the manager about the accident. He took the second night's room charges off as a courtesy. Gary helped Rick to the bell stand, and the man retrieved Rick's luggage and a large bag of stuff they had left behind, including the second bottle of Caymus Cabernet.

The man also wheeled down Chief's PVC bird stand on a cart. He didn't seem to know what it was; he must've thought it was a coat rack or something. Gary tipped him nicely, and then they were off to Cleveland, back to base camp at the Expo Center.

They arrived midafternoon and a meeting was set up with the FBI, Deputy Ron, and the crew. They all met at the Sheriff's Department at four o'clock. The FBI had reassigned their mobile unit, so now only Gary's bus and the EquuSearch rig remained, but they planned to leave soon. It seemed to Rick that they had given up on finding Tyler. At least there had been some movement on the case. Rick was ready to dive back in.

He had forgotten how bad his face looked; when he hobbled into the war room, he could see people's eyes get big at the sight of him. He had two black eyes, a large strawberry on his left check from sliding on the ground, and a cut above his nose right between his eyes.

"I know I look like death warmed over, but I'll be all right. What's new on the case?" said Rick.

"We're all glad you made it. I saw photos of that crash from the highway patrol. That Bronco was hard to even recognize," said Ron.

"Yep, I'm a lucky guy, they tell me. Now let's get to work."

"Okay, we placed two undercover guys at the cemetery on rotating shifts. They looked like regular maintenance crew. No one came the first day, and we had them work the opposite side of the cemetery in case they were being watched. On day two at around 9:00 p.m., a man walked into the back of the cemetery from the woods by Burrell

Bayou. We placed motion-capture video cameras all around the grounds. Here's what we got. Dim the lights, please."

Everyone turned toward the large TV they had set up. Ron pressed play on the video. It was a little grainy because it was so dark that night with no moon. A man wearing black leather gloves, a mask, and goggles was carrying some sort of device and looking down at it several times as he walked toward the crashed drone. It must've been his GPS locator for the drone. Something long was hanging from his shoulder. It was hard to make out. When he got to the drone, he thrashed his arms in the air a few times as if he was upset. He leaned over and picked up the package. A few bills fell out, and he tossed them to the ground in anger. Then the agents came running toward him with weapons drawn. The man reached down and grabbed a rifle hanging from his shoulder and started firing at the agents in a sweeping pattern. It was an automatic assault rifle of some sort. The agents hit the deck, and he began to run back toward the woods, firing behind him as he ran.

"He got away?!" exclaimed Rick. He couldn't believe this guy's luck.

"Yeah, we think he had a car stashed in the woods and took off down Marlow Road toward Ruleville," said Ron. "We are doing a house-to-house sweep of Ruleville now. It's not a big town, but there are at least sixty properties there. We found an abandoned wrecked Chrysler LeBaron, a black mask, cutoff sweatshirt, and black pants in a ditch on the corner of Marlow Road and Highway 8. We think he fled on foot from there. We ran the plates and found that the car was stolen. But here is the best part. Show him."

The agent backed up the video to where the guy began to shoot at the agents and zoomed in. When he swept left, he paused it. The fire from the rifle lit up the screen, and the faint sign of a tattoo on his right arm came into view. It was very grainy though and a little dark still. Another agent slid a manila folder over to Rick. He opened it and inside was a black and white eight-by-ten photo of the same angle on the video, only enhanced with more pixels. It was a trident, plain as day.

"Son of a bitch!" Rick shook his head. "It's him."

"We have a solid hunch it is. We've reopened the case file you worked on with him, and he is now ruled *not deceased* and a suspect in the kidnapping of Tyler Raynes," said the lead agent.

"Any hits on the Cadillac?" asked Rick.

"No, Rick, it's as if it disappeared off the face of the earth. We don't think the Cadillac was the car that slammed into you. We found some broken shards of turn signal glass about a half a mile from the accident and more on the side of the road, just beside where the Bronco was launched into the field. Several of the pieces fit together perfectly, so we are certain they came from the same vehicle. The FBI took molds of the tire marks left in the dirt beside the crash site. They can't match them yet, but they believe they came from a small truck or SUV, not a car. Didn't you say you saw square headlights behind you?" asked the agent.

"Yes, and they weren't high up like an SUV, so that's why I was thinking it was a car."

"Maybe it's from a dropped truck. It might not have anything to do with this case. Lots of punks drop their trucks.

Were you driving excessively slow? Maybe it was just a case of road rage."

"Slow? Hardly. I was at least fifteen above the speed limit. Please don't write me a ticket now," said Rick.

Deputy Ron just grinned and shook his head.

"Rick, I'm Agent Frank Foley," said one of the agents. "We haven't met yet. I was brought in because I am a specialist in tire tread forensics. I took the molds. I can tell you all with certainty: it wasn't a car.

"This is Jon Kohler; he flew in with me. He is one of the top computer science forensics men. He recovered the SD card from your Bronco that was filming behind you. It was burned badly, but he will try and rebuild it. If we can even get one image off of that SD card, it will be worth it. Currently, only thirty-one states require front and rear license plates. Most of the southern states do not. But we may get lucky. It may end up being a vehicle from one of the thirty-one states or some other vanity plate we can run. Or even get an ID of the driver."

Rick shook both Jon and Frank's hands and gave them his card. They wrapped up the meeting, and Rick and the crew headed back to the bus. Rick was frustrated and anxious. He kept thinking about the kid being buried alive somewhere. The morphine trip he'd had, combined with the movie *Buried*, didn't help things.

Gary had been on the phone so much his ear must've been hurting. He was on a mission though, and when they all sat down on the bus, he filled them in.

"Listen, y'all. I know Jules lost her ID, passport, and that cute little peashooter she just got."

"Hey! It's not a peashooter. It's a Smith & Wesson nine-millimeter M&P Shield."

"Well, pardon me, Lara Croft," said Gary with a chuckle. "Never mind, I'll explain later. Let's stay on point. Rick, luckily for you, your wallet was in your back pocket and not burned. But Ms. Juliana Castro, if that's her real name, has no passport, ID, or anything. The guns are easy. I already ordered duplicates of both of your pistols. Which reminds me, your new red Bronco with double thick roll bars should be arriving later today. Haha."

Rick gave Gary a look that meant, *Stop spending money!* Gary just blew off his glance.

"I've been on the phone with a friend of mine from Texas who now works in the State Department. He is getting Jules a temporary transit visa to Colombia to get a duplicate passport. I tried to do it faster, but they require her actual signature at the Ministry of Foreign Affairs located in Bogotá. We can fly there and be back in two days. I suggest that Rick, myself, and Jules make the trip while Possum stays here on point. What do you think?"

"Do we have to do this now? In the middle of an investigation?" asked Rick.

"No, not really, but I was thinking if we did, and it is actually Dale Clemens doing all this, he will most likely be made aware of it. He has to have some inside people in Miami at immigration. How else would he have gotten here in the first place with Feds all over his ass? Someone is helping him. That's why I want to route the jet into Miami and make sure his buddies are aware that you are leaving the country. If we can get him to think we are off the case, he may just make his final move. I can file a fake manifest for two weeks. We'll be back in a day and a half. He'll never know it."

"Won't he be tipped off when we check back into the United States?" asked Rick.

"Yeah, but we ain't gonna check in. We're gonna stop in Grand Cayman, refuel, and fly straight to the Cleveland Municipal Airport. Fuck it! I'll deal with immigration later."

"I like it! I like it a lot! This might actually work." said Rick. They might finally draw Clemens out into the open. Rick was itching to confront him face to face. "Is your pilot okay with it? I mean, his license is on the line."

"The amount I'm paying him, he'd pretty much fly any route we choose. Plus, he has plausible deniability. I told him I'm handling the paperwork and to just not worry about it. He winked at me. I think he's like a monkey that sees no evil, hears no evil, speaks no evil. The perfect pilot."

"When will y'all leave?" asked Possum.

"Now, and Jules, bring at least one outfit for you and Rick that are showstoppers. We're going clubbing," said Gary.

Rick looked over at Jules and just gave her that *what is Gary up to now* look, and she immediately started packing a bag. It would be a quick turnaround, so she just packed the essentials. Possum would take care of Chief. He was happy to get a little bonding time with his white-feathered friend.

They loaded up Gary's Bronco and headed to the Cleveland Municipal Airport. Next stop, Miami.

When they arrived in Miami, Gary had them exit the plane, and they all took a car down to South Beach. It might have looked like a fun getaway, but he wanted to draw attention to their presence. Many of Miami's biggest criminals had their roots in South Beach. The ones in the know were the bartenders.

"Champagne, my lady?" asked Gary as they entered Mango's.

With the help of lots of Tiger Balm and the strong but loving massage hands of Jules, Rick was moving around much better already. He was living off Tylenol 3, chewing them like candy. With a strong shot or two of some good rum and a handful of Tylenol, he almost felt human. He knew mixing Tylenol and alcohol was really hard on the liver, but it was better than getting addicted to Tramadol or Oxy.

Mango's had a tropical vibe with salsa dancers on the bar. Gary passed out his and Rick's business cards to every bartender he met, bragging about going down to Colombia for two weeks. He reserved a table in the Mojito room and got bottle service. He was dropping hundreds to every server in the place and acting drunk as a skunk. Rick and Jules played along. Gary was pouring alcohol for the other patrons around them too.

"Let's go to LIV," hollered Gary. "Who wants to come with us? Woohoo! Follow me."

Several smoking hot young gold-diggers walked arm in arm with Gary to the limo he had arranged out front. LIV was Miami's biggest nightclub, and while it wasn't technically in South Beach, it was close enough to count. They booked the biggest acts and had the biggest celebrity cameos. You never knew who you'd see at LIV.

Gary had prebooked a huge bottle service table, and they came in through the VIP rear entrance. He gave the girls in tow a thousand dollars each and told them to go mingle and bring back more chicks. On the main stage was Deadmau5, one of the most famous electronic music musicians in the world. He wore a lit-up mouse head mask over his head on stage. His real name was Joel Thomas Zimmerman, and he was originally from Canada. But now everyone called him Dead Mouse.

The music made Rick nauseous. The pounding beat was nonstop with four-on-the-floor bass and near never-ending twenty-minute songs that blended from one into another. Jules couldn't stop dancing, and the black dress with the long slit up the side with the pumps she was wearing turned every head in the club. She danced with all the girls, and Rick tried to keep up, doing his best not to puke from the Tylenol, rum, and dope beats, as they were called. Gary made their presence known and made sure everyone knew what they'd be doing for the next two weeks.

At five in the morning, they closed down LIV and took the limo to the airport. Gary had the driver take the entourage of girls wherever they wanted. The girls were making out more with each other than they were with Gary, but he was a trouper and took one for the team. He had a tendency to do that. It was funny to Rick how money made everyone else see Gary, yet to him, he was still just a good ol' boy from LaBelle, Texas. And deep down, he really was. Money hadn't changed him, and in Miami, you could be anyone you wanted to be.

"We're here!" said Gary, waking everyone up.

Rick felt like a truck had driven over his liver and a skunk had shit in his mouth. Jules looked a little worse for wear too. They hadn't pulled an all-nighter in a long time, and it took its toll.

Gary instructed the pilot, Clay, to file a flight plan for Bogotá, then Barranquilla, which was the closest airport to Jules's hometown, followed by a deadhead maintenance run to Grand Cayman.

Jules, Rick, and Gary reboarded the plane. It had three sleepers in it and was quite plush but it didn't appear on the design blueprints. To anyone inspecting the plane, it was merely a hydraulics and cables area.

Once they landed, they exited the plane and took a car to the Ministry of Foreign Affairs, and Jules signed the papers and got her new passport. Next stop was Licencia de Conducción Bogotá, aka the DMV, where Jules would get a copy of her driver's license. Unlike some places in the states that took forever, this DMV was fast and professional. They printed her one on the spot. They reboarded the flight for Barranquilla and landed a short time later.

"Jules, I have a surprise for you," said Gary.

"What?"

Gary pointed out of the window, and standing on the tarmac were Jules's mother and father. Tears began to flow down her cheeks, and she gave Gary a big bear hug.

"I don't know what to say. How did you...?"

Gary shrugged and grinned. "I have my ways. I talked to Rick, and he did the research and I contacted your parents. They speak quite good English."

"Yes, they do. I can't begin to thank you enough."

"There's more, Jules. I booked us a waterfront Airbnb for a week. We'll only be there today, but your parents can stay the entire week. It's my gift." Gary glanced at Rick. "I guess it's time to meet the parents, Rick. You nervous?"

"I'd be lying if I said no."

"Rick, because I love you, they will love you. I promise," said Jules as she kissed him on the cheek.

The visit was magnificent. They all sat out on a huge veranda overlooking the Caribbean Sea. Jules slipped in and out of English, telling her dad and mom about all their adventures. She told them all about Chief and how she couldn't wait for them to meet him. Rick promised to have them up for a visit once they solved the kidnapping case. They talked until the wee hours, drinking aguardiente and wine and eating an amazing Colombian meal Gary had had catered.

Jules explained to her parents that they had to leave and couldn't tell them where or why. They seemed to understand and sort of saw Rick as a secret agent. Once the parents went to bed, Rick, Gary, and Jules headed for the airport.

A fuel truck was just unhooking from the jet, and Gary paid a guy to roll them down to the plane in a container. Once they got to the plane, he cracked open the bottom of the container, and they slipped out and climbed up into the cargo hold of the jet and into the cubby space he had designed. The man loaded some luggage, several bottles of aguardiente, and some coffee beans into the hold and closed the door. The pilot signed off on the fuel. The immigration official just glanced into the back of the empty plane, signed off, and stepped off, closing the door behind him. Once they were airborne, they all climbed up into the main cabin.

"Rick, we have six hours on Cayman. You wanna do some snorkeling with the stingrays?"

"Stingrays?!" exclaimed Jules.

"Yep, it's pretty cool."

Jules clapped her hands. "Yes, let's do it."

"Whatever you want, baby," said Rick as he took her hand, leaned back in his seat, and rested his eyes.

CHAPTER FOURTEEN

It was still dark when they landed in Grand Cayman. Rick was a little nervous. The last time he'd been here, he was being chased by the police and still wanted for a robbery and B&E over on the west end. Gary kept telling him to relax and that he had it all under control. As the plane taxied to the executive side of the airport, Gary got everyone's attention.

"Okay, since we technically aren't here and we are still in Barranquilla, I got us these. Try not to laugh. Here, you are Valentina Salsa, and here's yours, Roja Bronco."

He handed them Colombian passports with their pictures and the fictitious names.

"What the fuck? Valentina Salsa and Roja Bronco? Are you serious?" asked Rick.

"Well, mine's even funnier—McLovin'."

"McLovin'? Just McLovin'?" Rick burst out laughing.

"Yeah, they don't give a shit here. We are ghosts." Gary chuckled. "Let's go rest for a bit before we hit Stingray City.

I got us adjoining rooms at the Grand Cayman Marriott. Clay is way over his legal flying time, and while he doesn't mind, that's the one thing we can't have. He needs his crew rest before we fly again."

They stepped off the plane, each carrying a small backpack with just the day's necessities and their fake IDs. A van took them to the hotel, and they all decided to nap until nine that morning, meet in the lobby for breakfast, and then head over to Stingray City. Some water time would do them all some good, especially Rick.

It was Sunday, and the Marriott offered a Sunday brunch. Since they were all still a little tired from clubbing and planned on being in the water soon, they decided to forgo the bottomless mimosas and Bloody Marys and instead ordered off the main menu. The meal was fantastic. Rick insisted on paying the bill. Gary had been dropping coin like it was going out of style, so he relented and let Rick pick up the check. The Sunday brunch was very popular on the island, and lots of tourists and locals partook.

On the way out of the front door, Rick spotted two police officers and a plain-clothed guy walking toward the restaurant in their direction. He tried to look away but locked eyes with the detective. It was Sergeant Jefferson, the same man he had locked horns with when he was arrested the last time he was here.

The sergeant squinted, as if he was trying to place Rick's face but just couldn't. Rick covered his mouth and faked a yawn as he passed him by, trying to hide most of his face with his hand. Jules and Gary were oblivious to the whole scene.

As they got in the car Gary had arranged to take them to Stingray City, Rick got their attention.

"Listen, y'all, I just spotted the detective who arrested me last time I was here. I don't think he recognized me. Keep your eyes open."

"Rick, I'm nervous. Is he gonna come after you?" asked Jules.

"I don't think so, Jules. I just wanna be precautious."

Rick noticed Jefferson turn back around one more time and give the car they got into another glance. Then he turned around and proceeded into the restaurant. He probably thought it was a case of déjà vu.

"Let's pet some stingrays!" hollered Gary.

Jules clapped her hands again, as giddy as a schoolgirl, but Rick still noticed some nervousness in her eyes. Gary had booked a private four-stop tour with George's Watersports that included all the gear, lunch, and beverages. The first stop was a snorkel on the big reef. The water was spectacular with visibility easily over one hundred feet. Every so often, Jules would grab Rick and startle him to point at a fish and tell him the species. She totally knew her fish.

"Look, Rick, a French angel."

She's so cute.

"Rick, Rick, look—a juvenile fairy basslet."

"Mm-hmm," Rick responded though his snorkel.

They continued to snorkel, then Rick pointed out one just to mess with her.

"Ooh look, Jules, a squirrel!"

"That's a longspine squirrelfish or *holocentrus rufus,* silly."

Rick just shook his head and stuck his face under the water again.

After about an hour, they climbed back into the boat.

"Our next stop is Starfish Point," the captain told them. "The name is a bit of a misnomer because—"

Jules interrupted. "Because there is no such thing as a starfish. They are actually known as sea stars."

"That's very good. How did you know that?" asked the captain.

Jules beamed. "I studied Zoology and Botany in college. I also took several courses in Oceanography and made it a point to memorize as many fish names as I could."

"That's great! As I was saying, it should really be called Sea Star Point, but everyone likes Starfish, so the name stuck. Starfish Point is a beautiful spot with very shallow water and sand covered in starfish, ahem, sea stars, and a sudden ten-foot drop on the edge. If you are a good snorkeler, you can dive down the wall. Friendly octopuses and several types of eels are often spotted there. We saw some on yesterday's morning trip."

Again, Jules was the first person off the boat. She swam over and put her knees in the sand and delicately picked up the starfish. Gary took a few pics of her with his iPhone he had put into a plastic baggy.

Meanwhile, Rick swam along the edge of the ledge, not too interested in starfish. Jules was doing great on her own and wouldn't even notice if he was there or not. He took several deep breaths, then held the last one and pointed his body straight down to the bottom of the wall and threw his fins skyward. In seconds, he was at the bottom, scanning the wall for an octopus. He saw a spotted moray and several types of cleaner shrimp but no octopus.

He went up for another gulp of air and dove down again. He looked in the cracks and crevices and then he saw it. It was a little guy. He looked timid at first. Rick held out his hand, and the octopus slowly wrapped one of his tentacles around Rick's little finger. Then another tentacle. Soon his entire body came out of the hole and was wrapped around Rick's hand. Rick was slowly ascending. The little guy wouldn't let go.

"Jules, come see this."

Rick waved her over with his other hand, keeping the little guy underwater by his chest.

Jules kicked with her fins and when she got close enough, she pulled his hand to the surface so she could get a good look.

"Oh, Octopoda."

"Is that Spanish for octopus?" asked Rick.

"Haha, no, that's the order, Octopoda. Kingdom: Animalia, Phylum: Mollusca, Class: Cephalopoda, Family: Octopodidae, Subfamily: Octopodinae, Genus: Octopus," she said with a smirk.

"I should have known. You are too smart, Jules."

Jules reached over and touched the octopus, and it changed colors. She rubbed its head, and it wrapped one of its tentacles around her finger, then another, and eventually moved over to her. The octopus was holding both Rick and Jules's hands at the same time and refused to let go.

"Aww. I think he wants us to stay with him," said Jules.

Both Jules and Rick played with the octopus for a while. They moved closer to the boat to show Gary, who had climbed back into the boat to air dry. It took a lot of coaxing, but they eventually were able to get the octopus to let go and swim back to the wall. They both climbed aboard, and the captain throttled the boat back onto plane bound for Mangrove Forest.

"Okay everyone, here at Mangrove Forest, you will see almost every fish, invertebrate, and crustacean in the ecosystem. It's a favorite for bull sharks and barracuda as well."

"Y'all have fun," said Gary as he sat back down and cracked open a Caybrew beer.

Rick and Jules did a little snorkeling at the Mangrove Forest. It really was a lovely spot; he thought it would be wonderful to come back and go kayaking there at some point. It reminded him of the mangroves in the Keys. They did spot a few large lethargic barracuda but nary a bull shark was to be found. They were more excited about the final stop—Stingray City.

"*Ay, Dios mío!* Look how big they are!" yelled Jules as the boat approached the sandbar.

She was the first one in the water again. The tour guide gave her a little baggy of squid to feed them. Rick followed her in, smiling as he watched her. She was like a little kid in a candy store. Some of the stingrays grabbed hold of her long, flowing hair. They were gentle though, and caused no damage. Gary found the biggest one and fed him nearly an entire baggy of squid. They took turns taking pictures with Gary's iPhone.

After an hour on the sandbar, they were all pruned up and ready to head back. They all rinsed off in the beach showers.

"I've gotta use the men's room," said Rick. "Be right back."

"We'll wait for you at the car," said Jules.

While Jules and Gary waited for Rick, a car pulled up right in front of them. The same sergeant they had passed back at the restaurant stepped out and approached the car at a fast pace. Jules's whole body tensed.

"Good afternoon. I'm Sergeant Jefferson. Where is the man you were with at the Marriott brunch? I have a couple of questions for him."

Jules's eye instinctively looked toward the bathroom, before she could stop herself. The sergeant took notice.

"Wait here," he said.

He began to walk toward the men's room.

Jules looked at Gary frantically. She was freaking out and wanted to scream at Rick to hide. "What do we do?" she said.

Rick had already changed into shorts and a t-shirt when he looked up and spotted the sergeant. Their eyes locked again, and this time the sergeant reached down for his revolver on his hip.

"Shit," mumbled Rick.

Outside, Gary yelled, "Back to one!"

It was a code they used that meant they needed to get back to the first place they had been. Rick wouldn't make it back to the car. His only chance was to split up with Gary and Jules and rendezvous back at the airport. He motioned at Gary to leave. The driver smoked the tires and drove out of sight.

Rick started running in the opposite direction. The pain in his back was masked by the adrenaline rushing though his veins. Even with all his injuries, he was faster than the sergeant.

He ran around the building and doubled back toward the sergeant's car. It was still running. The guy must've been in a hurry. Rick jumped inside and squealed the tires. The sergeant fired at him, sending bullets ripping through the front windshield. Rick ducked and avoided the shots. He passed Jefferson, who continued to fire but just hit the trunk and broke one of the taillights. Rick looked in the rearview and saw him grab his handheld radio. Over the car radio, he heard:

"This is Sergeant Jefferson. We have a possible fugitive southbound on Harbour Drive. He's in my stolen unmarked cruiser."

Rick quickly turned onto the first road he came to, which was Goring Avenue. Without his cell phone or GPS, he had no idea which way the airport was. He heard sirens from several directions. Then he saw a sign with an airplane on it and a left arrow. He turned left, nearly missing the road and landing in the ditch. He spotted another sign but pointing straight ahead. He had somehow gotten lucky and turned onto the road to the airport. Then he floored it.

Flashing lights behind him were gaining on him. Rick put the pedal to the floor. He was approaching the airport, and several more lights were coming his way from that direction. He looked out of the passenger's window and spotted the small terminal for executive jets. He didn't see Gary's plane. It wasn't where it had been parked.

Where the hell did it go?

Then he spotted it, out on the tarmac taxiing to the end of the runway. He ripped the steering wheel to the right and slammed into the grass. He headed straight for the cyclone fence and drove right through it. The car came to a sudden stop when he hit the soft dirt on the berm built around the airport.

He grabbed his backpack from the seat and began to run toward the plane. He had a good head start. The door of the plane was opening to let him inside.

Behind him, a police car hit the berm and stopped at the edge when it got stuck. Two men jumped out and started running toward Rick.

"Stop, stop!"

It was Jefferson. Rick heard a shot and felt a bullet graze his right lower leg. He didn't stop. He remembered he had his wallet and ID in his back pocket. He threw the backpack and continued to run.

He got to the plane and was running beside it. Gary leaned out and stuck out his hand. Jules was crying and didn't know what to do to help. Rick reached up, and Gary pulled him into the plane and shut the door. Breathing hard, Rick looked out of the window and saw the men stop and pick up the backpack. Jules wrapped her arms around Rick, nearly pulling him to the ground.

The pilot gave full throttle, and they were off in the air in seconds. Rick was trying to catch his breath. He looked down at his leg and saw the bullet had left a long red mark on his calf where it grazed him. No entry wound.

"Look, Gary," said Rick between breaths, "next time you want to stop, refuel, and go snorkeling, can we pick another place besides Grand Cayman? I ain't ever coming here again."

"What about your passport in the backpack?" asked Gary.

"I'm not real fond of Roja Bronco. Please let me pick my own name next time."

Rick just shook his head as the jet rounded the tip of the island, banked left, and pointed north to Mississippi.

Not long after Gary, Jules, and Rick had left for Colombia, the EquuSearch crew had also pulled out. The case hadn't exactly gone cold, but there had been a mass shooting in Texas, and it took priority over one missing kid.

Now, Gary's bus sat alone in the Expo grounds. A small FBI team remained behind but had moved their base to an Airbnb in town. There still had been no contact from the kidnapper, and Possum was beginning to think he might be getting cold feet because of the drone crash. They'd left it there so he would find it and think it was just a regular crash and that the dye pack had nothing to do with it. By staking out the cemetery and not catching him, though, that might have made him think it was a setup. By now, Dale would've gotten word that Rick and the gang had gone to Colombia. All they could do was wait for Dale to make his next move, if he was in fact the kidnapper.

Possum's phone buzzed. It was Deputy Ron.

"Hello, Possum. We just got a call from the kidnapper. He used a modulator to change his voice on the phone. He's figured out that it was a setup and somehow, he knew we caused the drone crash. He's threatened to cut off one of Tyler's hands if we don't deliver the five million dollars this time. He's not stupid. Leaving a few hundred-dollar bills scattered by the crash site didn't fool him at all. It actually insulted him. He's going to call back shortly with instructions. Keep your phone handy."

"Thanks, Ron. I'm on the bus, and I'll be here until I hear from you."

After hanging up, Possum went over every scenario in his head. He wasn't sure when Rick and the gang would get back, and they planned to stay out of sight regardless. There was strength in numbers, and if Dale was going to strike, it would be while Possum was alone. Possum was nervous, but planned to be prepared.

Deputy Ron called back a few hours later.

"Okay, Possum, we heard from him. He wants the money and he means business. I've spoken with Mr. Raynes, and he wants to pay it this time. Once I told him about the threat to cut off his son's hand, he was adamant. He's flying up from Biloxi, and we're gonna have him drop the money with you at the bus. We know Dale will be watching, but he hasn't given us any exchange details yet. Also, we still don't think he is aware of the value of The Black Strat. If he did, he would find a buyer on the black market, and we haven't gotten any intel of a purchase, according to the FBI."

"So, what's the plan?"

"Mr. Raynes will land near the bus, carry the money over to you, then leave. You'll have backup from the FBI in case Dale tries to interfere. Mr. Raynes has required proof of life before he does anything, though. The kidnapper said he will be sending it over soon. I gave him my email and the FBI's. Hold on."

Ron covered the mouthpiece of his phone, and Possum could hear muffled speech on the other end. Ron got back on the phone.

"Possum, I'm going to text you a photo he just sent us. Give me a second."

Possum waited for his phone to buzz again. When it did, he moved the phone from his ear and looked at the text. It was small, so he forwarded it to his MacBook. It was a picture of Tyler holding the Bolivar Bullet newspaper. His right hand was bandaged and the date of the newspaper was today. He was definitely alive. Possum's chest swelled up. At least for now, they weren't looking for a corpse.

"That's great news, Ron."

"Yes, we are all excited. I forwarded the photo to Mr. Raynes. He is arranging now to get the money. I've explained to him that once the kidnapper has that money, there is no reason for him to keep Tyler alive. There's a strong chance he will tie up loose ends and murder him. He won't listen. So, I'll keep you posted on his approximate time to get to you. Just stay put and we'll go from there."

"Okay, Ron, I'll be here awaiting instructions."

Possum knew Dale would be casing the bus to make sure the money was delivered. But he would be hard to detect. Since he flew drones, that was one way he might be watching. Possum decided to set up two motion detection cameras on the main road that sat in front of the bus at the Expo Center. These tiny cameras were amazing and could record forty-eight hours straight to a microSD card on one charge. He set one up on the fence facing the road, then walked across the street and hid another one on the post of a mailbox facing the direction of the other camera. Any person or vehicle that crossed the path would be clearly recorded. They recorded at 6K and had a 180-degree angle.

On the walk back to the bus, Possum's phone buzzed again.

"Possum, I just spoke to Mr. Raynes and he will be en route to you within the hour. He should arrive sometime between 5:00 and 5:30 p.m. Be ready."

The FBI positioned two snipers behind the bus in two vantage points in the Expo Center, in case there was an incident during the transfer.

Possum kept eyeing his watch. At 5:15, he heard the whirring of helicopter blades. He looked at the road. A few cars were passing by in both directions, but none were slowing down. A kid was kneeling next to his bike putting a chain back on that had slipped out of the gears. Nothing seemed out of the ordinary.

The chopper touched down, and Jack stepped out carrying a large black duffel bag. He set it on the ground on front of Possum and unzipped it. Possum picked up the bag and pulled out a few stacks of bundled bills in two-thousand-count increments.

"Get my boy back. Please."

"We will."

They shook hands, and Jack climbed back into the chopper and was gone in less than thirty seconds. The boy on the bike fixed the chain and rode past, never even looking toward the bus. Possum climbed inside and stuck the money in his bunk. He called Ron.

"Hi, Ron. I have the money. Now what?"

"We wait. Keep a weapon on you at all times."

CHAPTER FIFTEEN

Rick, Jules, and Gary landed at Cleveland Municipal Airport close to midnight. They took an Uber to the Cotton House Hotel where Gary had made reservations for adjoining rooms under the name Valentina Salsa.

Jules used her fake passport and paid cash for the room and deposit. They were doing everything in their power to stay under the radar. They got settled in their rooms, and Rick called Possum. He used the house phone and called a burner number Gary had given him after he picked up one from Walmart for Possum. He had instructed Possum to go by MJ, and Rick would be Roja in case the kidnapper had a phone scanner.

"MJ, it's Roja. Did you get the pizzas?"

"Yes, the pizzas have been delivered. All five of them."

"Did they get the order right? Any mix-ups?"

"Nah, they arrived just as I ordered them."

"Okay, well, y'all enjoy. If you need anything, I'm just a phone call away."

They hung up, and Gary handed Rick his sat phone.

"Okay, call him back on his cell number with this and be yourself. We are having a great time in Colombia, remember."

Rick waited about fifteen minutes, then called Possum again.

"Hey, Possum, it's Rick. I hope I didn't wake you. I'm not sure what time zone we are in here. Colombia is such a beautiful place. We are staying with Jules's parents in an Airbnb. It's spectacular."

"I'm good here, Rick. I was up. It looks like this case is gonna solve itself. Jack has given me the money for the kidnapper, and he will probably release Tyler once he has the money. We got a photo of him proving he's still alive."

Rick had a feeling Possum was just saying that in case his phone was being monitored. The likelihood seemed higher that once the kidnapper got the money, he would just kill Tyler rather than let him go—which meant they had very little time left to take down Clemens and get the kid out alive.

But Rick played along for now. "Oh, that's great news. I guess we're not needed after all. You hold down the fort. If anything changes, let me know. We'll be here for another thirteen days. You know how to reach me."

"Sounds good, Rick. We've got it covered here. I think it will be over soon. I'm gonna hit the hay soon. Have a good night. Say hi to everyone for me."

Rick hung up and sighed, running a hand through his hair. Possum was taking a big risk keeping the money on the bus with him, and he was uneasy about it. But he also knew it might be their last chance to draw Clemens out. The trap was set, and all they could do now was hope it would work.

After hanging up the call with Rick, Possum walked to the street to retrieve the motion cameras. He had a gun in his waist holster and paused a few times to check the street around him for any sign of movement, someone lurking in the dark. His heart was beating fast, but no one seemed to be out there.

Back inside the bus, he set the gun on the table beside him to keep it close. He popped the SD cards into his MacBook and used a program that would let him zoom in and out of anything on the cards. He took notes of each car that passed and easily got the license plates. None of the drivers even paid attention to the Expo. One was an old lady in her seventies at least. The other was a young man who was moving his head to loud music, oblivious to the chopper landing. The camera across the street had caught the chopper and the exchange perfectly. No cars passed during the drop, and the only other motion was the kid on the bicycle.

Possum zoomed in, and as the kid looked away from the Expo toward the field across the street, he saw it. His whole body stiffened. The kid wasn't a kid after all. It was Dale Clemens. He could see the eye patch clearly under his sunglasses. He switched to the other camera and sure enough, just under the cutoff sweatshirt on his right bicep was the bottom of the trident tattoo.

"Son of a bitch! He was casing the place."

Grabbing his phone, Possum stepped outside to call Deputy Ron. Just as it hit him that he'd left his gun on the table beside his laptop, a dark figure approached him.

Shit, thought Possum.

"Put down the phone and step back inside."

The man was wielding a sawed-off shotgun.

Shit, shit, shit.

Possum put his hands up and slowly backed up to the bus.

"Where's the money?"

"It's in my bunk."

"Kneel down and turn around."

"Look, you don't have to shoot me. You can have the money, Dale."

"Shut your mouth!"

He was wearing a black ski mask, gloves, and solid black clothing. There was no way for Possum to be certain it was him, but since he'd called him by his name and hadn't been corrected, and by the tone of his voice, Possum was pretty sure it was.

"Now put your hands behind your head and cross your ankles."

Possum reluctantly did as he was told. The man used zip ties to tie up Possum's wrists and ankles.

"Look, Dale, you're not gonna get away with—"

Thwack! A pain hit the back of Possum's skull and he fell forward, smashing his nose onto the floor of the bus.

When Possum awoke, he was in a daze. He wasn't sure how long he'd been out. He looked at his watch through blurry eyes. There was a small puddle of blood on the floor where his face had hit the tile. His head was pounding. He was dizzy and still in zip ties.

He struggled to the galley and stood up, using his balance, leaning against the wall and pushing himself up. With his back against the counter, he managed to get his wrists under the edge of the wall-mounted beer opener. He busted the tie after a few hard pulls. He took a knife out of the drawer, reached down, and cut the ties from his crossed ankles.

He was still in a daze when he dialed Gary's cell, forgetting that they were trying to keep the crew's whereabouts unknown. Gary didn't answer, and Possum's burner phone started ringing. It was Gary's sat phone. Coming to his senses, he remembered that Gary, Rick, and Jules were still supposed to be in Colombia.

"Gary, it's Possum. He took the money."

"Oh, so they did the exchange already. That was fast. Did he release the kid?"

"No, you don't understand. I was about to call Deputy Ron, and I was ambushed. He was casing the place on a bicycle, and when I stepped out of the bus for some air and to make the call, he pulled a shotgun on me. I was stupid and I forgot my own weapon. He must've slammed the back of my head with the butt of the gun. Knocked me out cold. When I came to, he and the money were gone."

"Son of a fucking bitch! That's not how this was supposed to go down. Fuck. There's no sense in pretending we are in Colombia now. He got the jump on us. We'll be right over."

They hung up, and Possum called Deputy Ron and told him what had just transpired.

By the time Rick, Gary, and Jules pulled up, Ron and a team from the FBI were already there. Forensic guys came onto the bus and made everyone wait outside while they took photos, dusted for prints, and swiped for DNA.

"Are you okay, Possum?" asked Rick, hurrying over to his friend.

"I've had better days, hombre. My head feels like it's gonna explode."

"We need to get you checked out. You might have a concussion."

The lead FBI agent questioned Possum. "Did you get a good look at the guy?"

"It happened so fast and it was pitch black out, but I did get him on my motion cameras. The cameras are sitting on the dinette beside my MacBook."

The agent leaned his head into the bus to ask the others inside to retrieve them. A moment later, he pulled his head back.

"They're gone. Are you sure you placed them on the dinette?"

"Yes! Fuck, I just bought that MacBook. It cost like $3,300! Now all video of him casing the place is gone too!"

The agent sighed in frustration. "We're gonna have to bring you in for questioning, Possum. You were the last person to see the five million dollars. How do we know you didn't make up this whole story?"

Rick opened his mouth to speak up for Possum, but Gary got to it first.

"Wait a minute!" said Gary, pushing his way forward. "I had fourteen hidden cameras installed on my coach. They are all being recorded to a two-sided DVD drive in the top left cabinet above the fridge."

Once the forensics team gave the all clear and left, everyone entered the bus. Gary pulled out a remote control and pushed a button, and a big-screen TV started folding down in the front of the bus. He scrolled back on the DVD, and there it was. Clear as a picture. Everything Possum said happened in 1080p full color. Possum folded his arms and shot the lead agent an *I told you so* look.

"We're gonna need that DVD now."

"Can we get a copy, at least?" asked Rick.

"Yeah, once Quantico gets it, we'll shoot you over a copy."

Rick called Jack Raynes and told him what had happened. He could hear the anguish in his voice.

"Will he let my boy go?"

"I hope so, Jack. I hope so."

The FBI and Deputy Ron stayed on the bus for several more hours going over the ambush again and again. It was obvious from the DVD that Possum was telling the truth, but in the eyes of the law, they didn't know who that guy was who'd hit Possum over the head. It could have been an accomplice of his in a ruse to steal the money.

Possum went along with their repeat questions. He knew how this worked and was prepared to be a person of interest. Once they were all satisfied, they left, asking Possum to come back to the Sheriff's Department in the morning to corroborate his story officially one more time on camera. He didn't mind. He knew what had happened. He was so upset that he'd taken down the motion cameras. He should've just swapped out the SD cards, but what was done was done. The great videos that came from Gary's surveillance cameras were a lifesaver for sure.

The drab paint on the walls depressed Possum as he sat down behind the metal desk facing a camcorder the next morning. Two FBI agents came in to question him. It was the same routine as the night before, and he went through the motions. He wasn't concerned or even bothered by it. He was clean as a whistle, and they knew it.

After an hour and a half of boring repeat questions, he was free to go. Rick took him back to the bus in his new red Bronco that had arrived that morning. Gary had driven up to Memphis with it to pick up Rick and Jules's new iPhone 13 Pros. Rick had given Jules his iCloud password so she could set up his new phone for him.

On the ride back, Rick asked Possum a few questions, and Possum knew why. He was trying to find something the FBI might've missed.

"Did anything stand out that struck you as odd about the guy? Anything at all?"

Possum thought for a while. "No, not really. He had the same build and height as Dale Clemens. He had an eye patch. Even with his ski mask on, I could see that."

"Any jewelry you could see on his hands, or markings?"

"No, Rick. He caught me by surprise big time. It was so fast. He was in and out in under a minute."

"What a damn shame," said Rick, shaking his head in anger.

"I'm so glad I'd put Chief in the rear master bedroom and shut the door. He may have taken him for insurance in case you came after him."

Rick's eyes darkened even more at that suggestion.

Possum's phone buzzed. "It's Ron," he mouthed to Rick. "Hey, Ron, what's up?"

"We got a call from the kidnapper. He said he's releasing Tyler today. He said he'll send an automatic email with GPS coordinates shortly. We are on full alert. Stay by your phone."

"I'm here and we're ready," said Possum. He hung up and looked back at Rick. "Dale is letting Tyler go today. I hope alive."

Rick was beside himself with frustration. He wanted to bust Clemens more than anything. It was personal now. He had managed to injure everyone on Rick's gang, and he wanted Clemens to pay for it.

They drove toward the bus and were on pins and needles waiting for the call from Ron. Seconds turned to minutes; minutes turned to hours. They were back at the Expo and pacing inside the bus when Possum's phone finally pinged. It was a text from Deputy Ron. Rick read it over his shoulder.

> We got him. He is dehydrated
> and en route to Bolivar
> Medical Center. I'll call
> with more details soon.

"Woohoo!" shouted Possum. "It's over!"

They ran outside and jumped into the Bronco. Rick floored it, bound for the hospital.

"Call Gary and tell him the news," said Rick.

Possum called Gary. While they were talking, his phone pinged again.

> Jack Raynes flying in to
> hospital now.

When they arrived, several press vans were outside of the hospital entrance. The kidnapping had made national news, and what was an edge-of-our-seat victim story had turned into a feel-good ending. Rick and Possum made their way through the crowd of reporters and into the waiting room of the ER.

"How is he, Ron?" asked Rick.

"He's gonna be fine. He has a black eye and a few bruises. "His right hand was infected a little where his ring finger was removed, but he is on a strong antibiotic now and will regain the use of his hand. Though he'll have to learn to strum without his ring finger. They have him on a saline drip. The Feds want a first crack at him, so we'll have to wait to talk to him. The doctor makes the decision when anyone is allowed in. Jack just landed and will be down shortly."

Everyone paced the floor, waiting for any news. The ER doctor finally came out. He asked for Mr. Raynes. Jack walked over to him and waved Rick and Ron over.

"Mr. Raynes, I'm Dr. Oliver. Your son is going to be fine. He was severely dehydrated and we gave him a sedative for his nerves. He seems in pretty good shape mentally. He said he was treated pretty good and only got the black eye, a minor cut, and some bruises when he tried to escape. He said overall he was well taken care of. He was locked inside an old, abandoned farmhouse off of Highway 8. You know, the one with the massive fireplace that faces Little Talla-hatchie River. Oh, I forgot you're not from here. Anyway, it's a few miles past Dockery Farms. He was within thirty miles of us the entire time."

"When can I see him?"

"I've asked the FBI if you can visit him first before they question him. They agreed, so you can go in now. Only you, Mr. Raynes."

Jack followed the doctor through some automatic doors and disappeared.

Rick went back to pacing as he waited for Jack to come back out. He was extremely anxious to speak with the boy.

"Son, I am so happy to see your face," said Jack. "I have been worried sick. Everyone has been. How are you feeling?"

"I'm fine. Just a little tired. I feel better than when I first came in here."

Tyler was lying on his hospital bed with two extra blankets pulled up to his chin. His dad had paid extra for a private room. His eye was black and he had a few scratches on his face. He looked thin and tired.

"Are you cold, son?"

"A little. I guess because I was so dehydrated, my internal thermostat is off."

"Yeah, that makes sense because to me it does seem a little stuffy in here," replied Jack.

They talked for a few more minutes and then Jack let Tyler rest. He had been through an ordeal and seemed out of it still. Rest and lots of water were what he needed most now.

Rick stood up as soon as Jack returned to the waiting room. "How is he?" asked Rick.

"He looks tired, but I think he's gonna be fine. I'm gonna speak to the doctor. It would probably be good if he spoke to a therapist. He's probably suffering from PTSD. He wasn't the jubilant guy I remember. The only time I've seen him that lethargic was when he was coming off of drugs. He has the same sunken-in dark circles under his eyes as when he was an addict. I think he just needs some time. I know the FBI will question him now, and I wish they'd give him some time, but I guess the sooner, the better, so we can still catch that son of a bitch before he flees the country. I don't care about the money; that's why I paid it. I just wanted my son back. But he needs to pay for causing him so much suffering."

"He will pay, Jack. We are going to stay on the case and catch that scumbag. Right now, we all need to be strong for Tyler. We're gonna head back to the bus, but please let me know when it's a good time to talk to him. I can follow up with the FBI. They aren't as compassionate as me, and I know the first forty-eight hours are important. His memory will be sharper the sooner he can be questioned. We need to get a track on Clemens before he slips through the cracks."

"Thank you, Rick. I appreciate all you have done so far. You have already earned the reward, and I will have my secretary make the necessary arrangements for the deposit."

"No, we're not done with the case," said Rick adamantly.

"I know you wanna keep working and I want you to as well, but our agreement was for any info leading to the return of Tyler. He's back, thanks in large part to you and your crew. That fucker still has The Black Strat, so I will make a new contract for you regarding returning The Black Strat and catching the guy who took Tyler. There will be a bonus for both."

"Whatever you decide is fair, Jack. We want to be a part of it regardless."

"You will be."

They shook hands, and Jack walked out of the hospital ER and ran his hands through his hair. He looked extremely stressed out. It was probably more relief mixed with shock that Tyler was back and safe.

Rick walked back over to Possum. "All right, man, there's nothing more we can do here. We may as well head back and rendezvous with Deputy Ron and the FBI tomorrow."

"Jules and Gary are on their way here. I'll call them and have them meet us at the bus instead," said Possum.

Rick drove in silence after Possum got off the phone with Gary. Neither one of them felt like talking. It was as if a heavy burden had been lifted, only to be replaced by the next challenge: finding Dale Clemens and bringing him to justice.

CHAPTER SIXTEEN

Gary and Jules arrived at the bus about forty-five minutes after Rick and Possum did. Gary pushed Rick's new phone over to him on the dinette.

"Thanks. Man, that screen is huge. I thought old iPhones had a big screen."

"Yeah, flip it over. It has four cameras."

"Damn, homie, that be fancy like," replied Possum.

"Remember when we used phones to call people?" asked Rick sarcastically.

Rick played with his new phone for a while, trying to get used to it. Gary showed him most of the ins and outs. Ron called and said that everyone should meet back at the Sheriff's Department around 3:30 p.m.

"Let's celebrate Tyler's return. Is everyone hungry?" asked Jules.

"Does a deer...?"

Jules interrupted him before he finished. "Stop, Possum. I know it's a bear!"

They all laughed.

"How about I make something special for lunch?"

"Jules, while I appreciate the offer, baby, how about I just spring for some pizzas and beer? I think the weight of this whole ordeal has been a lot for all of us. Maybe we all should just chill out and veg a little until we need to go meet with the FBI."

"You're right, Rick. I'm pretty drained myself," she said with a light laugh. "I'm not sure if I have the energy to be creative in the kitchen. Pizza it is!"

"I'll do the honors, Rick. I have it on speed dial. Ron told me the best place in town: Lost Pizza Company. They don't deliver, but I'll go pick it up if Gary will let me drive his Bronco." He grinned.

Gary tossed Possum the keys, and Possum rang up the pizza place to put in their order before heading out the door. They had plenty of beer in the fridge; Gary grabbed some for himself, Rick, and Jules.

Jules rubbed Rick's back with more Tiger Balm. He was feeling almost like his old self again, only sore like he had been to the gym and overdone it a little.

"That feels great, baby. Thank you," said Rick.

"I just want you to feel better. I'm here for you, Rick."

For a short while everyone did their own thing, and Jules and Rick went to the master for a quick nap. They didn't really sleep, just held each other in bed without talking. There was a strange somber vibe in the air. When they ate the pizza for lunch, it was supposed to be a celebration, but with Dale still out there and his presence lingering, it felt like the opposite.

Everyone started milling about around 2:45 p.m. to get ready for the FBI update. They all decided to ride together in Rick's new replacement Bronco. Of course, Gary had to make a few smartass comments about the roll bars he'd had custom-installed. He only did it for the comic relief. It cost more than fifteen hundred dollars, but to Gary, the harmless joke was priceless. He definitely got more of a kick out of it than Rick, who mostly rolled his eyes at each of Gary's snide comments about keeping the shiny side up and the dirty side down. Rick took it in stride, mostly because he knew Gary loved him like a brother, and the feeling was mutual. Rick always said, if Gary wasn't giving someone shit, then he didn't like them. Razzing his friends was a sign of respect.

They pulled into the Sheriff's Department, and the press was there but in fewer numbers. The crew made their way back to the war room.

"Rick."

"Ron."

Everyone shook hands and got down to business. The lead agent began.

"Mr. Tyler Raynes is in fair spirits, considering his ordeal. His overall health is good now. We photographed him, and other than a bandage over his right bicep from a cut he received while trying to escape, and a few other minor scrapes and bruises, he's actually doing well. Oh, and a nice shiner over his right eye."

"How is he holding up mentally?" asked Rick.

"Surprisingly well, I'd say. He gave somewhat of a description of the kidnapper. Pretty unimpressive really. He didn't know his name. We asked him if it was Dale Clemens. He said he had never heard of a Dale Clemens before. He said the kidnapper told him to call him Jake, just Jake, so he did."

"Do you think he can identify him in a lineup? Did you show a photograph of Dale to him?"

"Yes, but he said he only really saw him once and the man kept a black bag over his head most of the time except when he was allowed to eat, and his food was always served on a tray he pushed through the door while wearing an IT mask."

"An IT mask? Like from the movie *IT*?" exclaimed Possum.

"Exactly, just like the red balloons from the first drop. He has some connection to the movie, or it's just a diversion and means nothing. We're not sure yet."

"Does he know about the money?"

"He never mentioned the ransom and we are only feeding him information that he asks for. There's no need to upset him any more than he already has been. As far as we know, they could've been in on it together. It's highly unlikely, as we have no reason to believe Tyler ever knew Dale before the kidnapping. His story has checked out, and we had two different agents ask him virtually the same questions an hour apart, and he was spot on. Jack Raynes has flown back to Biloxi to take care of some business at his casino, but will return once we are finished with Tyler and he gets a clean bill of health from Bolivar Medical. We're expecting him to be released in a few days, as long as his psych eval is done. If he gets a clean medical and mental evaluation, we can't by law have him stay any longer, nor would we want to. If he decides he wants further mental help, he can pursue that in Biloxi."

"When can I speak to him?" asked Rick.

"Probably tomorrow after his psych eval, but we want to approve the questions before you go in, and one of our agents will accompany you. We don't want to tip any hats here."

"I understand. I'll write down what I want to ask him and give you a copy before we leave," said Rick.

"Any theft over a thousand dollars is considered grand larceny, and of course, we take kidnapping extremely seriously. We want Dale on much more than that, as you probably know. He is under investigation for drug trafficking, racketeering, and falsifying a passport, as well as attempted murder. The list is quite long. Needless to say, we have a vested interest in bringing him in. The only reason we are cooperating with the local police and you, Mr. Waters, a private eye, is because Jack Raynes is a very powerful man with lots of friends in DC. No offense, but we usually don't commingle this much."

"I get it," said Rick.

"Don't forget, we asked you to help with the drop because of time constraints with our drone tech. I have no interest in getting into a pissing match. We all have the same goal. Nail that fucker to the wall."

"Agreed."

"We have extra reinforcements in all major airports. Now that he has the five million dollars, we are sure he will try to get out of the US as soon as possible. We know he has a lot of support in Miami, so the bureau is on full alert, as well as local agencies down there. He's gonna make a mistake. We will get him. He can't just disappear."

"He's done pretty well so far," said Gary with a look of disappointment.

"We know what he likes. He has a passion for Maseratis, so every damn Mazzy dealership from here to Miami has been faxed his image. That won't stop him from acquiring a used one, though, and it's a long shot anyway, as we think he will try to leave the country as soon as possible. He can get as many Maseratis as he wants in South America, and we can't touch him down there. I honestly think if we don't get him within the next three to five days, he's gone. So, as usual, time is against us."

The meeting ended, and Rick and the crew headed back to the bus. He continued to go over the case files and talked to Jack and Deputy Ron as often as he needed to. Rick had a score to settle with Clemens, and he had every intention of doing so. He'd do whatever it took to bring him in, dead or alive.

The next day, he got the all-clear to speak with Tyler. He went alone and met an agent at Bolivar Medical who went inside Tyler's room with him.

"Hi, Tyler. I'm Rick Waters, a private eye from Destin. Your dad hired me to help find you."

"Oh Destin, yeah, I've been there. I used to play a few gigs over on Fort Walton. I can't wait to get out of here and start jamming again. I'm gonna blow them away when I get my band back together."

"That sounds great, Tyler. You'll have to let me know when you're playing down our way. Me and my crew will come out and support you."

"Thanks, man, I appreciate that."

Rick took out a copy of the preapproved questions he had written down and started to go down the list. He motioned to his phone and asked the agent if he could record. He nodded in agreement.

"All right, Tyler, I'm sure you've been asked some of these questions already, and I'm sure you're sick of answering them over and over, but maybe you missed something."

Tyler shrugged. "Shoot, man."

"Okay, before you were abducted, had you ever met Dale Clemens before?"

"Nope. I hadn't even heard of his name until one of the agents told it to me. I thought his name was Jake."

"I understand. The night you disappeared, did you see anyone else at the crossroads except the kidnapper?"

"You mean besides the devil I sold my soul to? Hahaha."

"Yeah, ha, except the devil."

"Nope, he was the only one."

"You're doing great, Tyler. Why do you think he wore an IT mask? Does it have anything to do with the case?"

"That's one question they haven't asked me yet."

The agent perked up and leaned in to listen more intently.

"I have no idea what his deal was with that stupid movie *IT*. He had it playing on a loop on a TV in the corner of the room. The old farmhouse had no electricity, but he brought in some battery-powered CD player or something. It was only the audio from the movie. Through the black bag he had over my head, I never saw light flicker—you know, like when a TV plays in a dark room. I always knew when the sun was coming up because I could see small amounts of light through the bag. The only reason I know it was audio from the movie *IT* is because I had just seen it two nights before Halloween at the Suds and Cinema with a friend of mine there in Fort Walton. It was still fresh in my mind. I thought the movie was stupid then, and just as stupid as he played the damn audio of it over and over. He's a weird dude. I think he thought it scared me. Like he was using it as a fear factor to control me. He just had no idea I thought it was an idiotic movie."

"All right, Tyler, just a few more questions and I'll leave you be. Did you ever see a guitar there, anywhere in the farmhouse?"

"Like I said, I always had a bag over my head except when I was eating. Then the idiot sat there and watched me with a shotgun pointing straight at me, wearing that stupid IT mask. He did the same thing when I used the bathroom. He kept me handcuffed the entire time except when I ate or did my business. I mean, look at my damn wrists. They are still raw from those damn cuffs."

Tyler pulled his arms out from under the bedsheet and showed Rick his wrists.

"What's up with your right arm?"

Rick pointed at a bandage all the way around his right arm on his bicep.

"Oh, it's just a cut I got when I tried to escape after eating once. He slammed my face with the shotgun, and I fell into the fireplace and cut my arm. It'll be fine."

Rick frowned. "That bandage looks a bit worn. You want me to call a nurse in to change it before we continue?"

"Nah, man, I told you. It'll be fine." Tyler climbed back under the covers and seemed a bit perturbed. "Can we just finish the questions? I'm kinda tired."

"Sure, son, no problem. What did his voice sound like? I mean, was he a tenor or did he have a low voice?"

"I have no idea. As I've already answered many, many times, every time he spoke, he used a little handheld thing that made his voice sound freaky. I think the FBI called it a voice modulator. Any other questions?"

After a few more questions, Rick looked down at his list. He had reached the end. He leaned over and whispered something to the agent. He thought for a second and then nodded.

"I know you are stoked to get out of here, and you joked about selling your soul to the devil to become the greatest guitar player in the world. You don't really believe that horseshit, do you?"

"I wasn't joking, you'll see," said Tyler with a wicked, evil-looking grin.

"Well, thanks for your time, Tyler. I'll let you rest now."

Tyler closed his eyes as a sort of dismissal to Rick.

Both he and the agent walked out of the room.

"What do you think about that selling your soul to the devil nonsense? Do you think he really believes that crap?" asked the agent.

"Who knows what he believes. He's a young guy with a long history of drug abuse. Maybe he was whacked out the night he was taken and thought Clemens was the devil," replied Rick.

"That's true. Could be."

They parted ways, and Rick headed back to the bus. As soon as he arrived, Jules gave him a big hug with a glass of rum in her hand for him. It was exactly what he needed. Chief was hanging from a makeshift perch Gary had made from some sticks and twine he'd found and tied to the rooftop air conditioner. There was a newspaper on the floor under him covered in spent peanut shells and grape skins. It looked like Chief got more on the floor than in his mouth.

"How'd it go, Rick?" asked Possum.

"The same way it did every time the FBI questioned him. The only difference is he gave a little more detail about the IT mask. The freak played the audio of the movie over and over in a loop. I think it was just a scare tactic. The kid wasn't scared though, so that kinda backfired. Also, the night he was taken, he really believes he met the devil and sold his soul. The agent thinks he was whacked out on something, and I tend to think he's right. So, all in all, I didn't get anything new that would help us, really." Rick sighed. "I've got a bad feeling Clemens has fled the country already. I hope I'm wrong."

"That's too bad, man," said Gary as he patted Rick on the shoulder.

Two days turned into two weeks, and the FBI pulled out of Cleveland altogether and focused more of their agents in Memphis and Miami. Jack refused to give up and tried to talk Rick into staying in Cleveland, but Rick eventually was able to convince him that Dale was long gone from Cleveland and probably the US, for that matter.

"We'll keep the case open," Rick told him one afternoon over the phone, "but I think it's about time the crew and I return to Destin."

"I guess I can't blame you for wanting to go home," said Jack.

"How's Tyler doing?"

"He's coming along nicely. I had him meet with a counselor several times for PTSD and he seems to be adjusting well. He's been clean and sober and has been practicing with his band. It's a blues power trio, actually. He's totally committed to taking it to the next level, and I plan to help him."

"That's so good to hear, Jack."

"Yeah, I bought him a new PA system and a van and trailer. He plans to go on tour. He's doing a show here in Biloxi before they head out. I'd love it if y'all could attend."

"Sure, we'll come down to the show," Rick told him.

Gary had Rick's Bronco trucked to Destin, and he hooked up his own Bronco to the motorhome and they planned to leave in the morning. Biloxi wasn't that far from Destin, and they all wanted to see Tyler.

"Maybe we can roll some bones, Rick," said Gary.

"Yeah, it'll be nice to be home, but one more night away won't hurt us, I guess. Actually, there is one more thing I think we should do before we leave."

"Oh yeah?"

"I think we need to check out that farmhouse where Tyler was kept. Make sure the Feds didn't miss anything that could help us track down Clemens."

"Sounds like a good idea."

They headed over to the farmhouse before the sun went down. The place was dingy and damp. The huge fireplace along the wall was made of large river stones. Rick ran his hand along the mantel, trying to find anything left behind. He had to give it one more shot before returning home.

"Possum, didn't the police report say that Tyler was found inside the house bound to a chair, and there was a padlock on the door outside?" asked Rick.

"Hang on, I have a copy of the report on my phone. Let me double check."

Possum scrolled through his phone for a minute.

"Yep, here it is. That's exactly right. Why?"

"Well, I was just thinking that if I was locked inside on a chair, I'd try to find a way out one way or the other. The door is super thick, and if it was padlocked from the outside, that exit would be useless. Do you see another way out of here?"

Possum scanned the room. There were no windows. He looked slowly and methodically then stopped and pointed at the fireplace.

"Bingo!" said Rick.

They all approached the fireplace.

"Close the door, Possum," said Rick.

Possum shut the heavy door, eliminating the only source of light in the house. Rick waved his hands in front of his eyes and couldn't see anything. Slowly, his eyes adjusted to the darkness, and a sliver of light could be seen emanating from the fireplace. He moved toward it.

"Gary, turn on the light on your phone and hand it to me please," said Rick.

Rick took Gary's phone, kneeled down, and shined the light up the chimney. It was full of cobwebs and dusty.

"Do you think a man could fit through this chimney?" asked Rick.

Gary dropped to a knee beside him and looked up.

"Not a man our size, but yes, a thin kid like Tyler could. I wonder why he didn't at least try to get out that way?" asked Gary.

"That's the sixty-four-dollar question, and that's also a question I'm going to ask Tyler," said Rick.

"If only we had someone small enough to try," said Rick as he shined the light toward Jules.

"Are you serious, Rick? There are spiders up there!" exclaimed Jules.

"Come look, Jules, it's just old webs. I see no spiders whatsoever."

She kneeled down and peered up. The chimney was definitely wide enough for her to get into, and the rough masonry on the bricks would give good handholds.

"I need gloves!" she demanded.

"We can go back to the bus and get gloves, but remember, Tyler didn't have any gloves. If you're scared or uncomfortable, we can go back to the Sheriff's Department and find some skinny officer who will do it," said Rick.

"I ain't scared. Move over," said Jules confidently.

"Now, Jules, I have to turn off the light to recreate exactly what Tyler would've faced. Are you okay with that?"

"Yes, yes, just do it. You're gonna owe me one, mister!"

"Whatever you want, baby," said Rick.

Jules began to crawl up. She was almost to the top when she yelled, "Rick, I found something. I'm gonna drop it."

She dropped the object, and it hit the bottom of the fireplace. A few moments later, she called down, "I did it! I'm on the roof!"

Possum opened the huge heavy door, flooding the room with light. Rick leaned down and picked up what Jules had dropped. It was a small notepad. They all stepped outside, and Gary and Possum helped Jules down from the roof.

Rick flipped through the pages of the notepad. Various names and numbers were scribbled on the paper. Most had a 305 area code, and some had Brazil's country code of +55, which was the area of Iguaçu Falls in the state of Paraná, an area frequented by Clemens. Rick continued to scroll down the list. Then he came across a number in Miami that was circled with a date just two days past. This was a big clue.

Rick wrapped his arms around Jules and swung her around. "Jules, you found Clemens's notes. This is huge!"

She was grinning from ear to ear like a Cheshire cat.

"We need to talk to Tyler ASAP. How in the hell did this notepad get lodged in the fireplace chimney?" asked Rick.

"Let's hope Tyler can tell us that."

CHAPTER SEVENTEEN

The Red Ruby Casino was bustling with excitement. Gary parked the bus under the parking garage in a dedicated area for oversized vehicles. Since they had been on the bus for so many days, they opted to get rooms for a change. Jack insisted on paying and set them up in the presidential suite. It had three bedrooms and was massive.

It was still early, and they had four hours until Tyler's show in the main lounge area. After Rick and the gang got to the rooms, Jack made an appearance and offered to show them some behind-the-scenes stuff in the casino. He took them to the surveillance room, which Rick had already seen, as well as his gun collection and range. Possum and Gary were beside themselves.

"Hey, Jack, can I speak with Tyler? Is he around?" asked Rick.

"Let me give him a call. He's probably rehearsing for tonight at the warehouse. It's just down the street."

Jack hung up after he spoke to Tyler.

"He's finishing up and will be heading here shortly. He wants to see you anyway and thank you again. In the meantime, let's play with some guns, shall we?" Jack grinned.

Jules chose a new gun to replace the pistol she had lost in the accident. She went for the Springfield Hellcat nine-millimeter this time, as Jack was fresh out of S&W M&P Shields. Rick chose a Springfield Garrison five-inch .45 ACP 1911 pistol. He insisted on paying, and Jack finally relented, but the price he offered them was far below retail. Rick paid him and slipped him a few extra hundreds to thank him. He didn't even bother counting the money.

After a little fun shooting some fully automatics in the range, they all headed down to the main casino, where Jack had put together a private poker room for them and brought in some of his friends to have a little mini-tournament before the show.

He showed them the front-row VIP section he had set up in the lounge for them for Tyler's show. The trio had just finished sound check, and all their gear was set up and shiny under the lights. Jack pointed out the two new guitars that Tyler had purchased for his tour. One was a cherry-colored 1976 Gibson ES-335TD, which he played slide on mostly and had a little higher action than the other guitar, a mid-eighties Fender Strat. The color really caught Rick's eye. It was plaid like a lumberjack shirt. He thought it looked very chic.

The drummer wasn't flashy and had a small compact Pearl kit with a hi-hat, a large ride cymbal, and a splash cymbal. The bass player's rig was solid. He played Fender Precision bass through a Mesa/Boogie Subway TT-800 Lightweight

800-watt Bass Head sitting in a four-by-ten cabinet. Tyler saw Rick and waved him over.

"Jack, I'll catch up with you in a few. I'm just going to speak with Tyler. I'll meet you in the poker room shortly," said Rick.

Rick followed Tyler into the greenroom.

"Hi, Tyler. How are you feeling?"

Tyler shook Rick's hand.

"I'm doing great, Mr. Waters, thanks to you."

"It was a group effort, son. We're just glad you're doing so well now. Listen, I have a question that might help me find Dale Clemens. You got a minute?"

"Sure, grab a seat."

Rick sat on the couch, and Tyler spun a chair around and set it across from him. Rick reached into his front pocket and pulled out the notepad.

"You recognize this?"

Tyler leaned in and squinted.

"Is that Clemens's notebook? I saw him fumbling with it a few times. I think that's it. It was kinda dark in there, but it looks like it. Where'd you find it?" asked Tyler.

"Well, that's the strange part. It was found near the top of the inside of the chimney, which leads me to my next question. Why didn't you try to escape through the chimney?"

Without hesitation, Tyler answered.

"I tried. I really tried, but I was so dehydrated and weak from lack of nourishment that I just couldn't pull myself up. Clemens did go up on the roof several times. I have no idea why. I thought maybe he was trying to get a better view to see if anyone was coming. I could hear him stomping around up there, and one day, he started cussing like crazy up there. I never saw the notepad after that. I bet he dropped it accidentally down the chimney. I wish I could tell you more, but that's all I know. I hope that helps."

"It makes sense. I'm sure Clemens was nervous about getting caught, and from the roof you'd probably be able to see the main road, especially with binoculars."

"He did have a pair of those. I saw them several times."

"That's about all I have, Tyler. We're looking forward to your show. See you out there. Break a leg."

"Thanks, Mr. Waters, and please thank everyone else for me."

They shook hands, and Rick proceeded to the poker room.

"Let's play some cards," said Jack.

Rick sat down and they all settled around the table, and Jack introduced everyone. He had set up a private dealer for them and a cocktail waitress. Hors d'oeuvres were laid out on the table, and they all had a plate and a couple of drinks before the game started. Jack excused himself to attend to some casino business. He planned to meet them in the VIP section for Tyler's show. They were playing with real money, and the buy-in was ten thousand dollars each. Winner took the pot plus a fifteen thousand-dollar bonus.

After two hours of play, it was clear who was way ahead—Jules. Rick had never played cards with her before, but had figured she knew her way around the table, since she had once been a dealer. He just had no idea how good of a player she was. She knew when to bluff, how to bluff, and her charm and good looks kept everyone guessing.

In the end, Jules won the mini-tournament. She got a trophy and walked with sixty-eight thousand dollars. She was beaming with pride. She had never had that much money at once, and asked Rick to help her do something with it when they returned to Destin. Rick had the cashier make her out a large check and give her five thousand in hotel credit for shopping. The last thing they needed was to be walking around with that kind of cash again after what happened the last time they were there.

"It's almost showtime, y'all. Let's head to the lounge," said Rick.

"I can't believe I won," said Jules several times, grinning.

"I can. You were fierce and cunning in there. Remind me never to piss you off. Haha. Actually, I was holding pocket kings on one hand, there was an ace, two, four, five, and seven on the table, and I folded when you went all in. Did you have the straight or pocket aces?"

"A lady never tells. That's why it's called gambling." Jules winked at him.

"What are y'all drinking? How about champagne?" asked Gary.

They all thought about it and agreed champagne made perfect sense to drink while seeing Tyler's new debut band. Rick loved power trios. It took very solid musicians to pull off a three-piece band. Each guy had to sing and be a master of his instrument. Some of Rick's favorite trios were Rush, ZZ Top, and Triumph. The British metal band Motörhead and Robin Trower. Also, Green Day, and in the blues arena, Stevie Ray Vaughan and Double Trouble, who sometimes were a band but often performed as a trio with Vaughan on guitar and lead vocals, Chris Layton on drums, and Tommy Shannon on bass. Based on the reviews Rick had read about Tyler's past performances on Facebook, Instagram, and other social media sites, he wasn't expecting much, but he was there to support him regardless.

After they'd had a few glasses of champagne, Jack showed up, and the lights dimmed. Tyler and the boys took the stage.

"I want to thank you all for coming tonight. This is our last performance locally for a while. We're doing a small circle tour of the Midwest and then heading down the East Coast. We'll be swinging back through Florida and then home to Biloxi around January. Then we'll regroup and head west."

There was a smattering of applause from the people in the lounge. Most were chatting away with each other, too involved in their own stories to pay much attention to Tyler. Rick hated that. That's one of the reasons he never really played his guitar outside of the yacht. Today's bar scene was less than supportive, and most people were just too cool to clap. Rick made up for them by clapping loudly and whistling, showing Tyler some love.

Tyler started the first song. It was "Stormy Monday," a standard blues tune that most bands covered. He played it quite well and was fluid on his solos. It wasn't a particularly hard song to play, yet he did it with ease and confidence.

"That boy's been practicing," Rick whispered into Jules's ear.

She looked up and nodded in agreement. "He's good."

The next song was a medley—or as he called it, a mash-up—of three songs by Robert Johnson. The first part was "Hoochie Coochie Man," followed by "Come on in My Kitchen," and he rounded it out with "Crossroads." He started with the Strat, then switched over to the Gibson midway through and grabbed his slide, as the bass player took the bass for a walk. Rick had seen a lot of bands before and wasn't expecting much, but by the time he had finished the medley, he was a fan. Tyler had a gift. His vocals were amazing for such a young guy, and his guitar playing was far above what Rick had read about.

"Has he always been this good?" Rick leaned over and said to Jack.

"Not even close. Since he got back from his ordeal, all he does is play. He's been practicing ten hours a day. I'm very proud of him."

Tyler started playing the next song, and Rick immediately knew it was a tune from Hendrix. He closed his eyes and could hear Hendrix playing the notes exactly the same. Rick sang along.

As soon as Tyler finished that song, he went into a Joe Satriani song called "Satch Boogie." This playing was at a level most people could never dream of. He immediately went into a Steve Vai song, and then folded that into a Dream Theater song. Rick's jaw was touching the floor. Dream Theater was one of the most technically perfect bands in the world with some of the most difficult and varying time signatures ever recorded. Tyler played it all with ease and finesse. He was flawless. The less-than-responsive crowd had changed. He won them over, and they were completely in his control. They stood there with bated breath, waiting for each song to begin, and Tyler had their complete attention.

After his hour-and-a-half-long set, he thanked everyone to cheers and approval and slipped away backstage.

He patted Jack on the back and said, "Jack, your son has become one of the best guitar players I've ever seen live. Is he planning on recording?"

"Well, that's his dream, of course. He told me that after his East Coast tour he plans to go out west and try to get a record deal. We all know how difficult that is, but it's what he wants to do. I've at least gotta let him try. I hired him a driver for the tour. I'm, of course, a nervous dad and don't want him to disappear, so the driver is a friend of mine. He's ex black ops and runs a protection detail in Mexico. I paid him a huge sum of money to keep my son safe and pretend to be a regular Joe tour bus driver. I'm starting them in a Sprinter Van, but I told Tyler if he stays clean and really takes this music seriously, then halfway through the tour I'll get him a real bus. I'm really proud of him."

"You should be. Can we talk to him?"

"Yeah, he's changing backstage. Let me see if he's ready."

Jack walked around the stage though a door at the side and came back a few minutes later, opened it up, and waved them all over. The backstage was nothing more than a small changing room with an old couch and table and a broken TV. Tyler was sipping on a Kombucha when they stepped inside.

"Hey, Mr. Waters. Did you like the show?"

"Like? More like love! You are very talented. How'd you get so good?"

"I told you, I sold my soul to the devil. Haha."

"Okay, well, I'm starting to believe you. You are really good, man."

"Thanks, Mr. Waters. I'm super stoked about going on tour."

"Call me Rick. Oh, forgive me. This is Jules, my better half, and this is Possum and Gary. You said you planned to swing through Florida. Any chance you'll play in Destin?"

"Actually, yes, on January ninth, we have a date booked at Club LA."

"We'll be there!" replied Rick.

Tyler shook everyone's hands and then introduced the band to them all. Jack had arranged for dinner for Rick and the crew. Tyler would not be joining them, as he needed to pack for the tour. They planned to leave at sunup. Their first stop was Jackson. Tyler was polishing his Gibson, and Rick was admiring his Strat.

"That's an interesting guitar. I've never seen a plaid guitar before."

"It's a regular old Stratocaster. I wrapped it with some plaid. I wanted something that would stand out and kinda be my signature look. Kinda like Eddie Van Halen's striped Frankenstrat or Brad Paisley's paisley-painted Tele."

"Good thinking. I like it," said Rick.

They all left the back room and headed to the steakhouse with Jack leading the way. Jack had recently decided to try converting his restaurant, at least on the weekend, to a Brazilian-style steakhouse where gauchos would bring different cuts to the table on skewers. It was unlimited and one set price. Rick had been to a similar restaurant in Orlando called Fogo de Chão. Possum and Gary had both been to one in Houston called Texas de Brazil. It was Jules's first experience with such a meal. She had a great time. She only tried a small piece off each skewer at a time so she could enjoy as many as she could. Rick mostly stuck to small cuts of filet mignon and lamb. The dinner was filled with fun and laughter, and at the end, Jack brought out an expensive bottle of port. The conversation changed to Dale Clemens.

"Do you think we'll ever find him, Rick?"

"I honestly don't know, Jack. I truly think he's slipped through the cracks and crossed the border into Mexico. If he got there, it would be no problem for him to get back to Brazil. When I get back to Destin, I'm going to follow up with the FBI and US Department of Homeland Security. If I get an inkling that he is indeed in Brazil, we will go after him. I just want to bring him back to US soil, dead or alive. I know it's a long shot, but it's a shot worth taking," said Rick.

Jack took a sip of his port and sighed. "This whole thing with Tyler's disappearance, the money, and The Black Start has been a lot to deal with. It's affected me and my job performance. I wanna put it all behind me. I know you have continued to search for Clemens, and I know I've racked up quite a bill with you. So, with that being said, I'd like to terminate the contract. Now, before you get excited, let me explain. I should've said, I want to renegotiate the contract. Here's what I have in mind. Before I tell you that, let me tell you why. Tyler's safe and making great strides in the music business. We had a bit of a setback relationship-wise. I sort of blew my top about The Black Strat. It was stupid and I tried to take it back, but what's said is said. I was upset that he took it in the first place, when he knew it was off-limits, and I guess I sort of took out my frustration of not being able to find Clemens or the guitar or money on him. He didn't deserve that. He's been through enough. We all have. Anyway, to make a long story short, I'd like you to just put finding Clemens on the back burner and focus on getting the guitar back. I think I am holding some animosity toward Tyler because of it, and that's the last thing I want to do."

"No offense, Jack, but I would like to continue to hunt for Clemens for my own reasons. I am always up for a treasure hunt, and if you want us to focus more on the guitar, we can switch gears. But I think dropping Clemens altogether would be a mistake. They are tied together, after all," replied Rick.

"I guess you're right, and that's kind what I was getting at. I wrote up a new contract. I put in a million-dollar bonus if you can recover the guitar in the same condition. I assure you, it has doubled in value since it vanished. My guess is now it's worth upward of twelve million dollars. So, a million dollars is a handsome but doable reward. What I'd like you to do is only report to me about leads on the guitar. I don't wanna fucking hear the name Dale Clemens anymore, if that's okay. If you wanna hunt for him, that's fine. I'll spit on his face with you if he turns up. Hell, I'll spit on his grave and help him to get there. How does that sound? Do we have a deal? Oh, and I will have a check drafted tonight for all your expenses and fees up until today. I've put you all up in suites for the night. I set up a five-thousand-dollar marker for each of you, and we'll just call the last contract completed."

"That's incredibly generous, Jack. You don't need to do the markers as a bonus though. That's too much."

Jack waved his reply away with a hand. "Nonsense. I've seen you play, Rick, so whatever you win is yours. Maybe your team is not so good, and I'll end up in the black. Haha. Either way, I don't care. Y'all just blow off some steam. I have to fly to Memphis soon for a meeting tomorrow morning. I'd join you if I could, but y'all are on your own tonight. Just see my secretary for the check. I'm good for it. I'm sure the new contract will be to your satisfaction. If you do end up going to Brazil, just keep track of your expenses and I'll do a per diem for you as well."

"You are so generous, Jack. Let's skip the per diem. I have a vested interest in getting that son of a bitch back myself anyway. After all, he did fucking stab me and shot at my first mate and nearly mortally wounded Chief the last time I went toe to toe with him back in Destin."

"I hope you'll find that piece of shit."

They finished their port, and Jack handed Rick a contract in a manila envelope. He told him to go over it in his room and sign it in the morning. He also said they could stay as long as they wanted, but Rick and the rest of the crew were ready to get home.

Jules stayed back and did some shopping while everyone else went to their rooms. Rick took a shower. She arrived an hour later with more bags than she could carry; a bellman helped her bring some up on a luggage cart. Rick had slipped into a hotel robe and was looking dapper with his hair slicked back. Jules had the bellman place all the bags on a table in the master bedroom. Rick tipped the guy and he left. Jules handed Rick a bag.

"Put this on while I shower," she said with a wicked grin.

She took a bag into the bathroom with her and closed the door. Rick opened the bag.

You've got to be fucking kidding me.

Inside the bag, wrapped in some tissue paper, was the smallest mankini he had ever seen. It was bright red. Nothing more than a banana hammock. At first, he refused to put it on, but he knew from that look that Jules would make it worth his while. Reluctantly, he slipped off his boxers and put on the tiny bikini briefs. That was an overstatement. He quickly put his robe back on and climbed into bed and covered up. Jules and only Jules would see him in these ridiculous drawers.

She came out a few minutes later wearing the most stunning negligee he had ever seen. She had a look in her eyes, and Rick knew what that meant. She crawled into bed and begged him to remove his robe. He finally relented and her eyes popped. She was on him like a kid in an ice cream shop. They rolled around in the bed forever and moved to the couch. It had been a long time since they had this kind of privacy.

"I need to take you to poker games more often, Ms. Castro," said Rick with a wink.

"No, all you need to do is wear those red knickers and I'll be ready! Rowrrrr!" she growled.

They made love for what seemed like hours and eventually made it back to bed and fell fast asleep in each other's arms.

The smell of fresh coffee awakened Rick, and he could hear the faint sound of the news from the TV in the living room. He threw on his robe, kissed Jules on the forehead, and proceeded to get some java.

Gary and Possum were leaning against the kitchen counter talking when Rick strolled in. He hadn't tightened his robe well, and when he walked toward the kitchen, it flung open, revealing his man-panties. Gary and Possum both applauded loudly and gave him a wolf whistle.

"Fuck! Not a word!" said Rick, his face heating with embarrassment.

"The things we do for love," said Possum, laughing.

"Not a word," repeated Rick as he poured a cup of joe.

Possum ordered some bagels, and Jules joined them not long after. She had already changed into shorts and a sports top. She planned to do a short workout in the gym before they headed for Destin.

Rick got everyone up to speed on the new contract, and Gary had his pilot deadhead the jet to Destin Executive Airport in case they did need to make a run to Brazil. The compensation package that Jack had set up was extremely generous. Rick would get $250k if he could find Dale Clemens and bring him to justice. By justice, to Jack that meant return him to the authorities or deliver him in a wooden box.

After Jules returned from her morning workout and showered, they all proceeded to the parking garage. It was just a little over a three-hour trip to Destin, and they were giddy to get home. Jack saw them off as Gary fired up the Prevost.

"Godspeed, Rick. Let's nail that bastard to the wall!"

CHAPTER EIGHTEEN

The traffic wasn't too bad as the bus entered the tunnel going under Mobile Bay, headed eastbound toward Destin. Chief was overly excited and bouncing up and down on the homemade hanging stand in the middle of the bus. Every time Gary would brake, the stand would swing and Chief would hold on for dear life. He was getting used to it and seemed to enjoy the thrill of the ride. As they came out of the tunnel, the sky was a deep blue, and the traffic on I-10 was still relatively spread apart. They decided to drop down on Highway 287 and go through Navarre, because the I-10 route was so boring and monotonous.

"Rick, can we stop at Navarre Beach? I've never seen it and you've told me so much about it," said Jules.

"Sounds good to me. You, Gary?" asked Rick.

"We ain't on no schedule, bro."

Neither Possum nor Gary had ever seen Navarre Beach either. It was the same beautiful white sand and blue water that Destin had, but it was far less jam-packed. The far end of it near Pensacola even allowed dogs on the beach, making it one of the only beaches in the panhandle of Florida that allowed pets. They stopped by Juana's Pagoda, a giant palapa on the sound just over the bridge to Navarre Beach. Possum jumped out and grabbed everyone a huge piña colada in a souvenir cup. He ran back to the bus and nearly tripped and fell, but caught his balance and saved the drinks. That would've been alcohol abuse, and no one would've tolerated it.

Gary pulled the bus out of the parking lot and turned right. The water was perfect. He found a long open right-of-way, turned around, and parked the bus with the door facing the Gulf. He turned on the generator, opened up the bus-length awning, and set out chairs for everyone. This was the first time they had actually used the bus for its full potential. It had a sixty-five-inch big-screen TV on the outside, and Gary had a massive slide-out fridge underneath that pulled out and was full of Coronas.

They all kicked back and sat on the chairs. Everyone except for Jules, who had already changed into a bikini and run to the beach and waded in the clear, cool, blue water. She was wearing a white string bikini; it looked neon against her dark tanned skin. It wasn't long before Rick threw his swim trucks on. He got Chief off of his hanging perch and put his flight suit on him.

On the way down to the water, he spotted a cheap boogie board some tourist had left behind and picked it up. Once in the water, he sat Chief on it. He was apprehensive at first, but he dug his claws in and seemed to get his balance. Rick tied the leash of the flight suit to the boogie board.

A tiny little wave came up, and Rick pushed him and walked along with it. Jules swam over to get a closer look. Chief seemed comfortable. The next wave came, and at first Rick walked with him, then let him go. He rode it all the way to shore with Rick following right behind him. Once he stopped, Rick grabbed the board and spun him around to try another.

"Good job, Chief! You did it, boy!"

Chief bobbed up and down, raising his crest with excitement.

"Chief, the surfing cockatoo! Yay!" exclaimed Jules.

Chief rode a few more waves and then Jules swam up behind Rick and wrapped her legs around him, and they just held Chief's board in position and enjoyed the water. It was a glorious day, and they would be home soon. It felt good.

"Come in, the water's fine!" yelled Rick to Possum and Gary.

They had switched from piña coladas to Coronas, and they were content to sit in the chairs, drink beer, and chillax. Jules, Rick, and Chief stayed in the water for an hour. Jules ran to the bus and retrieved them a few Coronas every so often. One they were adequately pruned up and Rick's forehead resembled a ripe tomato, they decided to head back to the bus and dry off.

It was around two o'clock now, and they realized they were starving. Gary knew just what to do. He opened one of the bays on the bus and pulled out an amazing Oklahoma Joe's half-smoker and half-grill. He had everything he needed for a quick fix of hotdogs with a side of baked beans. After they ate, they decided to head home. Rick gave Johnie a call to let him know their status.

"Nine-Tenths Charters, Johnie speaking, how can I help you?"

"Hey Johnie, it's Rick."

"Oh, hi, Rick. I'm in the engine room. You are on speaker. Can you hear me okay?"

"I hear ya fine. Listen, we will be home in about an hour. We'd like to go out on the booze cruise. Are there any spots open?"

"How many?" asked Johnie.

"Five, if you count Chief."

"Hang on. I have the manifest on the fighting chair. Let me climb out of here and check. Hang on, hang on."

A minute went by, and Rick could hear Johnie doing boat yoga to get out of the engine room.

"Yep, there's like six spots."

"You have music tonight?"

"Yeah, always. That's what makes us unique, remember? I have Zaq Stiles, a local guy tonight I saw perform at Tailfins. He does a lot of nineties acoustic stuff. Real good, you'll like him."

"We're en route and coming up to Mary Esther soon, so we ain't too far out. See ya soon."

"Okay, y'all be careful. I'll probably be down on *Nine-Tenths*. I have two more filters to change. Since y'all are coming, I'll join you on the party barge and it will be a full trip. Should be a hoot."

Gary continued driving east on Highway 98, crossed the Brooks Bridge in Fort Walton over to Okaloosa Island, then the long open stretch of rolling sand dunes until the Destin Bridge. They all gathered to the left side of the bus windows once they approached the Destin Bridge, to see

Crab Island. At least sixty boats were anchored there. It was high tide and the water was brilliant. Gary parked the bus in the oversized lot at the Palms of Destin.

"Where's my Ford?" asked Rick, noticing it wasn't in its usual spot.

"I sort of have a surprise for you. You'll see. Once we get to the HarborWalk," replied Gary.

Rick and Jules went to their condo to get cleaned up. Johnie had left the code to his unit for Possum, and Gary disappeared into his giant bachelor pad. After twenty minutes, everyone's phone pinged. It was Gary, asking everyone to come over to his place to see the renovations. They all made it over.

Gary had the door wide open. He had taken a three-bedroom unit and knocked down the wall next to it, which was a two-bedroom. Now he had a massive two-bedroom unit with matching master suites and a giant great room in the middle, complete with an indoor/outdoor waterfall and Jacuzzi. One entire wall had been turned into a bar with five draft taps and a full wall of the most premium liquor money could buy. Gary had fuck-you money now and it showed. They all had a drink and toasted in honor of Gary's new mega-pad, then Ubered to the HarborWalk.

"Look, Rick!" exclaimed Jules.

Just past AJ's sat Rick's red 1962 Ford F-100 Unibody next to a red and white TAB 320 teardrop trailer. On both the trailer and the truck window were Rick's logo and business names. Gary had already hired someone to sell tickets for both charter business. Jules planned on taking some days herself as well.

"I didn't have the heart to paint the old Ford. The red patina just looked too classic, so I had it polished with boiled linseed oil. It looks rustic and hip, don't you think?" asked Gary.

"I like it. Maybe I won't paint it after all. It looks pretty badass as it is," replied Rick.

They all strolled over to *Nine-Tenths* and met Johnie. He had already gotten changed into street clothes and was sipping on a Destin East Pass IPA. Chief was snuggled up with Jules as they stepped onto the sport fisher.

"Where's the party barge?" asked Rick.

"It's five slips down. But we don't call it a party barge. It's a sunset booze cruise with live music. Haha."

"Oh, I stand corrected," said Rick with a grin.

"Y'all ready to go? We have about thirty minutes before we push off, but we can go on early and have a few drinks, and I can show you the entire setup and you can meet the crew."

They all slowly moseyed down the dock toward the new charter. Johnie had turned it into a floating paradise. He'd added a full roof to the catamaran from bow to stern with tiki gods placed on each corner. The roof had been covered with thatch and resembled a palapa. The port-side bow had been transformed into a small raised stage good for solos or duos. It had lights and the EV Evolve 30 PA Johnie ordered. The mic stands were secured to the deck. The entire boat just oozed of fun.

"Wow, Johnie, you did a great job. I'm super impressed. I love the island vibe you gave it."

"Thanks, boss. It's meant for fun, to make memories and get return business. We do a limbo contest on the musician's break, and a conch-blowing contest at sunset. Winner gets one of these." Johnie opened a drawer full of gold medals on red, white, and blue ribbon. "Let me introduce you to the crew. Rick, this is Captain Jason Kaylor and his wife, first mate, and tequila girl Marissa, but she goes by Missy."

Missy had a leather tequila bandolier on her waist with a bottle of tequila on each side where pistols would be, and handblown Mexican shot glasses all the way around where bullets would normally be.

"I had it shipped in from a leather shop I know in Isla Mujeres," said Johnie.

"I like that we are using real glass. I hate plastic cups, and they are so bad for the environment," said Rick.

"Yeah, it takes a little extra time to shut down for the day, but check out the dishwashing station I had built."

Just behind the helm near the stern was a large flat table and cabinets. When Johnie raised the starboard lid, it revealed a double stainless-steel sink and an electric glass sanitizer. The boat even had two self-serve draft dispensers. One handle was Destin East Pass IPA, and the other was 30A Beach Blonde; both local brews. The pint glasses all had the charter logo on them and were available for purchase. The nicely equipped merch table also had t-shirts, caps, koozies, key chains and other logo items for sale. Johnie introduced everyone to Zaq, who was tuning up on the bow.

"Nice to meet you, Zaq. I'm Rick Waters, one of the owners. Johnie's told me good things about you."

"Hi, Mr. Waters, thanks for the opportunity."

"Call me Rick. We are informal here. I see you have a drink holder on your mic stand and no drink. What's your preference?"

"I usually drink IPAs, I guess."

Rick poured Zaq a pint and handed it to him.

"Y'all are so nice. I love working on this charter. I'll be here anytime y'all ask," said Zaq.

He continued to tune up as people started coming aboard. Once everyone was present, Captain Jason gave his safety speech through the Bose speakers mounted on both sides of the roof. The handheld fed into the sound system, which played island music when no one was speaking. The EV PA the musicians used also fed into the Bose speakers, giving the boat a clean, crisp surround-sound with plenty of bottom end.

"As Captain Ron says, if anything's gonna happen, it's gonna happen out there!" hollered Jason on the handheld mic.

The boat left the dock and started the circle of the harbor. Missy walked around offering tequila shots to any and all takers, as Captain Jason did his spiel about certain businesses and homes that surrounded the harbor. It was a who's who of Destin history, much of which Rick wasn't even aware of, and he found it entertaining and educational. Once they completed the full circle of the harbor, they passed Noriega Point and steered under the Destin Bridge toward Crab Island. Depending on tide and weather conditions, sometimes they'd venture out into the Gulf, but unless it was like glass, they preferred to stay in the bay, as cleaning up seasick customers wasn't just not fun; it was bad for business.

Once they passed under the bridge, they slowly motored around Crab Island as Zaq began singing. He started with a tune by Green Day and then moved on to some Blink-182, then "Say It Isn't So" by Weezer. He threw in a few Buffett and Bob Marley songs for the island vibe. All in all, his song selection worked well. During his one and only break, Missy brought out a limbo setup made of bamboo, and Captain Jason played "Limbo Rock" by Chubby Checker. Everything about the trip was fun. Jules even did the limbo. She could've won but let a kid get the gold medal.

"That was so fun, Rick!"

"Fun to watch for me. I would've knocked over the highest setting." Rick chuckled.

As the sun set on the horizon, the conch-blowing contest started. Missy passed the conch shell to each person who wanted to try and used a handheld timer. A woman from Indiana won. She blew for over fifty seconds.

Everyone left the boat with a smile once they were back at the dock. Both Zaq's tip jar and the crew's tip jar were full. Missy passed out a coupon for ten dollars off the next charter if they booked it within three days. It was a smart promotion.

Rick and the gang were all buzzed, and they invited Missy and Jason to come to dinner with them. Johnie offered to help clean glasses and get the boat put away. Rick and his entourage went ahead to secure a large table at Tailfins. He invited Zaq as well, but he had another gig to get to in Sandestin. They had a large table set up just below the bar on the first floor.

"Hi, I'm Bridget," said the waitress. "I'll be taking care of y'all today. What can I start you out with to drink?"

Rick ordered a round of Mermaid H2Os for everyone. That was one of the specialty drinks at Tailfins. He made Gary put his Platinum American Express Card away.

"It's my treat today, Gary! You've paid for enough stuff."

Gary relented and agreed to let Rick pay for once.

Once Bridget returned with the drinks and Johnie and the crew arrived, he ordered a Toms High Roller for an appetizer. It was a mountain of steamed seafood: Alaskan snow crab, mussels, clams, shrimp, and lobster tails served with new potatoes and corn on the cob. It was $195 just for the appetizer. Once it arrived, there was no doubt it was worth every penny.

After a few more rounds of drinks, everyone ordered an entrée except for Jules, who was a little full from the appetizer. She got a bowl of gumbo.

They all decided to walk their meals off when they were finished eating, and headed down to The Boathouse. A guy was playing, but Rick didn't care for his music, so they walked up the hill to The Red Door, one of Rick's favorite hangs. It was geared more toward locals. He was greeted by the manager, Sammy.

"Hi, Rick, long time no see. Where ya been?"

"Oh, we were in Mississippi working a case."

"Y'all want a table or you wanna sit at the bar? My husband Mikee is working, or my sister Mary can serve you at the round table on the end."

"Yeah, we'll take the round table."

Rick fist-bumped Mikee as they walked past the bar.

"Hi, Mary, can we get a round of Bushwackers?"

"Of course, you can, Rick! I'll be right back, and you can introduce me to everyone."

Mary returned shortly with tall, delicious Bushwackers, and Rick made the intros.

It was the perfect end to a perfect day. Everyone was fat and happy. They said their goodbyes to the crew, and Johnie walked with them back toward *Nine-Tenths*. Rick and the gang Ubered back to The Palms of Destin and called it a night.

The next day, Rick planned to set up a war room in his condo to go over every single piece of evidence to try and find Dale Clemens. He planned to travel down to Miami with Gary in a few days to follow up and see if Dale had made an appearance, and to try and find the person whose number he had circled in the notepad. He had a feeling it was a number for a fence.

Rick was certain he had left the country by now. He just wasn't sure which route he'd taken. He hadn't been seen or heard of since the day he took the five million dollars. That kind of money could hide a person really well.

CHAPTER NINETEEN

The heat in Miami was uncomfortable even in November. Rick called the number of the fence and told him he had some loose jewels he needed to get rid of. He said he was an old friend of Clemens and his name was Robert Frost. The man agreed to meet them the next day at Bayside Marketplace near the main stage. It was a get-to-know-you meeting in a very public place.

They arrived early at Bayside and grabbed some espressos from a kiosk near the entrance. They sat in the back row center stage, as they had agreed upon.

Twenty minutes later, a man walked up and sat directly in front of Gary and Rick. He leaned back in his chair and said, "Nice weather today."

"Yes, it's very warm, no chance of frost."

That was the line that would indicate who they were. The man relaxed a bit and turned around.

"How do you know Dale Clemens?" he asked.

"I've known him a long time. I know he had a meeting with you three days ago. He loves guitars."

"If you know him so well, then you also know that he never showed up for that meeting."

Rick frowned at that. "I apologize, I didn't know. I thought he was avoiding my calls. We were in on that deal together."

"Well, he no-showed. I heard the heat was on him, and he left for Brazil. I also called his number and got nothing. Okay, enough of the formalities. What do you have and what do you want for it?"

"I have a small bag of loose diamonds. We can arrange a time tomorrow or the next day to show them. I just want a fair price. Dale said you pay fair and are discreet."

"All right, let's meet tomorrow at 7:30 p.m. at the Monterrey Bar on Island Avenue. I'll have a private booth in the back."

"We'll see you then."

The man got up and walked away.

Rick had no intention of meeting him. He had everything he needed to know. He was sure Clemens had left the country with The Black Strat. They decided to focus their efforts on finding out how he'd gotten to Brazil. There was no way he'd flown commercial.

Rick and Gary went to every nightclub, bar, and speakeasy in South Beach and other parts of Miami, posing as possible clients to import drugs from South America. They dropped Dale's name a lot but never got anywhere. Finding

Clemens was turning out to be far more difficult than they'd ever imagined.

"Do we dare go to Brazil?" asked Rick.

Gary was up for it, but they decided to put out some bait down there first and see if they could get any bites on Clemens's whereabouts. They caught nothing. If he was hard to find in Miami, it would be even more difficult to find him in the rainforests of Brazil. If he was down there, he was lying low. Not too hard to do with five million dollars. Still, Rick was determined to give it a shot.

"Jules, we will be back in a few days. Everything's good down here. Just keep booking those charters, baby. You're doing great."

"Okay, my love. I want to run something by you and see if you're okay with it."

"Shoot."

"Well, I've been thinking, since we have the little office down on the HarborWalk and the new big office at The Palms... I was wondering if you'd mind if I got my bail bond agent license?"

"You wanna be a bounty hunter?" he asked, a little surprised.

"Well, yeah, but they are not allowed to be called that in the state of Florida. I've been going down to the courthouse and I met a guy who deals with bond jumpers. He says it pays really well, and I think it would be an asset to your detective agency. It's very safe. Most people just forget to show up to court and come in peacefully. I know I can do it. There's a course I have to take."

"It sounds okay, Jules. We can talk about it more when I get back. How long is the course?"

"About a hundred and twenty hours. I already signed up. I just need to turn the paperwork in. I wanted to make sure you'd be okay with it."

"Haha, you are something else, Jules. I guess it's better to ask for forgiveness than get permission, huh?"

Her eyebrows scrunched in confusion. "Huh?"

"Never mind, baby, you have my blessing. We'll see you soon."

Gary's jet landed in the mask of darkness the next night. The pilot stayed with the plane, had it serviced and fueled in case things went sideways. Rick rented a huge Mercedes-Benz G550 four-by-four, and they headed to Dale's last known hideout.

They cautiously approached the building. There was one armed guard sitting in a chair leaning against the far-left corner. Rick pointed at his eyes and then toward the guard. He would create a distraction, and Gary would take him out. Rick crept quietly toward the far side of the building though the heavy brush.

When Gary was in position behind the guard, Rick stepped out of the jungle and began to wave at the man.

"*Olá. estou perdido, estou procurando as Cataratas do Iguaçu,*" said Rick, trying to look like a lost hiker.

The Portuguese phrase he had memorized basically meant, *I'm lost, I'm looking for Iguaçu Falls.*

The man stood up and grabbed his rifle and began to walk toward Rick. Gary stepped up behind him and wrapped his arm around his throat in a choke hold. The man struggled but soon dropped the gun, unconscious.

Gary dragged him into the bushes, gagged him, and tied him to a tree. He removed his hat and fatigues shirt and put them on. He picked up the man's rifle and walked toward the main door, motioning Rick over. Rick opened the door, then raised his hands as Gary walked behind him with the gun in his back and the hat over his eyes.

"Who's this, Ernesto?" said a man behind a desk. He was busy weighing cocaine.

He was the only man in the room. His pistol sat on the corner of the desk. Gary stepped from behind Rick and aimed the gun at the man as Rick pulled his .38 snub-nosed revolver out from behind his back. The man lunged for the gun and Gary fired, hitting him in the shoulder. He fell backward in his chair.

Rick and Gary ran toward him, and Rick pressed the barrel of his pistol into his forehead.

"Don't even breathe!"

"Who are you?" asked the man, whose shoulder was bleeding profusely.

"Never mind that, I'll ask the questions. I know you speak English."

"No shite, I'm from England. Of course, I speak English."

"Where is Clemens? Dale fucking Clemens?" asked Rick.

"I have no idea. I swear. We haven't seen or heard from him in months. I know he went stateside. I haven't spoken to him since. I'm not lying. You may as well shoot me because I have no clue where he is. No one does."

"Let's just see."

Rick put the pistol against his leg and slowly moved his finger to the trigger. The man flinched, but said nothing.

Rick then moved the gun directly on his crotch. He cocked the pistol.

"Please don't. I swear I have no idea where he is. He owes a lot of people money, including me. If I knew, I'd tell you."

Sweat was pouring down the man's forehead.

Rick moved over to his desk, took the man's pistol, and stuck it into his waistband.

"If I find out you're lying, I'll personally come back here and castrate you .38 Special-style. You understand?"

The man nodded his head vigorously.

They slowly backed out of the doorway with weapons drawn.

"You might wanna untie Ernesto. I'd hate for the ants to eat him alive. He's tied to a tree beside the building. Oh, and I think I'd fire him if I were you. He's not a very good guard," said Rick, just before he slammed the door.

They hauled ass away in the four-by-four and continued their search for Clemens. Every sleazy bar they went to that was known to have ties to him revealed nothing. If he was in Brazil, he had to be in the jungle somewhere. But even that didn't seem like his style.

They decided it was a waste of time and headed back to Destin. The mystery of Dale's disappearance and The Black Strat were haunting Rick. He had to find that guitar, but he had all but exhausted every avenue. Clemens had already tried to kill Rick a couple of times, so it was more than personal. He was positive the car that ran him off the road had belonged to Dale as well.

Rick ground his teeth together as he stared out the window of the jet. *Where the hell are you, Clemens?*

With no other leads to follow, Rick tried to focus on getting things in Destin back to business as usual. Both charters were doing extremely well, and the new teardrop trailer office was a big hit. Rick took a few small local cases and brought Jules in on them. She had a keen eye and was sharp as a tack and turning into quite an investigator herself.

With Rick's help, she got her own private eye license and joined the team full-time. She no longer was concerned about returning to South America to work with the pink dolphins. Something had changed in her when she was carjacked in Mississippi. It lit a fire under her; she now wanted to be in control. She took several self-defense courses and acquired a few new handguns. Her bond recovery business was growing and growing fast.

The fact that she was beautiful and lethal now helped her a lot. She now feared no one and dressed the part. When she came to the office, she wore tactical gear. She was all business.

They both agreed that they would leave work at home. Rick had renovated another condo in The Palms of Destin on the first floor as a second satellite office from the harbor. While the HarborWalk mostly did the bookings of the charter tours, they also got leads regarding P.I. work and acted as an answering service for all the businesses. Anything not related to charters was redirected to The Palms office. Rick added lockers and gun safes to the office, and whenever they called it a night and headed up to their own condo, they always left it all behind in the war room downstairs and dressed Florida casual. They seemed to have perfect balance. Rick gave Gary any cases involving infidelity, since he enjoyed busting cheaters. It just wasn't Rick's cup of tea.

Possum continued to stay in Florida, returning back to Houston every so often to dust his house and check on things. He was kinda living in both places and mostly enjoyed helping Johnie on Nine-Tenths Charters. He was always reminding Rick to go treasure hunting when he had a free minute. They often went to the East Coast to search for Megalodon shark teeth. It was like they were all one big family. Life was good.

Rick kept an eye on Tyler's musical career, which seemed to be blossoming. He had worked his way through the Midwest and had been hitting the big clubs in New York, Boston, and Philly. He focused most of his dates in New York though. Mostly in the city with a few dates upstate. One day, Rick found an article about Tyler in the *Rolling Stone.*

> *Blues guitarist Tyler Raynes has been causing quite a stir in the music scene in New York City. He was recently spotted opening for legendary artist Eric Clapton at Soho's famous blues bar, Terra Blues. Clapton did a popup concert last week and touted Raynes as the future of the blues. Rumor has it, he's working with the one and only Mutt Lang on a new record and will be signing with a major label any day now. There's been a bidding war between Capitol Records on the West Coast and Columbia in the Big Apple. The announcement should be made soon, according to Raynes's spokesperson.*

"Jules, come read this!"

Rick slid his *Rolling Stone* magazine across the kitchen table for Jules. She read in silence as Rick watched her.

"Wow, he did it!" she exclaimed.

"It looks like it. I hope we get to see him again before he gets too big," replied Rick.

Jules and Rick's lives had become so intertwined now that they did the same thing nearly every day. Jules would work out with Rick and on certain mornings they would go jogging. After they showered, they'd go downstairs and check messages from the HarborWalk office. Jules would check with all the bonds companies, and on trial days, she'd go down to the courthouse in Fort Walton and see who had warrants put up for them for failure to appear, so she could be the first to offer her services to a bail bonds company. She was all over it.

As the months passed, Rick continued to keep an eye out for any leads on Clemens's location, as well as the location of The Black Strat. Still, nothing came up. Rick was experiencing a little burnout, and every time he saw a commercial for Dreams Resort in Tulum, he got an itch to go on a siesta in the Yucatán. Until he resolved Clemens's mystery though, a holiday was out of the question.

He remembered that Tyler would be coming to play in Destin the following week, at Club LA. The gang planned to check out his show and support him. Rick wished he'd have good news to give him by then, but at this point, he doubted it would happen.

Jules sat in her Bronco across the street from The Block with her spotting scope, waiting for a woman named Lindsey

McMann to appear. Lindsey had tattoos on her arms and legs and was super skinny. She had a serious addiction to meth and would do anything or anyone, male or female, to get her fix. A warrant for her arrest had been issued, and Jules had negotiated a twenty-five percent commission if she could bring her in. That would net her a cool $7,500 for an hour or two of work.

Lindsey not only had the drug charge against her but also a failure to appear and a felony for possession with intent to distribute. The judge set her bail at $33,000. Her boy-friend had cooked up a bunch of crack and meth and had Lindsey sell it in exchange for a place to crash and her own personal use. She was an addict. Her boyfriend was in jail with a bond fee he couldn't afford, so he was stuck.

This was Jules's first stakeout like this, and she was ener-gized. Rick had called to check in with her earlier and make sure she was okay, and she'd assured him she could handle it. She just wanted to bring this girl in tonight so that she wouldn't miss Tyler's concert at Club LA tomorrow.

At around 9:20 p.m., she saw an Uber pull up. She zoomed in with her spotting scope and immediately knew it was Lindsey. She wanted to catch her before she went into the club, but by the time Jules crossed the street, she had already gone inside.

Shit, I have to change now.

Jules ran back to the Bronco. She was wearing black tacti-cal pants and a vest. She would stick out like a sore thumb in that outfit. She climbed in the back seat and put on a knee-length red dress. She slid on a stretchable holster high up on the inside of her thigh. The only thing in Jules's unzipped purse now was a Taser and a pair of handcuffs. It was time to go clubbing. When she approached the doorman, he keyed in on her and walked toward her. She was afraid he was going to frisk her, so she batted her eyes and diverted his attention by remarking how much she liked his tattoo of a skull on his left arm. She flirted with him hard, hoping he'd just wave her through. It worked. There were no guns allowed inside, even with a permit. She could go to jail if caught.

She walked over to the bar and ordered a club soda with a splash of cranberry. She scoped out the entire bar and spotted Lindsey in the corner with two big black guys. She was rubbing her leg against one of them in a sexual way, obviously trying to either get some money or drugs. Jules moved closer, trying not to be too obvious. The man palmed Lindsey a little baggy. Jules had to get to her before she got whacked out on something. It would be easier to take her in.

"Kevon, is that you?" said Jules in raised voice.

The black guy next to Lindsey looked up, trying to recognize Jules. He was squinting like he couldn't figure her out.

"It's me, Jenny from Niceville."

"Oh, hi, Jenny. Come on over here, baby," said the guy, trying to pretend like he knew her.

"How have you been?" asked Jules as she gave him a hug.

Her perfume was wafting in the air. Lindsay gave her the stank eye as the black guy pushed her aside for Jules.

"It's not Kevon, it's Wayne."

"I'm sorry, Wayne. I'm terrible with names. I'm trying to score a little something-something. Can you help a girl out?"

"I just traded my last dime bag to her. I need to re-up."

Lindsey gave Jules a fake smile, like she had beat her out of something.

"When are you gonna re-up, Wayne? I need it bad," said Jules.

"In about an hour. I'm waiting for Pookie to show up. I can get you then."

"I can't wait an hour. I'm getting the shakes, baby. Hey, girl, I'll give you two bills if you'll give me yours. You can get more than that after Pookie gets here."

She stood there and thought about it.

"Are you a cop?"

"Fuck no, I hate pigs. Look, I have the money on the center console of my Bronco. You wanna follow me? I'll even let you have a hit."

She nodded and smiled, showing her rotten teeth. Jules told Lindsey where she'd parked and to meet her across the street in five minutes. She went to the Bronco and took two crisp one-hundred-dollar bills out of her purse and put them in the glove box. Then she waited.

About six minutes later, Jules saw Lindsey crossing the street. When she saw the Bronco, Jules waved her over to the passenger side. She climbed in. The only thing in Jules's unzipped purse now was a Taser and a pair of handcuffs. Her pistol was still on her inside thigh.

"Where's the cash?"

Jules opened the center console and it was empty.

"Oh, I'm sorry. I forgot it's in the glove box."

When Lindsey leaned forward to open the glove box, Jules slid her right hand into her purse. As Lindsey saw the bills and reached for them, Jules tased her. Her body starting shaking violently. Jules released the trigger on the Taser, jumped out of the Bronco, and ran over to the passenger side as Lindsey slumped over on the seat. She quickly handcuffed her behind her back and used the zip ties she always kept in the door in a tube to secure her to the seat-belt buckle. Now all she had to do was make the short drive to Crestview. She got back in the Bronco and texted Rick.

I got the bitch, it's Miller time.

You rock, baby!

CHAPTER TWENTY

Rick, Jules, and Possum pulled into the parking lot of Club LA, and Rick drove around the back. Gary had taken his jet to Costa Rica to check on a new business venture. He didn't tell them exactly what it was, but said it had something to do with coffee beans and Tungsten's two-hundred-acre farm.

Tyler had become so famous that he now had to use different entrances for most venues. He had arranged for Rick to come in the back way as well and had given his name to the doorman. Tyler had signed with Capitol Records in Los Angeles, and his CD debut would be launching the following Tuesday. It would probably be one of the last small venues he and his trio would play. Once the album hit the charts, Tyler's life would change forever.

Rick shook hands with Tyler and saw he hadn't changed much. He had dark circles under his eyes and wore a black long-sleeve t-shirt with a Highway 61 road sign emblem on it; a tribute to the great blues highway. He looked tired. The road did that to a person. He was still wearing the same black scuffed-up Converse shoes with the bright red laces that he'd been wearing the last time Rick saw him.

"How's the road been, Tyler?"

"It's been a whirlwind. Lots of shows all the way down the East Coast. Did you hear I signed with Capitol?"

"I did. We are all very proud of you. I'm sure your dad is beaming."

"I haven't talked to him much. We sort of had a little falling out. He's still pissed that I took The Black Strat and Clemens stole it from me. It all came out one day on the phone, and I haven't talked to him since."

"I'm sorry, Tyler. He did mention that y'all were a bit at odds. I'm sure it'll all be fine. He is your dad, after all. Are you gonna see him in Mississippi?"

"Most likely. We'll probably smooth things out then. Look, I got y'all front-row seats. It's mostly standing room here at this venue, but I had them curtain off a sort of VIP section with seats. My agent and PR person will be there, as well as a couple of the label folks."

"That's so kind of you, Tyler. Can we see you after the show?"

"Yeah, here, let me show you. This is the greenroom. Just knock when I'm done. We usually unwind a bit before I change and hit the road."

Tyler opened the door to a room with a couple of couches and a vanity mirror and a wall divider just to the right of it for changing. It wasn't fancy, but it served its purpose.

"When you start doing stadium tours, are you gonna have a concert rider that insists on no brown M&M's?"

"Haha, I'll have something like that."

When Van Halen was at their height in the early eighties, they'd had on their rider, *NO BROWN M&M's*. Most people thought they did it to be arrogant rock stars. The reason they actually put it in there, toward the bottom, was to make sure the promoters actually read their rider. It was a smart business move.

"Any news on Dale? Do you think they'll find him?" asked Tyler.

"I honestly have no idea at this point. I ain't giving up. It's like he's a ghost now. There has been no sighting of him in Miami or even Brazil. It's a mystery. It's like he is no longer on the face of the earth."

"That sucks. Well, good luck. I gotta get ready for the show. Drinks are covered in the VIP area, so y'all help yourselves."

Tyler bent down to retie his left shoe then stepped into the greenroom.

"That one always comes loose. I guess I need new shoes. Haha."

They all proceeded to the VIP area, and Rick ordered a light beer. He didn't feel like drinking anything heavy, plus he was the DD tonight. Jules got a Tito's and soda, and Possum went for a Maker's Mark neat. There was a buzz of excitement, and it was obvious to Rick that Tyler's fan base had grown. He saw several people with his band t-shirts on, carrying signs from *Will You Marry Me Tyler* to *I Love You Tyler*. The venue was filled with energy and anticipation.

The lights dimmed, and Tyler stepped through the curtains. Everyone cheered, and there was loud thunderous applause as he picked up the plaid Stratocaster. The room went black except for a huge spotlight on Tyler. He hit the first note, and Rick immediately recognized it as "Little Wing," a song written by Jimi Hendrix and covered by every blues man ever since. Tyler's version of it seemed to go from Hendrix to Stevie Ray Vaughan plus some of his own unique style. He hit every note with speed, finesse, and confidence. He made it look so easy.

Damn, he's good.

"Now, I'd like to play a song I wrote and recorded for my debut album. It will be coming out next Tuesday. This will be the first single. I hope you like it. It's called 'Now You Have the Blues.'"

Everyone in the venue listened and grooved to the song. It was a medium-tempo twelve-bar blues song that had a similar vibe to "Perpetual Blues Machine" by Keb' Mo'. It had an instant and distinguishable hook and was catchy from the start. Rick thought it would do well on the blues charts. When the song finished, the crowd erupted with approval. He then played another original, this time a ballad that would definitely work on the pop charts. It was a great song, and Rick could imagine John Mayer cutting it. It had that "Gravity" feel. The trio did several medleys and a tribute to Robert Johnson. Tyler closed the show with one of the most downright radical versions of "Crossroads" he had ever heard. He thanked the crowd and came back for two encores. The show was magical.

Once the lights came on and people knew he was done, they clambered to the merch table to get anything and everything Tyler Raynes. Rick, Jules, and Possum made their way backstage. He knocked on the door and Tyler opened it.

"What did you think?"

"Oh my God, dude. You have it going on," said Rick.

"I loved it!" exclaimed Jules.

Possum gave Tyler a big thumbs-up. They chatted a bit and drank some more. Jules was rehashing every guitar solo as if Tyler wasn't there. He obliged her and let her gush.

"Hey, guys, excuse me for a second, I'm gonna change really quick."

"Do you want us to step out?"

"Nah, I can change behind the divider. Have a seat on the couch. I'll just be a minute and then maybe we can grab a bite before we hit the road?"

"Sounds like a plan, blues man. We'll be right here."

Jules sat on the couch in between Rick and Possum and thumbed through a magazine. Rick grabbed a guitar pick sitting on the coffee table and bent it to see how thick it was. It was a Dunlop 73. The same kind found where Tyler was abducted. They were very common and used by lots of players.

When he bent it, it slipped from his fingers and flew across the room toward the vanity. Rick walked over to pick it up and caught a reflection of Tyler changing shirts behind the divider. On the table behind him was a syringe and a spoon. Rick wasn't spying; it just happened. His brow furrowed. He was disappointed that Tyler was again doing drugs.

What he saw next stopped him in his tracks. On his shoulder was a trident tattoo.

He walked stone-faced back to the couch and pulled out his iPhone. He scrolled to the surveillance camera close-ups he had blown up from the bus cameras the day the five million was taken. He turned white as a ghost. He whispered something to Jules, and she stuck her hand into her purse. She whispered to Possum, and his body stiffened.

"Why'd you do it, Tyler?" asked Rick.

Tyler stepped out from behind the divider.

"Why'd I do what?"

"Why did you kill Dale Clemens and then steal his identity to steal the money?"

A look of horror and fear overcame Tyler, and he looked around the room as if he was looking for a weapon or something.

"You have no proof. I didn't do anything!"

Rick turned his phone around, facing Tyler, and pointed at the bottom of the screen at the shoes. The man in the still shot was wearing black Converse with bright red laces and the left one was loose and hanging, exactly as it was that very moment on Tyler's foot.

"How'd you know?" asked Tyler, as he moved toward Rick in an aggressive manner.

Jules pulled out her pistol and aimed it at him.

"Don't even think about it, Tyler!" she said fiercely.

The life looked like it just drained out of Tyler's eyes. He sat down on the chair in front of the vanity, defeated.

"What now?" he asked.

"Now we call the police. You will be brought to Okaloosa Corrections in Crestview and processed then transferred to Bolivar County, Mississippi, to answer for your crimes."

Possum was already dialing the Sheriff's Department.

"It's all over, Tyler. You may as well just sit still and wait. Jules has a trigger finger. If you lawyer up, you will get a fair trial. If you return the money or what's left of it, your dad may not seek to press charges on that. Where's the body? Cooperating will go a long way for you. There's no love lost, now that Clemens is dead. I'm sure you had your reasons why you did what you did."

"How did you know I killed him?"

"I didn't at first. It was a hunch. Something about your shoes was bothering me, but I didn't know what it was. Then I remembered the shoes from the surveillance video and when I saw your tattoo when you were changing, it all came together. The way he disappeared off the face of the earth made no sense to me. I started thinking maybe he was dead. The tattoo sealed the deal for me."

Rick raised the sleeve on Tyler's right arm, and there it was—the trident. He walked over to the plaid Stratocaster sitting on a guitar stand, while Jules kept the gun sighted on Tyler. Rick reached down, grabbed the plaid cloth, and ripped it. Underneath the cloth was the unmistakable Black Strat. He flipped the guitar over and peeled off an oval Fender "Made in the USA" sticker revealing a serial number. On his phone, he opened the notes app, and the number matched the famous stolen guitar.

"I'm gonna give you a bit of advice, Tyler. Don't say anything until you speak to a lawyer. As much as I wanna know where the body is, use that to your advantage. You can use it help you with a plea. I don't want to scare you, but Mississippi has the death penalty. Being a kidnap victim, I can't see a D.A. going after murder charges. I'm sure you would plead not guilty anyway and argue that it was self-defense. That doesn't look good for you. If you were just a kidnap victim, you would have fled and found the police. If you play your cards right and your dad hires the best lawyers money can buy, you can walk away from this case."

Tyler just sat in silence with his head down.

A short while later, the Okaloosa County Sheriff's Department took him into custody. It was now time for Rick to do what he knew had to be done but damn sure didn't want to do. He had to call Jack before the press got to him.

Rick stepped outside alone and made the somber call. Jack took it well, all things considered, and told Rick he'd transfer his fee once the money was returned and Clemens's body was positively identified. It was over. Rick hugged Jules, and they walked toward Rick's Bronco with Possum tailing them. They climbed in, and Rick set the key fob in the cup holder but didn't push the ignition button at first; he just sat there.

"I think we all a need a vacation. How about Mexico?"

EPILOGUE

Tyler Raynes spent a week in Okaloosa Country Corrections, aka the Crestview Hilton, as it had been nicknamed, before being transferred to Bolivar County, Mississippi. He was released on a $350,000 pre-trial conditions bond and made to wear an ankle monitor and stay on house arrest at his father's estate in Biloxi. The district attorney dropped the charges of grand larceny when his dad refused to press charges against him, and most of the money was returned.

In light of Tyler burying and hiding Clemens's body, the D.A. wanted to pursue second-degree murder charges. The maximum penalty Tyler could receive was forty years. Tyler drew a map to the body. It was a mere seventy-five yards behind the old farmhouse he'd been found in. He had used a backhoe to bury the Cadillac in an overgrown field behind the house. The badly decomposed body was found wrapped in a blanket in the trunk. It was positively identified through DNA to be, in fact, Dale Clemens. The cause of death was ruled to be blunt-force trauma to the front of the skull. The murder weapon was in the trunk. It was a claw hammer. Both Tyler and Dale's DNA were recovered from the hammer.

Tyler's first album debuted at number one on both the blues and pop charts. The news of his arrest wasn't made public until after the album dropped. There was still speculation that money had been paid to keep it from the press. No proof had been provided, since he was arrested on a Saturday night and the album dropped the following Tuesday. His fans supported him through the entire trial, and a Facebook page was created called "Tyler Raynes Is Not Guilty." His record label didn't drop him because of the charges, and before the trial even started, he had sold over six million copies.

Tyler pleaded not guilty to the second-degree murder charges. His team of lawyers put together an obvious case of self-defense. There was never any way to completely confirm that Tyler was the one who took the money from the bus. He claimed he'd originally met Dale in Fort Walton, where he had scored drugs from him. He continued to buy from Dale and got to know him, and when the money ran out, he hatched the plan with Dale to fake his own kidnapping. Once Dale found out the value of The Black Strat, he got greedy. Dale decided to keep both the ransom money and fence the valuable guitar on the black market and eliminate Tyler. He went on to say that Dale forced him to get the tattoo, then dress like him and purchase identical shoes to him when he made the heist on the bus.

Tyler's team put together an amazing defense. In a rarely used technique, Tyler took the stand himself, testifying that he was nothing more than the scapegoat for Dale Clemens and was being framed, and that after Dale took the money, he came back to the farmhouse to tie up loose ends and get rid of Tyler. He claimed that he got the idea from Dale himself about putting the body in the trunk of the Cadillac and burying the entire car. It's what Clemens had intended to do to him. He said Dale repeatedly told him he was going to bury him alive in that Cadillac once he had the money and used it as some sort of psychological torture, and that he was traumatized at the time and not in his right mind. A video surfaced of a man fitting Dale's description stealing a backhoe only a few houses down from the farmhouse. When Dale came back after the theft, Tyler slipped loose and hit him once in the head with the hammer. He got scared and did to Dale what Dale had threatened to do to him all along.

The fact that only a few thousand dollars of the original five million were missing went a long way in corroborating that the only reason he'd kept the money was because he was afraid the cops might think he did it with malice and he would need it to escape the country. He also got that idea from Dale. He testified that he'd planned all along to return the money once things returned to normal. In the end, the jury bought his story, and Tyler Raynes was found not guilty of all charges and released a free man.

Rick didn't believe him, but at the same time didn't care. Dale Clemens was no more, and that was enough for him.

Tyler went on to become one of the most famous blues guitarists in the world. When asked how he got so good so fast, he always answered the same way.

"I sold my soul to the devil at the crossroads."

The jury is still out on that one.

ACKNOWLEDGEMENTS

I want to thank my mom, Sylvia Stone, who inspired me to read at an early age when I wanted to just watch TV. She taught me how I could disappear in the books and take little cosmic journeys in my mind. I miss you mom. Thank you so much.

I'd like to thank my mentors Wayne Stinnett and Nick Sullivan.

Thank you to my editor, Stephanie Diaz Slagle, my formatter, Colleen Sheehan, my proofreader, Gretchen Douglas and my narrator, Nick Sullivan. He's a man with many hats.

Thanks to my awesome beta readers, Bavette and Dennis Battern, Mike Keevil, Carroll Scadden Shroyer, Chuck Springs.

Special thanks to all my readers who make doing this a possibility. I'm still blown away when someone tells me they just love my books and characters. It's incredibly humbling.

ABOUT THE AUTHOR

Eric Chance Stone was born and raised on the gulf coast of Southeast Texas. An avid surfer, sailor, scuba diver, fisherman and treasure hunter, Eric met many bigger than life characters on his adventures across the globe. Wanting to travel after college, he got a job with Northwest Airlines and moved to Florida. Shortly thereafter transferred to Hawaii, then Nashville. After years of being a staff songwriter in Nashville, he released his first album, Songs For Sail in 1999, a tropically inspired collection of songs. He continued to write songs and tour and eventually landed a gig with Sail America and Show Management to perform at all international boat shows where his list of characters continued to grow.

He moved to the Virgin Islands in 2007 and became the official entertainer for Pusser's Marina Cay in the BVI. After several years in the Caribbean, his fate for telling stories was sealed.

Upon release of his 15th CD, All The Rest, he was inspired to become a novelist after a chance meeting with Wayne Stinnett. Wayne along with Cap Daniels, Chip Bell and a few others, became his mentors and they are all good friends now. Eric currently resides in Destin, Florida with his fiancé Kim-Cara and their three exotic birds, Harley, Marley and Ozzy. Inspired by the likes of Clive Cussler's Dirk Pitt, Wayne Stinnett's Jesse McDermitt, Cap Daniels Chase Fulton, Chip Bell's Jake Sullivan and many more, Eric's tales are sprinkled with Voodoo, Hoodoo and kinds of weird stuff. From the bayous of Texas to the Voodoo dens of Haiti, his twist of reality will take you for a ride. His main character Rick Waters is a down to earth good ol' boy, adventurist turned private eye, who uses his treasure hunting skills and street smarts to solve mysteries.

FOLLOW ERIC CHANCE STONE

WEBSITE:

ERICCHANCESTONE.COM

FACEBOOK:

FACEBOOK.COM/RICKWATERSSERIES